Praise for Denise Patrick's
Gypsy Legacy: The Earl

"[This] is the third book in *The Gypsy Legacy* series, and I enjoyed it just as much as the first two. . . . This is a truly happily ever after story told beautifully by Ms. Patrick, and I would love to read more."

~ *Goddess Minx, Literary Nymphs Reviews*

"How easy it is to fall in love...while reading a Denise Patrick novel, that is. Having read the first two books in this series, I was so looking forward to reading *The Earl*. Ms. Patrick's crisp, engaging writing style makes it very easy to fall into this. . .very well written story with believable characters and a story that will touch your heart."

~ *Orange Blossom, Long and Short Reviews*

Look for these titles by *Denise Patrick*

Now Available:

The Importance of Almack's

Gypsy Legacy series
Gypsy Legacy: The Marquis (Book 1)
Gypsy Legacy: The Duke (Book 2)
Gypsy Legacy: The Earl (Book 3)

Gypsy Legacy:
The Earl

Denise Patrick

A Samhain Publishing, Ltd. publication.

Samhain Publishing, Ltd.
577 Mulberry Street, Suite 1520
Macon, GA 31201
www.samhainpublishing.com

Gypsy Legacy: The Earl
Copyright © 2010 by Denise Patrick
Print ISBN: 978-1-60504-738-6
Digital ISBN: 978-1-60504-644-0

Editing by Lindsey Faber
Cover by Natalie Winters

First Samhain Publishing, Ltd. electronic publication: August 2009
First Samhain Publishing, Ltd. print publication: June 2010

Dedication

To a great editor. Thanks, Lindsey. For everything.

Prologue

Lake District, August 1853

The two little girls traipsed blithely through the gypsy camp, giggling at some private joke. No one spared them more than a cursory glance as they went by in shifts rendered nearly transparent from swimming in the lake. The smaller of the two had golden ringlets streaming down her back, but the other's hair was the blue-black of a raven's wing.

Mira looked up as the two girls approached, and smiled. They had been camped in this place for nearly three weeks now and she was glad Caro had made a friend. 'Twas fortunate the other little girl did not know why her mother brought her to the camp each day then left her to her own devices, but Mira would not decry the fates who saw fit to provide Caro with a playmate.

"And what is so funny, little ones?" She greeted each girl with a length of cloth to dry themselves and their hair.

"A fish tried to eat Katie's toe," Caro told her with a big grin. "Didn't you hear her scream?"

"I did not scream," Katie interrupted in seven-year-old indignation.

"Yes, you did," Caro replied with all the confidence of one who was a year older. "And I'll bet Mira heard you too."

Mira had not heard any scream, nor had any of the others, she was sure. Otherwise the boys, whom she knew were not far away, would have gone to investigate. Sixteen-year-old JoJo was inordinately protective of his little sister.

"I heard no scream," she said now, and received a brilliant smile and adoring look from Katie's blue eyes.

Caro's eyes, a darker blue and more intense, studied Mira

for a moment before she conceded, "Well, maybe she didn't scream that loud. But it *was* funny."

Mira glanced up at the sky, noting the lateness of the day. They would break camp early tomorrow and leave this place. She hoped Caro would not miss her friend too much.

Katie sat on a blanket, accepted the comb Mira handed her and began working it through her tangled locks. Caro didn't bother with her own wild mane, but sat beside her friend and, using a comb, began to work on the other side.

It was a familiar ritual and Mira watched the girls fondly as they worked to restore order to Katie's long, golden tresses. Soon the hair was combed smooth and re-plaited into the same two plaits she'd worn when she arrived. A short time later, her shift was dry enough for her to put her blue and white dress back on, then her stockings and shoes. Suddenly she was a young lady again.

Across the camp, the *shuvani* emerged from her *vardo* and Caro got up and ran to greet her. Hair as black as Caro's flowed down her back, streaked liberally with grey. Old before her time, but wise beyond her years, Nona possessed high cheekbones beneath wrinkled brown skin and alert dark eyes. Nona was the leader of their small band—the final word on where they went and what they did. And she was Caro's great-grandmother.

As the two approached, Mira could hear Caro recounting the fish story to Nona, and was relieved when Nona did not laugh within Katie's hearing. "Now you must say goodbye to your little friend, Caro," Nona said as they stopped. "We will be leaving early tomorrow, for it is time for you to return home as well."

The two little girls dutifully gave each other hugs under Nona's warm regard and said goodbye, then Nona sent Caro off to find her older sister, while Nona sat beside Katie. She was holding a parcel, which she handed to the little girl. Mira left the two of them alone.

"I am sorry we must leave you, little Katie," Nona said, "but I have given you a very special present."

Katie unwrapped the heavy brown paper and found a small statuette of a black cat with green stones for eyes. "A kitty?"

Nona smiled. "Yes. A very big kitty. It is a panther—a big

kitty found in a faraway place."

"For me?"

"Yes." Nona's smile broadened. "It is yours. And it is magic too. Just as real panthers are fierce and protective, so will this one be for you. It will keep you safe, and some day it will bring you your prince."

"A prince?" Katie's eyes grew round with wonder, and Nona glimpsed the beauty she would become.

A feeling of *rightness* settled in Nona's heart. She had not wanted to come this far north this year. It was farther than her small band had traveled in a very long time, but the cards decreed they should come here, and now, looking at the small child beside her, she did not doubt the cards had been right again.

"Yes, a gypsy prince. He will be your destiny. When you get to be a big girl, you must only marry your gypsy prince."

Katie nodded happily. "JoJo," she stated. "I'm going to marry JoJo when I grow up. Then Caro will be my big sister." Setting aside her statuette for a moment, she gave Nona a hug.

Nona laughed and hugged her back, enjoying the feel of the small warm body. "You will know when you find him," was all she said.

Chapter One

London, April 1867

The Earl of Wynton was trapped.

Surveying the luxury around him, he had to admit it did not look like any prison he'd ever imagined. Royal blue velvet floor-to-ceiling drapes framed large windows overlooking the front of Waring House, yet he could hear none of the noise of the street. A plush cream-colored rug covered the floor, matching the cream and blue silk striped wallcovering. A large gilded mirror hung over the fireplace to his left, the mantel sporting a small gold and white porcelain clock which proclaimed the time as five minutes past six. Scattered throughout the room were various pieces of furniture, all upholstered in cream and blue. At the far end sat a piano, the bench with its back to the wall so the player faced the room. He wondered briefly if his sister had shaken her dislike of playing for large gatherings.

He should have recognized the possible trap in the carefully worded note he received earlier, but he hadn't. Instead he had blithely arrived for tea with his youngest sister, Felicia, Duchess of Warringham, only to find his other sister, Tina, Marchioness of Thanet, also in attendance. His jailers might be friendly, but they were still bent on his confinement.

He was slipping. Three years ago, before he left for a tour of the Continent, he would never have fallen for such a tactic. But returning to London after an extended absence, he had not questioned how his sisters knew he'd returned, nor was he suspicious of the invitation he received.

He mentally kicked himself for returning at this particular

time. Perhaps that's where he'd failed. But he had become restless. He was not willing to admit to being homesick, but the wanderlust which prompted him to pick up and go three years ago had waned and he found himself missing home and family. Now, however, he wondered if he should have resisted the pull—at least for a few more months until the Season was over.

Not that he didn't love his sisters. He did. He'd felt keenly the responsibility left to him to ensure their happiness, and taken it seriously. With Felicia it meant using force, as his great-grandmother had hinted, but the results were well worth the discomfort he had felt at the time at doing so.

"Jon!" His musings were interrupted by the object of his thoughts. "You are not paying attention."

Eyeing the figure perched across from him on a cream damask upholstered sofa, he was struck by the changes in her over the past three years. Her ebony hair was still thick and lustrous, blue eyes bright under dark winged brows in a creamy complexion. Physically, she looked much the same, but the young, insecure girl of nineteen he'd left behind had been replaced by a mature, confident woman of twenty-two. Secure in her position at the pinnacle of London society, she seemed to have shed her personal doubts concerning her background. He wished he could do the same.

"No, I'm not," he told her. Leaning forward, he replaced the gold-rimmed porcelain teacup on its saucer and set them both down on the low table before him. "I did not return home only to have the two of you immediately begin matchmaking. If and when I decide to marry, it will be to the woman of my choosing."

"What about your... What did Nona give you, anyway?" Having merely been a spectator so far, Tina finally joined the conversation, and Jon shifted his attention to her for a moment.

Petite and dark-haired like Felicia, but six years older, she was the calm one. The one who always seemed under control. If she was excited about something, her large aquamarine eyes would sparkle, but never did she radiate the same kind of energy Felicia did. Sitting on a blue sofa that matched the one Felicia occupied, she took a sip of her tea as she regarded him speculatively.

"Or, more to the point, what are you supposed to be looking

for?" Felicia asked.

He sat back in his chair and eyed the two of them warily.

"I don't know that I should tell you," he answered. "You'll only hound me for the rest of the Season."

"We wouldn't do that, would we?" Tina asked Felicia, and smiled serenely when Felicia shook her head emphatically, causing her dark curls to seem in danger of tumbling out of her elegant coiffure.

"Of course we wouldn't. But I'm sure we could be of some help. After all, we know most of the young women out now. I would wager we already know our future sister-in-law."

Jon could not dispute that statement, but the wide-eyed innocent look on her face set off warning bells in his head. He knew better than to trust either of them. Happily married, they only wanted the same for him, but their method of doing so would require that he fall in love with his future wife— something he had no intention of doing. He only needed to find the young woman who possessed the statuette and decide whether he would offer for her. His title and wealth ensured that whoever she was, if he offered she'd accept—or rather her parents would—and all would be well.

He was under no illusions about his value on the marriage mart. Most families would welcome him with open arms, regardless of his tainted background. He would be satisfied with that. Love, as he saw it, required letting go and opening yourself up to too much emotional instability. It made no sense whatsoever. As a man of science, logic and reason were his cornerstones. Things that didn't fit those models—like love and destiny—didn't belong in his world. He'd often observed that women who thought they were in love tended to become too dependent upon their husbands. Even his own sisters seemed to have succumbed at one time or another. He wanted someone he could hold an intelligent conversation with—not a limpet.

When his great-grandmother, a Romany *shuvani*, told him shortly before her death six years ago that she had given his statuette—the one she had promised would someday be his—to the woman she'd determined to be his destiny, he nearly swore in frustration. A firm believer in fate and destiny, her actions should not have surprised him. In fact, he should have expected that she would fulfill her promise in a roundabout way.

"Maybe it would be better if you let me find this person myself," he suggested now. "After all, Nona expected me to." Nona also expected him to marry the person. Something he was not inclined to do. He wanted a reasonable marriage built on mutual respect, and a wife who would not demand too much. While he expected to be faithful to his vows and expected his wife to do the same, it did not mean they had to live in each other's pockets.

"True, but maybe she knew you'd need some help," Tina reasoned. "That's why we had to be married first. So we'd be able to devote the time to helping you." He could not fault her logic, but could hear his mental teeth grinding.

It wasn't that he didn't want them to know. He'd actually considered how they could possibly help him identify the woman. The problem was that his goals were very different from what they expected them to be. If he didn't tell them, however, he'd never hear the end of the speculation and they might let something slip which would alert whoever had his figurine.

"So," Felicia repeated, "what are you looking for?"

Jon looked into her eyes, bright with curiosity, and barely refrained from shaking his head. He was convinced he'd never find the woman otherwise. After all, he couldn't picture any young lady carrying it about with her. It would never fit into a reticule. And there was no harm in looking around for what was left of the Season.

He sighed. "Very well, but if you know who has it, you have to promise not to tell me unless I can't discover it on my own."

Tina stared at him quizzically. "Then what would be the benefit of us knowing what you are looking for?"

His smile was more of a grimace. "Perhaps to let me know if I'm showing interest in the wrong person," he responded, then added hastily, "*when* I decide to be interested, that is."

"Very well," Felicia said at last, "but I reserve the right to tell you if I think it's best. After all, it might be better at the outset if you did your own discovering, but if complications arise you might need to know."

The clamor in Jon's head got louder with her last

pronouncement. "Such as?"

"Suppose she's already engaged or, heaven forbid, married. Maybe she's put whatever it is away somewhere, lost it, or doesn't remember it."

Jon admitted she had a point. What would he do if the woman hadn't waited? He'd consider himself lucky to have escaped. But he still wanted the figurine. He could not explain to himself why possessing it was so important, just that it was. So, how was he to get it without marrying the woman in question? Maybe if he found it, he could decide whether it was truly important enough for him to sacrifice his freedom. For that, however, he needed his sisters' help. He looked from one to the other. There was no way out. He could see his sisters were already well on their way to planning his downfall as he began describing the object Nona told him would someday belong to him.

"It's a statuette or figurine. A little larger than the teapot. Made of black onyx. It's a figure of a panther with emeralds for eyes." He nearly grimaced at the thought of Nona telling some impressionable young woman the panther represented himself.

Felicia briefly stilled at the description, but the pause was so slight, he thought he imagined it.

"Interesting," Tina commented. "And did Nona say how you were to find this person if you weren't able to see her with the statuette?"

"No, not really. As usual, she spoke in riddles." He refused to admit Nona had told him to follow his heart.

"Did she give you a description?" Felicia asked in a strange voice.

"A description?" he asked. "Such as...?"

"Remember what she told me?" Felicia reminded him. "Sun-ripened wheat and highland heather."

He chuckled with genuine glee at the memory. "The only time in your life you fainted that I can recall."

Felicia turned to her sister, who watched the two in perplexed silence. "Nona told me when I found the owner of the ring she gave me, I would be rewarded with sun-ripened wheat and highland heather. Unfortunately, I didn't know highland heather was purple—nearly the same color as Brand's eyes."

"And sun-ripened wheat is the perfect description for his hair," Tina finished in understanding.

"Well?" Felicia asked, turning back to her brother.

"It's possible it was buried in the conversation somewhere. I'll let you know if I think of anything that would fit. But as you can tell, it's highly unlikely I will find the statuette on my own, although Nona promised it would be mine one day."

"Unless it's on display in the sitting room during an at home or calling hours," Tina said. "Hmmm, I haven't seen anything like it." She looked over at her sister. "Have you?"

Felicia was silent for a long time. She poured herself another cup of tea. Jon noticed her hand shook slightly. But when she took another tart from the tray, nearly dropping it, he began to worry. She was staring off across the room as if deep in thought, and it occurred to him she was stalling.

"Felicia?" Tina finally said. "Where have you gone?"

She washed down the last of the tart with her tea and turned solemn eyes on them. "Yes," she answered. "I know who has it."

He quelled a groan. Should he ask her who? She was watching him sadly, but with an almost unholy gleam in her eye which did not give him any degree of comfort. It was almost as if she was pitying him, but was amused all the same. Maybe he didn't want to know after all. But perhaps he could ask a few questions to help him narrow his search.

"Where?"

"At Miss Ridley's Academy."

"So it's one of your school chums?"

She merely nodded.

"Then she shouldn't be too hard to find, unless... She's not already married is she?" The thought made him hopeful, but at the same time worried. Suppose he *had* waited too long to come back from his travels? If she was married already, how was he to get his panther?

"Thankfully, no," Felicia answered. "But like most of the young ladies you've met since I made my come-out, you've given her the cold shoulder. So now you are not high on her list of people to be cordial to."

Jon mulled over this statement for a moment. This might,

indeed, be harder than he thought. If the young woman wouldn't even speak to him, then what? It would be fine if he didn't plan on wedding her, but he still wanted his statuette. Perhaps he needed to know who it was after all.

"Then perhaps you'd better tell me."

Felicia shook her head slowly. "I'm sorry, Jon, but I don't think I should. I think you'd better figure this one out for yourself." He started to say something, but she continued. "I also won't say anything to the young woman in question. I think it's best if I just stay out of it."

Jon watched her with a measure of unease. Her sudden sobriety over the subject was both unsettling and a bit disheartening. He fully expected her to tease him unmercifully over this, but she seemed to be worried. And that, conversely, worried him. It also made him a little desperate.

"How about if you at least provide me with a list of young ladies you went to school with, including this person on it, and I will work my way through them?"

Felicia considered this for a moment, then nodded. "I see no harm in that. I'll have it for you by tonight. Will you be at the Marsdens'?"

"I can arrange to be."

"Fine."

He rose to his feet. "Then I will take my leave. I have mountains of correspondence to catch up on. Perhaps one day we will actually catch up on each other's news?" He sensed that right now was not the time. His revelation bothered Felicia, which, in turn, troubled him enough that he needed to escape.

Felicia stood and approached him. "I'm sorry." Then she hugged him.

"It's good to have you back," Tina said, also giving him a hug before he left.

Once he was gone, however, she turned to her sister.

"All right, out with it," she demanded. "What's wrong?"

"Wrong?" Felicia asked, one eyebrow arched innocently.

"Give over, Felicia. You really look troubled about this. Is it that bad?"

Felicia was silent for a moment, then she smiled sadly. "It would be funny, if it wasn't so ironic. The lady in question is seriously considering another offer right now, but I know she hasn't definitely said yes yet."

"Why didn't you tell Jon that much, at least?"

"Because then he'd be able to figure out who it is almost immediately once I give him the list I promised. And quite frankly, I want him to worry over this a bit. You know how his mind works. I'd wager you next quarter's allowance he's thinking he can find this woman, make an offer—how many marriage-mart mamas do you think wouldn't make their daughter accept?—marry her out of hand, and never become emotionally involved." She paused for a moment to give her words a chance to sink in. "I don't think Nona wanted a loveless marriage for him any more than she did for us, but that's exactly what he would get if he didn't have to work for it. It may even be what he thinks he wants, but I don't want that for either of them."

"And the young woman?"

"Well, she's known him for a long time. And she must know what the statuette represents because she chased him all through her first Season and never seemed to understand why he wasn't interested. And now that I know what he's looking for, I even know when Nona gave it to her. But there have been times when he was just short of rude to her. I can't imagine what happened at my wedding, but they were distinctly ill at ease in each other's company." Felicia shifted in her seat, staring off across the room for a moment, then continued. "I even tried to warn her off. I didn't know what he was looking for, you see. I've seen that statuette so many times, but never once did I ask her where she got it—or even wonder why she had it."

Tina was silent for a long time, obviously waiting for Felicia to continue.

"Are you going to tell me who she is?" she finally demanded. "I don't want you to have all the fun watching the two of them."

Felicia's smile was suddenly mischievous as she answered, "It serves him right. She'll make him work for it—her parents are probably the only ones I know who will let her say no if she wants to. He won't be able to just offer for her and expect her parents will make her accept."

Silence fell again.

"Well?" Tina's voice was pure impatience.

Felicia relaxed against the back of the sofa and laughed. "It's......"

Lady Amanda Cookeson looked up from her book as her father, the Earl of Barrington, entered his library. Comfortably ensconced in a cushioned window seat, she hadn't expected him to return until much later and had decided to indulge herself with her favorite pastime before tea. He noticed her as he rounded his desk.

"Ah, so this is where you've been hiding," he said affably. As he glanced down at her lap, his smile dimmed. "What are you reading now?"

"Oh, just a book I found in here," she answered, dismissively.

"What book?"

She regarded him warily as she closed the book. "Why do you want to know?"

"For the same reason you don't want to tell me."

She fidgeted on the seat. She knew he hoped it was one of those gothic novels or pieces of fluff normally enjoyed by women, but as usual he was to be disappointed.

"Honestly, Papa. There's nothing wrong with me reading Homer. He just writes stories, after all."

The earl rolled his eyes heavenward. "Yes, but his stories are written in Greek."

"Yes, well—" she licked her lips, "—that's true, but—"

"Amanda, I've told you before. If your reading habits get out, no man will want you."

"I know, Papa. But if a man can't abide a woman with a brain, then maybe *I* don't want *him.*"

The door to the library opened, interrupting the long-standing argument.

"Here you are." The Countess of Barrington looked in.

Amanda looked away from her father and addressed her

advancing stepmother. "Were you looking for me?"

"Oh, no," the countess replied, shaking her golden head. "I was looking for your father, but I'm glad I found both of you together." Glancing down at the book in Amanda's lap, she looked into her husband's annoyed countenance, slipped her arm through his and said, "It's time for tea. I told Barrons to put it in the drawing room."

The earl looked down into his wife's eyes. "I only stopped in the library to check on some papers, and found Amanda here instead. But I can attend to them later." He smiled and, turning, allowed himself to be led toward the door.

"You must join us as well, Amanda," the countess said. Looking back over her shoulder, she winked conspiratorially at Amanda and towed her husband from the room.

Amanda sank back against the cushion and sighed. Saved again. Thank heavens her stepmother came in when she did. Her father did not approve of women knowing too much. He was constantly telling her she would never land a good husband if she knew too much. Men, he insisted, didn't want bluestockings for wives.

Picking herself up, she followed her parents out, stopping only long enough to entrust her book to a footman to ensure that it found its way to her room. She would be better off if she confined her reading to her room, or at least one of the sitting rooms, from now on. Every time she had a discussion with her father over her reading habits, she promised herself to do just that. Unfortunately, the library was a much more comfortable place in which to indulge and she found herself there often, regardless of her decision to avoid her father's book-lined sanctuary.

"I heard a rumor the Earl of Wynton has returned," Eliza said casually over tea. "I would guess his sisters are glad to have him back."

"Most likely," the earl agreed.

Amanda said nothing, although she noticed her stepmother looking her way. Putting down her teacup, she took a bite of their cook's delicious seed cake to cover her agitation. She refused to let her unease show.

Fourteen years ago, she had fallen hopelessly in love with

her best friend's brother. At age seven, however, it was little more than hero worship. When she was presented to him at her debut three years ago and discovered he was an earl, it was as if the intervening time never happened. Chasing him through that one Season had shown her that feelings weren't always reciprocated, but naïvely she was determined to wait him out. Sooner or later he would realize they belonged together. Instead, after one disastrous encounter at his family seat, he left the country.

She still had feelings for him, but resolved to treat them impassively. She should have given up on the elusive Earl of Wynton by now. He had been gone from England for three years. She was now in her fourth Season, and tired of waiting. She wanted a home and family of her own. She would bestow her favors on someone more appreciative. Like Viscount Thurston.

As if he read her thoughts, her father asked, "Have you an answer for Thurston yet?"

The word yes was on the tip of her tongue, but she couldn't utter it. "No," she answered.

Her father frowned. "If you wait too long, someone else will come along and divert his attention."

Amanda wondered if her father knew he made men sound like capricious, but pompous, idiots.

"I think tonight I will ask him if he likes Homer."

"You will do no such thing!"

"And why not?" she asked, ignoring his bluster. "If I accept him, I will have to live with him. It would be nice to know whether his views on reading material for women coincide with yours."

"And...?"

She smiled at the curiosity in her father's voice. "If they do, then my answer is no."

The countess's laughter broke into their squabbling. Amanda knew her stepmother considered both of them stubborn and recalcitrant. Like children who liked nothing better than to bicker.

"Stop it, you two," she scolded. "Trent, you must leave Amanda to her own pursuits, and Amanda, you must not bait your father that way. We have been over this before and neither of you will relent, so why do you continue?"

Amanda sighed and sat back. "I'm sorry, Eliza, Papa. I shouldn't have said that last. Lord Thurston has given me until the end of the week. I will give him my answer on Friday as I promised." Then she excused herself and went up to her room.

Ringing for her maid, she shed her dress and corset for a comfortable gown and wrapper, then declared her intention to rest until it was time to dress for dinner. Trying to continue reading, she found she couldn't concentrate on the words before her. Instead the past rose to taunt her.

Three years ago she had been eighteen, full of wonder and promise, naïve, innocent, and in love. At least she thought she had been. It was her first Season and her come-out had been a success.

Her best friend, Lady Felicia Collings, had been in her second Season and the two of them had been nearly inseparable. Felicia's oldest brother, the Marquis of Thanet, had taken his wife to Italy to recover from the loss of their second child, but her other brother, the Earl of Wynton, had been initially attentive, but no more so than any other young man. And that was where she'd made her mistake.

She glanced at her bedside table, on which sat the black statuette Nona had given her. In the aftermath of her mother's death less than a year later, she had retreated into her own world. Lost and uncertain, the panther had become her protector, and with the faith of a child, she always felt safe with it near. Through her fertile imagination, she had woven story upon story around the prince Nona had told her about and how he would someday come and rescue her.

From the moment she had been reintroduced to Felicia's brother, she had known her panther represented him—that he was the only one for her. Hadn't she told Nona JoJo was her prince? So what if he was an earl now?

It didn't help her imagination that he had hair as black as the onyx her panther was carved from, emerald green eyes, and moved with the easy grace and self-assurance of one who knew his place in the world. She'd also learned, as the Season progressed, that many viewed him as a sleek jungle cat—

graceful, but deadly if provoked. It was common knowledge he was a crack shot and could regularly be found at the boxing salon.

Unfortunately, he had not returned her feelings and when it was obvious she had him in her sights, he began to avoid her. It was also evident he didn't remember the seven-year-old girl who, as a youth of sixteen, he had taught to swim one magical summer in the Lake District. He wasn't likely to remember her name. Katie had been a nickname her mother used, and he and Felicia both hadn't used their own names. She'd learned from Felicia that Nona insisted on using short names for them so they could not be identified.

Then an old scandal had erupted around them with the return of her stepmother's brother, his subsequent marriage to Felicia, and the death of their father, all within a month's time. Ironically, it was during the time before Felicia's wedding that her own hopes and dreams were brutally crushed. Closing her eyes, she could believe it only happened yesterday.

It was the day before the wedding. Immediately after luncheon, she had been at loose ends. Eliza was closeted with the dowager Countess of Wynton, the Duchess of Westover, and the Countess of Weston, finalizing wedding arrangements. Eliza's stepmother, the Duchess of Warringham, was nowhere to be found. Felicia and her fiancée had disappeared, and so had the rest of the men. Finding a book to read seemed the best course and with everyone gone she thought there would be no one in the library.

As she descended the grand staircase in the front hall, she had envisioned herself as mistress of Wynton Abbey, the earl's family seat. It was a beautiful home built on the ruins of an old Cistercian Abbey with extensive grounds. She could easily see herself conferring with the cook on the week's menus, the housekeeper on which rooms needed refurbishing, the gardener on which flowers to plant, and so on.

The library door stood slightly ajar, leading her to believe it was empty. Slipping inside, she closed the door quietly behind her. Her father often scolded her on her voracious appetite for books, so she never allowed anyone to catch her reading.

The library was immense. Floor-to-ceiling bookshelves lined

the inner wall as well as the outer wall, only broken up by the tall windows interspersed between them. Standing just inside the door, she looked around her in wonder, eyes alight at the thought of having all these books at her disposal. When she was mistress here, she promised herself, she'd read every single one. Moving into the room, she approached a nearby bookshelf, scanning the titles.

With the heavy burgundy drapes pulled back from the windows, she needed no light to peruse the shelves. The Aubusson carpet muffled the sound of her footsteps as she moved further into the room, her eyes picking out titles on the shelves.

She had stopped before a shelf, her eye caught by a specific title, when she sensed she was no longer alone. The hairs on the back of her neck rose and, spinning around, she came face to face with the earl.

"Oh." It was all she could think to say as that hooded emerald gaze raked her from head to toe. Sun-browned skin stretched over high, carved cheekbones, with ebony hair and brows, and a straight nose over full lips. He was too handsome for his own good, she thought. She knew she wasn't the only one interested in him, but she already considered him hers— she had prior claim, after all. It was unfortunate he didn't seem to realize it.

"Looking for something?" His smooth, rich voice was like velvet in her ears.

"I-I," she had stammered, searching for an excuse to be there. She refused to tell him she had come for a book, so she took the only other out she could think of. "I was looking for you."

One dark eyebrow rose. Crossing his arms over his broad chest, he rocked back on his heels and regarded her suspiciously. "Well, now you've found me. How can I be of assistance?"

Nervously licking suddenly dry lips, she said the first thing that came to mind. "Why don't you like me?" And instantly wished the floor would open up and swallow her whole. It took a supreme effort not to clap her hand over her mouth. Instead she looked away, across the room—and spied the small table covered with papers and the chair beside it at which he had obviously been working.

There was a huge cherrywood desk at the other side of the room. She'd noticed it—and the fact that it was empty—when she entered. Why hadn't he been working there?

Rooted to the floor by nothing more than severe embarrassment, she jumped when she felt his hand beneath her chin, turning her face around and up to his. He suddenly seemed closer and the room much warmer.

"And what makes you think I don't like you?" His voice deepened and it took all her willpower to stay upright.

"You avoid me all the time," she said faintly, and felt her insides curl at the patronizing look on his face.

"I don't think I avoid you any more than anyone else."

The hand under her chin trailed down to the base of her throat, one long finger resting on the furiously beating pulse. For a moment she was deliciously lightheaded as blood pumped through her whole body. Even if his finger hadn't been resting on her pulse, he had to know how fast her heart was beating. She was sure he could hear it.

"Don't speak to me like that." She barely kept her voice even.

He smiled, his eyes warming, and her senses shifted into high alert. "Like what?" Now she knew why he'd been likened to a predator.

"Like you speak to Felicia." She lifted her chin. "I'm not your little sister."

His eyes burned into hers for what seemed like an eternity, then he bent his head. His mouth stopped less than a hairsbreadth away, and she allowed her eyelids to drop.

"No, you're not, are you?" he murmured, then he crushed her lips beneath his.

Her world careened out of control in an instant. His lips were cool and firm against hers and his hand slipped around to the back of her neck, cradling it, as his other arm circled her back, holding her motionless against him. At the first touch of his lips, her hands moved upwards, ostensibly to steady herself. Resting on his solidly muscled chest, she could feel the rapid tattoo of his heart beneath her palms. She wondered vaguely if it always beat that fast.

The touch of his tongue along her lower lip had her gasping, parting her lips in surprise, and moments later he swept in to taste. There was no quarter asked, and none given as Jon kissed her with a passion that curled her toes. Her blood heated and warmth gathered in her lower belly. She forgot to breathe until her lungs forced her to draw air from him.

This was what she had been waiting for. What she had been born for. What she had been promised by his great-grandmother. Despite all that, nothing could have prepared her for the feeling of melting into him, of nearly being absorbed by him, and the feeling of loss which occurred when he raised his head.

She barely heard the strangled groan that came from his throat before her shoulders were grasped and she was unceremoniously pushed away from him and held at arm's length. The hands gripping her upper arms were bruising in their intensity, but she was thankful for the discomfort, for it allowed her mind to return from wherever it had wandered.

I love you—the words were on the tip of her tongue, but never uttered. At least she had been saved that final humiliation, for the earl had blasted her with a freezing glare from his emerald eyes, then let go of her as if she were suddenly a red-hot coal. She nearly collapsed, so weak were her legs.

"Get out!" he bit off savagely, turning away from her. "And don't come near me again or I won't be responsible for my actions." He was struggling with himself, breathing heavily, and she wondered if he was unwell.

Yet she had stood there, knowing her heart was in her eyes, unable to stop the gathering of tears. And when they began to slip down her cheeks and her hard-won control deserted her altogether, she fled to her room, leaving the library door standing open.

"Never again!" she vowed. Never again would anyone hurt her like that. She would marry because she wanted to, but she would not allow herself to love again.

After Felicia's wedding, she had returned to London and thrown herself back into the Season, yet maintaining the brittle facade she'd developed was exhausting. She was almost thankful for the mourning period she had been required to observe in the wake of Eliza's father's death. It allowed her to firmly cement her new persona in place. That the earl left the country not long after the duke's death made her transformation easier.

He had been gone for three years. She had nearly accepted at least two proposals in that time, but each time just couldn't convince herself to say the word, still yearning for something she told herself she should not want and could not have.

And her panther mocked her for trying to run from her own destiny.

Chapter Two

"Here you are." Felicia handed Jon a folded slip of paper. "There are ten names there. All young women who were at Miss Ridley's when I was."

Jon looked down at her as she stood beside him watching the dancers dip and swirl across Lord Marsden's ballroom. In a pink watered-silk gown with sapphires flashing at her neck and in her ears, she looked like a sweet confection. He did not doubt hungry eyes followed her about the room, but was equally as sure no one dared poach.

Unfolding the sheet of paper, he scanned the names. Catherine Hargrave. Susanna Marsden. Theresa Winston. Beatrice Wyndham-Smythe. Amanda Cookeson. Elise Harbington. His heart suddenly stopped and his eyes moved back up one name. Amanda Cookeson. He nearly groaned aloud and wondered if his sister had developed a mean streak in the last three years.

Refocusing, he forced himself to finish the list. Ellen Stimpingston. MaryAnne Lester. Carol Tinning. Sophie Lawrence.

Forcing his voice into a calm he didn't feel, he said, "No one too onerous. Did you cull the list?"

She grinned as he folded the paper and slipped it inside his coat. "Don't forget. I know who you're looking for. So I thought I could at least leave off the worst of the possible candidates."

"Such as...?"

"Did you really want to spend time with Diana Houghton?"

"Good God, is she still around?"

Felicia nodded. "And worse than ever."

Jon visibly shuddered at the thought of the red-haired harpy whose sharp tongue and hateful disposition had reduced more than one debutante to tears. She was pretty enough, but he didn't want a hateful shrew for a wife.

"And have you had many run-ins with her?"

"No." A slightly naughty smile appeared. "She gives me a wide berth these days."

"Why?"

"Because she wants to continue to enjoy the good graces of most of society's hostesses. It would only take one encounter with me, and she'd never receive another invitation," she replied with the confidence of a duchess.

Jon was still laughing when Felicia's husband appeared. Brand Waring, Duke of Warringham, was slightly taller than he was, with dark gold hair and violet-hued eyes. His large but lean frame moved with a casual grace, but Jon knew how fast he could move when necessary. Felicia and her friend, Geri, the Duchess of Westover, often referred to him as a lion, an apt metaphor.

"So," the duke began, "now that you're back, I understand you've consulted my wife on matchmaking."

"Brand!" Felicia rounded on her husband. "Don't tease."

Brand chuckled. "Sorry, love. I couldn't resist."

Jon grimaced. Scanning the floor, he thought he recognized a number of the young ladies on his list, but couldn't be sure. There were at least three he didn't know at all and a fourth whose name was familiar, but her visage was lost. Before the night was through, he planned to at least get a look at all of them. He'd worry about talking with them in the coming weeks.

He suddenly stilled as his eyes met a pair of sky blue ones across the room. Her eyes widened but she did not look away. Instead she openly inspected him for a moment before turning back to her companions.

"You do remember how to dance, don't you?" Felicia's voice brought him back to the present. Frowning at his inattention, she glanced in the direction of his gaze, then turned back, speculation in hers.

"Of course," he replied automatically. Offering her his arm, he said, "Shall we?"

He was out of practice, but the steps came back easily enough. "So, when do you plan to start?" she asked him when the pattern of the quadrille brought them together.

"Perhaps tonight," he answered. "I am acquainted with the first two on the list. Perhaps I will dance with each of them once." He reminded himself he wasn't looking for a wife, but it would do no harm to be charming to a few young ladies. If he spread himself thin enough, no one would know he was looking for someone in particular.

When they returned to Brand's side, Tina and her husband, Jay, had joined him, along with Brand's sister, Eliza, and her stepdaughter, Amanda.

"I wasn't sure the rumor was true," Eliza said to him in greeting. "But I'm glad to see it is."

"I'm afraid even unwelcome gossip occasionally turns out to be so," he replied smoothly, bowing over her hand. Then he turned to greet Amanda.

Her tension was palpable and he wondered why no one else seemed to notice, yet she curtsied and greeted him in a normal voice. She hadn't changed much. She was still stunningly beautiful with large blue eyes in a heart-shaped face, an elegantly slim nose and bow-shaped mouth. He tried not to remember how soft that full bottom lip was. Yet he had not forgotten how perfectly her curves had fit against him, or the softness of her skin. The scent of honeysuckle wafted to him and he breathed deeply, the fragrance calming his racing heart.

Their small party stood together chatting, with Eliza asking him questions about his travels and whether he intended to stay put this time. He could feel Amanda's eyes on him as he tried to concentrate on Eliza's questions and wondered why it was suddenly so warm in the room.

He knew he hadn't changed much in the three years he'd been gone, but he wondered all the same what she found so interesting. He'd always towered over his sisters, but now he seemed to tower over her as well, although she was taller than both Felicia and Tina. Perhaps it was just his imagination.

A young man approached the group. Amanda smiled at him as he spoke to her, then turned and excused herself. A waltz was beginning and he watched as she went gracefully into the young man's arms. Gritting his teeth, he turned back to answer another of Eliza's questions about his travels.

Felicia and Tina spent most of the evening watching Jon and Amanda. They both noticed Amanda did not return to their small group until Jon left, and she managed to disappear whenever he was there. They found her actions curious.

"I could have sworn she had feelings for him three years ago," Felicia said to Tina as they climbed the stairs to one of the withdrawing rooms.

"Perhaps she did. But three years is a long time—and you said yourself you thought something happened between them at the Abbey."

Felicia didn't respond as they entered the brightly lit room. They were silent as they checked their hair and gowns for dangling curls and threads, and applied cool towels to faces and throats.

On the way back to the ballroom, Tina turned to Felicia. "How long do you think it will take him to figure out he's looking for Amanda?"

"That depends. He already knows I only gave him a select list. There was no use putting women on it I knew didn't belong there and might be more trouble than they were worth."

Reaching the top of the stairs, Tina looked out over the assemblage. As with most entertainments, it was a veritable crush on the ballroom floor. She found her own husband instantly, his chestnut hair gleaming in the candlelight. Brand stood beside him. They were deep in a discussion which, no doubt, concerned their joint shipping business. She could see Jon dancing with a tall brunette, but Amanda was nowhere to be found. She frowned.

"Do you see Amanda at all?" she asked Felicia.

"No," was the reply after a cursory sweep of the room. "Why?"

"Curiosity. Who is Jon dancing with?"

Felicia scanned the room and found the pair. "That's Susanna Marsden." She chuckled. "At least he hasn't lost his common sense. I put Susanna on the list precisely because we would be here tonight."

Tina frowned. "I heard a rumor she might be spoken for already."

Felicia nodded. "It's true, but everyone who went to school with her knows she can't abide cats in any shape or form. Even mentioning them in her presence is likely to provoke a distinctly hostile reaction. You should have seen the scene she caused over Amanda's panther at school. She absolutely refused to enter Amanda's room again after that."

"Do you think she'll remember and say something to him if he mentions a panther?"

Felicia seemed thoughtful for a moment before replying. "I suspect she's forgotten. At least, I'm hoping she has." She lifted a shoulder in a small shrug. "If she does, then he'll know that much sooner."

The set ended and Jon and his partner began to stroll the perimeter of the room, stopping to talk briefly with others as they moved.

Descending the staircase, Felicia and Tina met them, spoke briefly, then moved on, reaching their own husbands just as the band was striking up another waltz. Leaving Jon to his own devices, they danced with their spouses and left soon afterwards.

Jon threw himself into a corner of his carriage as the door shut behind him. Moments later the conveyance began to move and he let out a huge breath, relaxing into the velvet-covered cushions. If tonight was anything to go by, he'd be a candidate for Bedlam well before the end of what was left of the Season.

He pulled out the list Felicia had given him. Why he'd asked her to provide him with a list, he wasn't sure. Perhaps he thought she'd give him a clue as to who he was looking for on it. Maybe she had and he hadn't discovered it yet. What she had given him was a variety.

Blondes of every shade, redheads, brunettes and all the colors in between. Blue eyes, grey eyes, brown eyes, black eyes, and even one with eyes that mirrored his own. Tall, short, average, pleasingly plump, slim, svelte, rounded and not so rounded. She must have worked long and hard on the list in order to ensure there was little to do in the way of comparison.

She had been right about one thing, though. He had only spoken directly to two of the women on the list, but their reactions had not been very welcoming. Susanna Marsden openly took him to task over his near-rudeness three years ago, then informed him she would be returning to the country after this Season to marry a neighbor with whom she had a long-standing acquaintance. Thank God she wasn't who he was looking for. A passing reference to a cat had elicited a visible shiver of distaste.

Lady Catherine Hargrave was an empty-headed piece of fluff. She hadn't even known what a panther was, and her large grey eyes went completely blank once she was no longer the topic of conversation. She would make someone who was looking for a biddable but simple wife the perfect spouse. Thankfully, not him.

His eye unerringly went to one name on the list.

Amanda.

He'd hoped three years would have dimmed the attraction he felt. Had thought it had—until tonight. Seeing her again brought back all the memories he'd suppressed. Touching her, even momentarily, was enough to cause him to react physically. But the worst had been watching her walk away on another man's arm, smiling up at him as if she hadn't a care in the world, when only moments before she'd stood tense and stiff beside him wishing, he was sure, she was anywhere but there.

She had looked at him like that once upon a time. Before he'd kissed her. Before he let his emotions get the best of him. Before he'd destroyed her hopes and dreams. He'd watched them crumble in the aftermath of that kiss and known he was responsible. She had not forgiven him—probably never would.

Perhaps it was for the best. She was the only woman who had ever gotten under his skin. The only one who could provoke a reaction in him. He didn't need that kind of attachment. Not only did he not want a clingy, dependent woman as a wife, he didn't want to become emotionally attached to the woman he married, either.

He wondered briefly if Felicia hadn't put her on the list to torture him. But Felicia hadn't known about the encounter at the Abbey. Amanda had avoided him once Felicia and Brand were gone, pleading a headache in order to retire early in the evening. Even later, at The Downs for Brand's father's funeral, she made excuses not to be in his company. The one time Felicia and Eliza had thrown them together had been distinctly uncomfortable.

He may as well cross her off the list now. Yet somehow, he couldn't. He'd promised himself this afternoon he would work through whatever list Felicia gave him in an orderly fashion, eliminating candidates only after speaking to them personally, until he found the one he was looking for. He owed Nona, and himself, that much of a search. Not that he intended to fall in love with the woman with the statue—he just wanted to know who she was.

There was no doubt he would eventually marry. He was the last of the Kentons, and possibly would be the last Earl of Wynton if he didn't marry and beget an heir. There had been a time when that wasn't true.

The coach slowed and came to a stop. Moments later the door opened and he stepped out and climbed the steps to his home. Sending his butler to bed, he headed for the library and poured himself a large brandy. Holding the balloon-shaped glass in one hand, he idly flipped through the correspondence on his desk as he sipped.

Finding nothing that couldn't wait until morning, he left the room and headed upstairs. He was tired, but would get little sleep tonight. Amanda had done that to him.

His valet, on his orders, hadn't waited up for him. Undressing, he shrugged into a dressing gown of black silk and went to the window. Still sipping his brandy, he stared into the darkness and relived his past.

He could admit to himself now that he had fallen for Amanda. She was a breath of fresh air in the stale world of London society, yet the embodiment of all that was English. All that he was not. Young and innocent, her wide blue eyes made promises she had no idea how to keep. He'd wanted to be the one she kept those promises to. But he'd been afraid to acknowledge his attraction.

At the time, he told himself he wasn't looking for his figurine. He still had to make sure Felicia found the person who could identify her ring. When it became obvious Amanda had him in her sights, fear had kicked in.

Then came the disastrous meeting at the Abbey. The taste and feel of her was permanently imprinted in his memory. Burned into his senses. He'd spent the last three years trying to forget her. Trying to lose himself in other interests and pursuits.

Instead, she haunted him. In Italy he saw her magnificent eyes in the intense blue waters of the Mediterranean. In Greece he saw her in the golden sand of the sun-washed beaches. In France he saw her in the beautiful gowns of the women of the French court. No matter where he went or what he did, something reminded him of her.

Resisting the impulse to ask Felicia directly about her in their correspondence, he had, nevertheless, scanned his sister's letters avidly for news of her. And even though Felicia never mentioned a marriage, he had been convinced Amanda would be married with a babe in arms by the time he returned.

Only she wasn't. And she was on his list.

What if she had the statuette? The thought came out of the blue like a bolt of lightning. He froze at the possibility. It couldn't be. Fate could not be that cruel. But Nona said the woman with the statuette was his destiny. His mate. Could that explain his attraction to her?

He didn't want his destiny. He only needed a wife to give him sons to carry on his title. Then she could go her way and he could go his. If he married his destiny he suspected that would not be possible.

Despite his scientific and logical bent, he knew better than to underestimate his great-grandmother's otherworldly intuitiveness. Marrying someone destined to fall in love with him would cause untold misery to that person if he did not reciprocate.

Turning from the window, he put down the now empty glass, shrugged out of his robe and slipped between cool sheets. And wondered what he would do if it turned out Amanda was the person he was looking for.

Amanda stared at the canopy above her head. She had done well. The earl had not noticed her nervousness tonight. Neither had Lord Thurston. So far, so good. But how long could she keep it up?

Avoiding Jon all evening had turned into an exhausting endeavor. There had been one moment when she thought she could face him again. Their eyes met across the ballroom. She had been caught watching him. Instead of looking away, she'd stared at him for a few moments, before casually turning back to respond to a comment. It had given her the courage to accompany Eliza across the room while Jon and Felicia danced. But she underestimated the strength of the feelings she still harbored.

Tense and uncomfortable, she had stood beside him, outwardly calm but surreptitiously studying him, while Eliza peppered him with questions about his travels. Ordinarily she would have been interested in his replies, but she hadn't been able to think clearly enough to pay attention.

He had not changed much in the three years he'd been gone. Perhaps it was just her vulnerability which made him seem taller than before. His skin, tanned to a healthy golden hue, might be repugnant to some, but not her. She had to stop herself from remembering the feel of his lips on hers, from wanting to repeat the experience once again.

When Lord Thurston appeared to claim her for a set, she had been relieved, smiling up at him with a warmth she hadn't quite intended.

Now she was torn. She had promised Lord Thurston an answer by the end of the week. Three days away. Then what? Or, more to the point, could she say yes as she originally planned?

"Why now?" she demanded out loud in the darkness. "Why couldn't you have waited another week to return?"

In another week, she would have been happily planning her wedding. All thoughts of him would have been unimportant. She and Eliza would be making lists, planning food, deciding where and when, making appointments to begin the fittings for her wedding dress, and all those other myriad things that seem to need to be done when planning a wedding. She wouldn't have had time to think about the Earl of Wynton.

Liar!

The whisper seemed to come from beside her and she turned, only to have her gaze fall on the statuette. Reaching for the figurine, she dragged it into bed with her and cuddled it close.

"You were supposed to keep me safe, JoJo," she whispered to it. "But who was supposed to save me from you?"

No one. She knew it without the words having floated through her head. No one should be needed to save her from him. He was her destiny. Nona said so. She didn't need to be saved from him. So, why couldn't she just accept it and wait for him to realize it?

For how long? How long should she wait to see if he came to his senses? What if he never did? She was tired of waiting. She wanted a home and family of her own. And what if she waited and he married someone else? How long was she willing to give him to realize Nona's dream?

She stroked the smooth surface of the panther's back and closed her eyes. She could still see him at sixteen. Already tall and lanky, with a gentle kindness in his manner toward a perfect stranger—and a little girl at that. The sight and smells of the Lake District returned. She could almost feel the cool water as it sluiced over her skin. The smell of sunshine and the forest.

JoJo was her prince. Hadn't she told Nona so? So, what should she do about it?

She had three days to see what happened, then she would decide whether she would marry Lord Thurston, or consider the Earl of Wynton worth waiting for.

Jon spent most of the next two days closeted with his solicitor and secretary, receiving an accounting of his properties, making decisions, and signing orders. Three years was too long, he decided. He'd never leave for such a long period of time again.

Finished for today, he pulled his watch out of his pocket to check the time. The fob caught his eye and a piece of his last conversation with Nona floated through his head.

"I have much to tell you," Nona said in a soft voice. Gesturing to the chest beside her bunk, she had him find and remove a small, intricately carved box. On the top was etched the figure of a panther in motion, its sleek grace almost lifelike. The sides showed the same jungle cat in various poses, including at rest on the back.

The box reminded him of something else and he looked around the *vardo*, seeking, but not finding, a particular object.

"It is not here," Nona told him. "It has not been here for many years."

He turned back to her, surprise in his eyes. "But you promised—"

"I promised it to you, yes, but you must seek out your destiny. When you find her, you will find all you have been promised."

The box Nona gave him that day had not been empty. Inside he discovered a gold watch fob in the shape of a large cat. To remind him, Nona had told him, of his destiny.

White's was quiet during the late afternoon. Jon liked the solitude of sitting and reading *The Times* while sipping a glass of Madeira. He hadn't been there long when he heard someone take the chair across the small table from him. Lowering the paper, he discovered he had been joined by one of his brothers-in-law.

"Anything interesting in there?" Brand indicated the paper.

Re-folding the sheet and putting it down, Jon shook his head. "No. Just the usual." He was surprised how little had changed in three years. Two afternoons of reading the paper reminded him of that.

A waiter approached and asked Brand if he wanted anything. Brand declined and turned to Jon.

"I'm assuming you didn't do anything too scandalous on the Continent, or we'd have seen you long before this."

Jon chuckled. "It depends whether you consider consulting with doctors and visiting hospitals from Paris to Athens scandalous."

A golden eyebrow rose. "Did you at least meet some

interesting people?"

"Vienna was lovely. I happened to be at the home of the English Consul when an invitation arrived for an Imperial ball. He invited me along. It was an interesting evening."

"So, is the empress as beautiful in person as the stories say?"

Jon shrugged. "She is certainly lovely, but very unhappy I would guess. She made a token appearance, spoke to a few people, then left as early as decently possible."

"And you?"

"I enjoyed myself, but if I'd wanted to spend all my time at balls and parties, I'd have stayed home. I spent most of my time tracking down and speaking to Semmelweis's colleagues. I'd read some of his studies, but he died the year before I made it to Vienna, so I had to console myself with meeting people who'd known him. Unfortunately, they weren't very complimentary about his research and findings. Too bad. I think he had something."

"Semmelweis?"

Jon grinned. "Felicia would tell you not to get me started talking about medicine. It's probably the only topic I find wholly fascinating, but most would consider either boring or beneath me."

"Perhaps some would, but I know Felicia regards your medical skills highly."

"Sisters tend to do that."

Jon emptied the rest of the liquid from the decanter into his glass.

"You still haven't answered my question," Brand said, adding, "and, before you consider it patronizing, yes, I'm interested."

Jon took a sip of his drink. "Very well, without going into too much detail, Semmelweis was a physician at the Vienna General Hospital who did some experiments regarding the relationship between cleanliness and childbed fever. He concluded that just the act of washing your hands between patients could cut down on the mortality rate caused by infection. I found his work interesting, so I wanted to speak to him about it."

"Then it's too bad he died before you got a chance."

Jon nodded. "Despite that no one paid him any heed, I think he had a good point. And Dr. Lister at King's College Hospital agrees."

Chapter Three

Viscount Martindale's mansion in Mayfair was ablaze with light, the glow so bright it could be seen from a considerable distance away. Jon encountered Felicia in the crowd shortly after his arrival. Tonight she was attired in sapphire blue. Her dark hair was piled artfully atop her head, diamonds winking from the coiffure like stars in a night sky, complementing the necklace and earbobs she wore.

"Jon! I'm glad to see you." She slipped her arm through his. As they strolled, she pointed out a couple of the women on his list.

A young woman stepped into their path. She hadn't done so deliberately as she was looking the other way, but Felicia spoke to her, nevertheless.

"How nice to see you again, Miss Harbington."

Elise Harbington spun around in surprise and Jon found himself looking at a woman nearly as tall as himself. Somewhat pretty features combined with brown hair and eyes made her not quite memorable, but he nevertheless spoke politely to her once Felicia introduced them, even garnering a promise of a cotillion later in the evening.

"You'll like her," Felicia said as they moved away. "She might not be beautiful, but she's not an idiot."

Jon's chuckle had her turning to look up at him. "As opposed to Catherine Hargrave."

She sputtered. "I'm sorry about that, but I wanted to come up with an even number. It was either her or Diana Houghton and I wasn't sure you'd forgive me if I put Miss Houghton on the list."

Jon slanted a surprised glance in her direction.

"You might be right."

"Have you met Theresa Winston, yet?" she asked and, when he shook his head, offered, "I'll introduce you. She's Martindale's oldest, but tonight's ball is for her younger sister, Lillian."

Although he knew who she was, he had never been introduced to her. As Felicia performed the introductions, a country reel was forming and Jon took the opportunity to try to speak with her while dancing. He found, however, that it was extremely disconcerting to dance with someone who insisted on searching the rest of the dance floor for someone else. His prepared remarks, designed to direct their conversation in such a way to ask about a small statuette of a panther, fell on deaf ears. In the end, it was with severe frustration he mentally crossed her off the list without an affirmative declaration she did not have what he was looking for. Perhaps he'd try again another time.

Returning Miss Winston to her mother's side, he took his leave and headed for the refreshment table. He needed a drink.

"Wynton! How are you? I heard you were back." Jon looked up from the glass of champagne and spied an old friend from Oxford approaching. The two men spent some time catching up on each other's lives until he remembered the promised cotillion.

Elise Harbington was an interesting young woman and he discovered he actually enjoyed their time on the dance floor. Intelligent and articulate without the artifice many young women cultivate, once he discovered she did not have the statuette, he was a bit disappointed. But not for long as it occurred to him that once he found the woman with the panther, Elise might make a very nice choice for a spouse. She was everything he sought in a wife—amiable, intelligent, somewhat attractive and, most importantly, she did not incite an ounce of passion in his blood. The possibility had him smiling as, after returning Elise to her chaperone, he came upon Felicia and Amanda with a group of acquaintances.

Amanda stood chatting with Felicia, Lord Thurston and three other friends when she felt a presence behind her. A small shiver of awareness snaked down her spine, as Felicia looked up and smiled at whoever approached.

Jon did not seem to notice her paralysis as Felicia drew him into the group to stand between her and Amanda. He greeted her and the rest of the small group evenly as Felicia performed the introductions. Charity Bascomb, a petite redhead with large green eyes, did nothing to disguise her interest, and Amanda bristled at her bright smile. Martha Danvers did little more than mumble her greetings and present an awkward curtsy. Viscount Thurston and Lord Carver greeted him enthusiastically, launching into a discussion of the political situation on the Continent until Felicia cut them off and steered the conversation back into more general topics. She noticed he smothered a smile at the adroit way Felicia handled the two young men.

Standing beside him, Amanda was keenly aware of him. When someone jostled her from behind and her shoulder brushed his arm, a tingling began in her shoulder. For a moment, she forgot she was in the middle of a crowded ballroom and nearly clutched at him for balance. Curling her hands into fists to prevent herself from acting rashly, she tried desperately to concentrate on the conversation swirling around her.

A quadrille began forming on the dance floor, and Jon turned to Martha. Amanda watched, attempting to conceal her jealousy, as he escorted Miss Danvers onto the floor. Martha was an excellent dancer and Amanda was aware that on the floor she was often a different person, her face lighting up and somber dark eyes sparkling with excitement. Upon their return to the group, she would once again become silent and withdrawn. Lord Thurston often remarked on the transformation. She wondered what Jon would make of it.

The next set was a waltz. She'd already danced an earlier waltz with Thurston, so she was not surprised when he solicited Miss Danvers' hand, while Lord Carver turned to Miss Bascomb. That left her with Jon. She waited for what seemed like eternity for him to turn to her.

"Shall we?" His deep voice invaded her befuddled thoughts.

Tongue-tied, she merely nodded and put her hand on his

arm.

"You are looking quite lovely this evening." The compliment rolled off his tongue as they whirled down the floor. Her heart was thumping wildly in her chest, the blood drumming in her ears. She still hadn't looked him directly in the face.

"Thank you," she managed breathlessly. His breath, warm and moist, stirred the curls at her temple and she caught a whiff of soap and another scent she couldn't identify. A chuckle above her head caught her attention and she looked up into smiling green eyes.

That smile caused her heart to skip a beat and she had to blink to cover the awkwardness. She could not allow him to affect her like this. He was only being nice to her because she was his sister's friend. The same thing had happened three years ago. Only then she had mistaken his friendship for something more. She would not make that mistake again. This time she was certain he had nothing more than politeness on his mind. Unfortunately, her heart stubbornly refused to believe it.

Heat washed over her, causing her to catch her breath and miss a step all at once. He caught her, momentarily pulling her closer. The hand on her waist burned her through the layers of silk and cotton, tendrils of heat radiating from that point to engulf her completely.

She should make some attempt at conversation, but she hadn't a coherent thought in her head. Her senses were caught up in his presence and the spell he was weaving around her. If this dance didn't end soon, she'd end up a puddle on the floor at his feet.

"Careful," he said when she missed another step.

She mentally shook herself, ruthlessly scolding her wayward emotions.

"I'm sorry. I'm being horribly rude."

He smiled again, flashing perfectly even, white teeth. That traitorous organ in her chest stopped beating for a full half-second.

"You are obviously distracted. But I don't mind. One does not always need to talk during a dance."

His understanding made her feel like an imbecile. Pulling

herself together, she asked him about his travels.

"Did you see anything particularly interesting?"

He blinked at the question, then answered smoothly, "Actually I saw quite a few things some might call interesting."

"Such as?" She was only partially listening. The sound of his voice was easy on her ears and she just wanted to listen to it.

"Hmmm." He seemed to be thinking for a moment. "In Rome I came across a small menagerie."

"A menagerie? What was so unusual about a menagerie?"

"This one had some unusual animals in it."

She tilted her head to one side, studying his face. "Such as?"

His eyes glinted in the candlelight and she thought she detected speculation beneath the surface before it became light and amusing again.

"Well, there was a monkey, a bear, a panther, an elephant..."

She didn't know why, but intuition told her there was more to this conversation than she understood.

She pursed her lips. "Interesting."

"Monkeys, bears and even elephants are common in menageries. But I found the panther interesting. Have you ever seen one?"

Her heart lurched in her chest. Why did he want to know whether she'd ever seen a panther? Did he know about JoJo? Had Nona told him she had it? She couldn't have. Nona had only known her as Katie. Besides, Nona was long dead.

"Only in books."

"The owner was selling small figurines of the different animals. He insisted some of his best customers came from England. I think he thought I was looking for items to ship back to a shop to sell. I wonder if they would have sold."

"I suppose that would depend on what animals they were."

"Hmmm."

She kept her features neutral under his thoughtful gaze.

"I suspect there are already shops on Bond Street selling such things. Have you seen any? Monkeys, elephants, panthers, or maybe even bears?"

"No." She was having difficulty concentrating. It was fortunate her feet knew the steps or she might have stumbled at the last question. Why would he want to know about animal figurines? "Not that I can think of."

"Relax," he said with a chuckle. "It wasn't a trick question."

She frowned up at him, but the twinkle in his eyes convinced her that her suspicions were unfounded, and she reciprocated with a smile of her own.

The waltz came to a close and Jon escorted her back to her friends.

As they approached the knot of people, Jon noticed Tina and Jay across the way. Excusing himself to go join them, Felicia excused herself as well.

"That was very nice of you," she told him as they left the small group behind.

"What was?"

"Asking Martha to dance."

He chuckled. "It was self-preservation. I would have never shaken Miss Bascomb."

"True. Martha has always been shy, but when Charity came to town this Season, she just seems to have gotten worse. They're cousins and Martha is the elder, but Charity has always outshone Martha. Sometimes I think she does it on purpose."

"It's difficult to outshine a person on purpose. It's usually an aspect of a person's personality."

"Not where Charity and Martha are concerned. The truth is that Charity is jealous, but Martha doesn't see it because she doesn't see herself as anyone to be jealous of. All she needs to realize is that Charity would kill for her brown hair and dark eyes rather than the flaming mop Charity calls her own hair, and she'd feel a lot better. Unfortunately, all she sees is Charity's personality, much of which is forced."

"You can't solve everyone's problems, you know."

"I know, but I can solve Martha's. She's in love with someone and I'm going to see that she gets him."

"Who?"

She shook her head. "I can't tell you. But as soon as I work something out, I'll let you know."

"Why is it I'm not sure I want to know?" They reached Tina and Jay as she responded.

"You should," she murmured.

Jon stood in the shadows of the terrace, staring off into the darkened garden beyond the ballroom. Having finally escaped his sisters, and danced dutifully with a number of matrons and another young woman on his list, he was enjoying the cool night air.

The doors opened and a couple exited the ballroom and slipped into the garden. Another couple did the same a few minutes later. Jon was about to go back inside when the doors opened and yet another couple stepped out onto the terrace.

"It's too important a decision to make lightly," Amanda was saying. "I will give you my answer on Friday, like I promised."

"What is there to think about?" Lord Thurston demanded. "Either you wish to become my viscountess or you don't."

Jon melted back into the shadows, unable to quell his curiosity.

"Is that what you think? That it's a question of whether I want your title or not?"

Jon wondered why Thurston didn't seem to notice the irritation in Amanda's voice.

"Of course. Isn't that what every young woman wants?"

"Not this one."

"Then what do you want?"

"I haven't decided yet." She turned and looked out over the garden and Jon openly studied her profile from his hiding place. The moon was playing hide-and-seek with the clouds, but the pale pink gown she wore shimmered in the faint light. "When I decide, I'll know whether you can give it to me or not. And then I'll decide whether I will marry you."

Thurston's disbelief was obvious. "And you'll decide all this by Friday?"

Amanda turned back to her suitor. "You don't think I will?" she asked, the challenge in her voice obvious.

The viscount must have seen something in her eyes, for he changed tactics. "Of course. I'm sure you will," he said placatingly. "It's just that I wouldn't want you to worry that beautiful head too much about all this. Once we are married, there will be so many other things to keep us occupied that we will wonder why we waited so long."

Amanda's back was to Jon and he noted the way she stiffened at the viscount's reply. The tension radiating from her was almost tangible. He wondered if Thurston was truly that dense.

"Such as?"

"I thought we might go to Paris," Thurston was saying. "You could do some shopping for some new gowns. Once we return, there would be redecorating to do and, of course, a nursery to set up."

The condescending tone in his voice grated on Jon's nerves. He could imagine what it was doing to Amanda's.

"I see." Amanda's voice could have frozen boiling soup, not that Thurston noticed. "And what of my charity work?"

"Well, you may continue to donate to the poor unfortunates, but I, of course, will have to oversee the amounts." He all but patted her on the head, so patronizing was his reply.

"I see."

One of the couples who had entered the garden earlier returned to the terrace. The young woman's eyes were bright, her cheeks flushed. Jon smiled to himself as he watched the pair enter the ballroom. Unfortunately, Amanda also reentered the ballroom in their wake, Thurston trailing behind her.

He nearly laughed out loud once they were gone. So, Thurston had asked for Amanda's hand. That was one arrangement that would never work. Of medium height with light brown hair and grey eyes, he supposed Thurston was decent enough. He didn't look soft and Jon guessed he could be considered handsome, but he wasn't right for Amanda.

Amanda was vibrant and alive, but Thurston was dull and boring. Pleasant, but still dull and boring. There was no other way to sum up the differences. He reminded Jon a bit of Amanda's father. He wondered if Amanda saw him that way too.

Heaven forbid Amanda should marry a younger version of her own father. That would be too much.

Too bad, he thought. If Amanda married Thurston, that would be one less problem for him. At least she didn't have the panther. He had noted the curiosity in her eyes when he told her that outrageous fib about the menagerie and the figurines, but it had been all he could come up with on a moment's notice. She would have seen through the story he'd told the other young women.

Reentering the ballroom a short time later, he was waylaid by Lady Barrington. While they conversed, Amanda and Lord Thurston joined them, Thurston taking his leave only moments later. When Amanda's father arrived to dance with his wife, he and Amanda were left standing on the side of the ballroom alone.

Jon didn't wait for an opening. "I understand felicitations may be in order soon."

Amanda stiffened, her eyes narrowing up at him even as her smile stayed in place.

"Who told you that?"

"Is it a secret Thurston has asked?"

"No, but I haven't given him my answer yet." She relaxed somewhat, but still seemed uneasy.

They stood in silence for a few moments, watching the progress of the cotillion. "And have you come to a decision?"

"Why do you want to know?"

"Curiosity."

Amanda looked up into his face, searching for...what? He wasn't sure, but he kept his expression carefully blank.

"Do you want my opinion?"

Startled, she couldn't hide the surprise in her eyes. "Why would I want your opinion? You don't even know him."

Jon smiled. "True. But as an unbiased bystander, I could give you my humble impression. That is, provided you are interested."

He knew her curiosity was aroused. She wanted to know, but didn't dare ask. Why he was teasing her, he couldn't have explained to himself, but watching the speculation in those lovely blue eyes kept him from backing off.

"Weelll, just for the sake of conversation, suppose I was? Interested. In your impressions, that is. Then what?"

"Well, just for the sake of conversation, I would say he seems like a nice young man." She relaxed slightly. "But he reminds me a bit of your father." Her eyes widened at that statement, but she said nothing, so he continued. "But I understand that sometimes young women prefer the comfort of the familiar when they marry, hence they are likely to marry someone like their own sire."

Jon knew he was gambling on her feelings for her father by his last statement. That Amanda loved her father was no secret. That he loved her and indulged her in return was also no secret. Which was why he was certain Lord Barrington would not force her to accept a proposal from just anyone. But Lord Barrington was a bit of a prig when it came to women and their place in society. And it was obvious Lord Thurston shared his views.

The music ended and her parents rejoined them. After a few moments, he excused himself and headed for the door. Tomorrow was another day and he still had four more women to question. Reaching the front foyer, he collected his hat and cloak from the butler and left.

Amanda stared into the darkness. Moonlight streamed through the open drapes on both sides of her bed, providing enough light to see the shapes of the furniture scattered around the room. The mirror above her dressing table reflected some of the light back, but she barely noticed it. Sitting up, the statuette in her lap, Jon's words came back to her.

He reminds me of your father.

Had she noticed the similarities before? Similar color hair and eyes. Facial features somewhat the same. The tendency to lecture and patronize. They even had similar views on women's reading materials.

Her father often objected to her choice of reading materials, but never had he gone so far as to suggest she should confine herself to novels and fashion magazines. She had casually mentioned to Lord Thurston tonight that she was reading *The*

Odyssey and his reaction had not been positive. She had been relieved when she realized he assumed she was reading an English translation. She had not bothered to correct him. Especially when, in the next breath, he suggested Homer was too difficult for her to understand and she should stick to novels and fashion magazines.

She did not want to marry her father. Eliza might be content with him, but she would not.

She looked down at her panther. The emeralds seemed to glow in the meager light. "I should never have danced with him," she whispered. "He makes me think about things which are best forgotten." Like that kiss. She stroked the sleek black figure as memories intruded. Dancing with Jon had resurrected memories she'd tried to bury. Being held in his arms reminded her of what it had been like. What it could be like.

She'd decided to move on with her life, hadn't she? She wasn't going to wait for Jon to realize they belonged together, was she? He would probably eventually marry, but she couldn't wait, could she? She wasn't getting any younger, and she wanted a home and family of her own, didn't she?

Why had he come back now? Why couldn't he have stayed away a little longer? If she had been married already by the time he returned, it would have been better. *For whom?* She didn't want to dwell on that question, or its answer. If she had already been married, she would have been content. She wouldn't have given the Earl of Wynton a second glance.

She sighed. "Why can't I just forget him?" she asked the statuette. "It's not as if he's ever paid me any particular attention."

Does it matter?

She wished it did, but she knew the truth. It didn't. She needed to learn to live with her own weakness. As long as Jon was present, no one else measured up. She had already told two others no while he was out of the country. What made her think she would be stronger now that he was back?

She had told David tonight that when she decided what she wanted, she would decide whether he could give it to her. If she hadn't danced with Jon, she might still be undecided, but now she knew. She wanted Jon, and David could not give that to her. It was as simple as that.

It had taken only one dance for her to realize that there would never be anyone for her but Jon. But what was she to do about it? How was she to persuade him that she was the right person for him? How would she convince him that they belonged together?

Nona promised her she would have her gypsy prince, but she knew that to mention anything regarding his background to Jon might cause more trouble than she was prepared to deal with. Jon was sensitive about his gypsy heritage. Too many matrons used it capriciously to categorize him whenever possible. So, how was she to let him know?

"I should have told him about you." But she didn't want him on those terms.

After Tina and Felicia, she had determined for herself what the panther represented. At first she had been ecstatic, nearly delirious with joy as she realized Nona had chosen her. But he had already been on the Continent for a year when she'd figured it out and the longer he stayed there, the less sure of herself she became. Besides, she didn't want him just because Nona might have told him to marry the person with the statuette. Despite that Nona had told her she should only marry her "prince", she wanted more than an arranged marriage. She wanted him to want her—not just her panther.

She sighed and snuggled down under the counterpane. Maybe she should have told him. But after the incident three years ago, she was afraid of his reaction. He hadn't wanted her then. Why would she think his feelings had changed in the interim? And if they hadn't, would she have him just because she had his statuette and he was following orders?

Hugging JoJo close, she burrowed deeper under the covers, seeking the solace she always felt with the statuette near. Tonight, however, it was elusive. Instead, she yearned for a strong pair of arms, a solidly muscled chest and tender smile topped by deep green eyes.

She groaned. Maybe she should marry Thurston after all.

Chapter Four

Amanda alighted from her carriage, glanced up and down the street, then crossed the pavement and entered the building before her. Unlike the hustle and bustle of the street outside, it was quiet inside. Heading down the darkened, but clean, hallway, she passed two doors before reaching the one she wanted and, opening it, stepped inside.

A middle-aged matron sat behind a small desk in a corner on the opposite side of the room, her dark grey dress nearly blending in with the drab walls. Two small, grimy windows, close to the ceiling, opened on to an alley, letting in very little light, but helping to alleviate the stuffiness. A brazier for providing heat in the winter sat in the corner near the door. On rows of benches, neatly lined up four deep, sat nearly twenty girls, aged ten to twelve.

Heads bent, the girls worked on slate tablets before them, copying the words from the large board in front. Slipping out of her dark blue cloak and hanging it on a peg by the door, she glanced at the board, and smiled. Mabel always used verses from the Bible when the girls needed to practice their penmanship.

"A good verse," she said to Mabel as she approached the desk.

Mabel gave her a gap-toothed smile. "It never hurts to teach from the good Lord's word."

"As long as it's plain, simple and easy to understand." She glanced at the board again. "Are they nearly finished?"

Mabel nodded. "What're ye teaching today?"

"Arithmetic," Amanda answered. "I think we will review

basic addition and subtraction, then start with multiplication."

"Good," Mabel approved. "Never know when the grocer or the draper will need an apprentice what knows their numbers. Jest don't let Mr. Cooper catch ye."

Amanda grimaced. "I won't. I'll make sure they have their needlework handy and if he asks, I'll tell him they need to know how to count their stitches if they are to turn out a decent product."

As a rule, Amanda hated deceiving anyone, but she considered this a necessity. Ever since a new headmaster had been put in place to run the Wynton School for Girls, the curriculum for girls had been severely curtailed. In addition, the Board that handed out the grant money which kept most of the schools in London afloat ordained that girls be taught more domestic subjects, including needlework. Unfortunately, that meant other subjects had to go in order to make room, and for Mr. Cooper, the school headmaster, the subject considered unimportant for girls was arithmetic. Amanda, however, had other ideas and Mr. Cooper rarely entered the classrooms. As a volunteer, a donor directly to the school, and a gently bred lady, Amanda was considered competent to teach needlework.

She knew Mr. Cooper would think long and hard before he asked her to leave. She brought sizeable donations with her to the school, and she worked for free. In addition, she had, with Felicia's help, convinced Jon's grandmother to set up and fund a foundation for the school. The Board had been so grateful they named the school after her. Amanda hadn't told anyone else, but she had begun to think the school should disassociate itself from the Board altogether. Just how she was going to accomplish that she hadn't yet decided, but she would discuss it with the dowager countess soon. Despite her plans, she did not like flouting the rules openly, so she went along as best she could, adding subjects when she saw an opening to do so.

Arithmetic and needlework went hand in hand. French went well with it too. And so did a little natural science and philosophy. She also had an agreement with Mabel whereby Mabel would teach the other domestic subjects when she was absent from Town. Since some of the girls were only there for four hours a day, they squeezed in as much as they could.

Mabel left and she turned to the class. For the next two hours she drilled the girls in numbers—first in English, then in French. Then they graduated to sums, and were introduced to the concept of multiplication. In between, she talked to the girls about their lives, hopes and dreams.

Most of the girls were orphans, residents of the orphanage next door. The school agreed to educate them provided they arrived clean and fed. It was a good arrangement, for it provided the girls with a needed education and saved the orphanage the expense of providing it as well as food, clothing, and shelter. To Amanda, it made perfect sense, and kept the girls from being shipped off to work in the factories too young.

The rest came from families who were not well-off enough to employ a governess, but could afford the small fee the school charged. These girls were often the daughters of merchants and tradesmen, and many went home in the afternoons to work in their fathers' shops while the girls from the orphanage returned in the afternoons to learn a trade.

In the two years since Amanda had discovered the school and become involved with it, it had changed dramatically. Gone was the dirt and filth which had been piled in the halls, the girls no longer were crammed into one or two rooms with little or no supplies and they now received a decent education from women with some education themselves.

"You have done well today." She praised the girls as Mabel returned, signaling the end of the morning. "Try not to forget everything before tomorrow."

A chorus of girlish laughter greeted her.

"We won't forget, Miss Amanda," one of the girls said as they filed out of the room. "You'll see."

Once they were gone, she turned to Mabel. "I'm afraid I won't be here tomorrow. I have a prior engagement. If I finish early, I will try to drop in, but I'm not sure it will be possible."

"'Tis all right. Ye know ye do too much as it is. Mr. Cooper takes advantage of yer good nature."

"It's no trouble at all. I enjoy being with the girls. Having been an only child for so long makes me love being around children all the more."

Mabel smiled. "What did ye think of Cassie?"

Amanda remembered there had been a new girl in the class today. She hadn't said much, even when Amanda tried to draw her out.

"She seems quiet, but maybe it's because she's new. Where'd she come from?"

"A woman brought her to the orphanage. Said her mum died an' she had nowheres to go."

"Poor thing," Amanda sympathized. "How old is she?"

"Ten."

"Was the woman who brought her a relative?"

"Said she wasn't, but ye never know. According to some of the other girls, Cassie talks and acts 'real fancy', an' I asked Granny about her. She says the clothes Cassie arrived in were well made and of good materials. The orphanage could clothe nearly a dozen girls if they sold the clothes Cassie arrived in and some of the other things what arrived with her."

"What does Cassie have to say about any family?"

"Nothin'. She don't talk much and don't cause no trouble, but the girls all say she cries a lot at night."

Amanda pondered Mabel's words all the way home. Orphanages, she knew, usually only took in children of a middle-class background. The poorest children often lived on the streets, faring the best they could. It was an untenable situation, but new groups were appearing almost daily, trying to alleviate the problem.

It wouldn't do to dwell too much on Cassie. She would adapt in time, but Amanda understood her loss. Having lost her own mother when she was eight, she often wondered what might have happened to her if she had lost her father as well. She wouldn't have ended up in an orphanage, but her life would have been very different.

"I've made my decision," she said to Felicia that afternoon as they strolled through Lady Warburton's gardens.

The majority of the guests at the garden party were clustered in small groups scattered across the lawns, but she and Felicia hadn't wanted to sit.

"And?"

"I can't," she said. "I just can't marry Lord Thurston."

"Why not?"

"It's all your brother's fault."

"Why is it Jon's fault you can't marry Lord Thurston? I'm assuming you're talking about Jon."

Because I've been in love with him since I was seven years old. But she couldn't tell Felicia that. Felicia might say something and try to fix it. It was fortunate Felicia didn't know what her panther represented.

"Because he pointed out Lord Thurston was too much like my father, and as much as I love my father, I could not be married to him. I would go mad in a very short period of time."

Felicia giggled. "Oh."

They approached a small pond and stood at the edge watching the ducks swimming to and fro. The sun overhead was hot, but the cooling breeze that fluttered the edges of her blue parasol made standing there bearable.

"Are you sure?" Felicia asked after a while.

"Sure? About what?"

"About Lord Thurston?"

Amanda sighed. "Yes."

"Good, then. When will you tell him?"

"I suppose I could tell him tonight, but I promised him an answer tomorrow at ten."

"Wait until tomorrow and tonight you can help me make the disappointment less painful."

Amanda glanced over at her friend. "What are you planning?"

Felicia's dark blue eyes sparkled as she looked up at Amanda. "I happen to think he and Martha Danvers will make a good match. So, tonight we will pair them up."

Amanda's laughter bubbled forth. "Felicia, you are incorrigible."

Felicia was unapologetic as she responded with a grin. "I am, aren't I?"

"Lady Huddleston must be ecstatic." Felicia met Amanda

near the top of the stairs leading down to the ballroom. "I wouldn't have thought she could squeeze so many people into one place."

"Let's hope the windows are open, otherwise we'll all be swooning before the night is over." Amanda used her fan vigorously. She was already warm and she'd just arrived.

Felicia grinned. "Knowing Lady Huddleston, she'll consider that the ultimate mark of success."

She nodded. "The Courtlands' wasn't nearly as crowded. By the time Eliza and I left to come here, most of the young people had already left."

They moved through the crowd discussing family, friends and Amanda's charity work. At one point, they stopped as a group of people all moved into their path at once. Another person collided with her from behind. Turning, she found Martha Danvers behind her.

"Pardon me," Martha stammered. "I didn't... That is, I wasn't watching..." Amanda thought she looked quite pretty dressed in a gown of pale peach.

Remembering her conversation with Felicia at Lady Warburton's earlier, Amanda smiled. "No harm done, Martha."

"Indeed," Felicia chimed in. "It's good to see you. How are you this evening?"

Martha dipped Felicia a curtsy and replied, "I'm well, Your Grace." She looked around as if searching for someone. "But I seem to have lost Charity."

The best thing to happen so far tonight, Amanda thought. "I'm sure she will be fine."

"Why don't you walk with us for a bit until we find her?" Felicia invited.

Amanda was stopped by a patron of the school who wanted to ask her some questions. Waving Felicia and Martha off, she turned to give Lady Atwater her full attention. Some minutes later, as she finished her discussion, the musicians struck up a waltz and she turned to find Jon beside her.

It would be churlish to refuse, she told herself. Especially considering the decision she'd made the night before. Yet she was still uneasy and unsure in his presence. Why couldn't she just put what happened three years ago behind her? He obviously had.

It was as they passed another couple on the floor that she spoke.

"I noticed you talking to Lord Thurston." She strove to keep her voice steady. "You weren't, by any chance, warning him off, were you?"

"Could I?"

"I don't know. I suppose it would depend on what you said."

"Are you not sure of his affections?"

She did not want to answer that question. It was not Thurston's affections she was unsure of. It was her own. And knowing she planned to tell him no on the morrow caused her to feel more than a little guilty.

They passed Thurston and Martha once again and she wondered how Felicia had orchestrated that. But she had to admit they made a fine couple. Thurston was smiling and Martha seemed to be conversing with him, something Amanda knew was difficult for her. Mayhap everything would turn out for the best after all.

"And why would I want to?"

"Want to what?"

"Warn Lord Thurston off, as you put it?"

Blood stole into her face as she realized how the question sounded. Once again, she had spoken before thinking. Why couldn't her wayward tongue keep still in his presence?

Jon watched the color suffuse her face, then recede, leaving huge blue eyes in its wake before she lowered her lashes, shielding them from him. For the first time since he was a green youth, he didn't know what to say to a woman. That Amanda was still wary of him was obvious, but how to alleviate it without touching on the source of the uneasiness eluded him.

Reminding her of the kiss did not bother him. In truth, he wanted her to remember that magical moment. However, he would prefer she not relive the hurt he had inflicted afterwards. If he closed his eyes, he could still see the pain and disillusionment which had filled her eyes before he turned away from her. The destruction of her dreams. Dreams he knew had been centered around him. It would serve him right if she never felt comfortable around him again.

Unfortunately, that wouldn't do. She was his sister's best friend. He had the feeling they would be seeing a lot of each other over the years and he didn't want one thoughtless act on his part to keep them from being friends. That was the least they could be.

"Relax. I don't bite."

Her head snapped up, her gaze colliding with his. "You'll forgive me, my lord, if I disagree," she responded tartly. "I'm afraid previous encounters are all I have to go on and they tell me something different."

"I wondered." His voice was low.

Her eyes narrowed suspiciously. "Wondered what?"

He wasn't sure how to answer her. "Three years is a long time to hold a grudge."

Amanda's eyes widened. He knew she had not expected him to acknowledge the incident. Perhaps there was hope after all. If they could get past that, then...who knew what could happen.

"I do not hold grudges. But I do learn from experience."

"Experience can, indeed, be an excellent teacher," he agreed, "provided one does not learn the wrong lesson from it."

The dance came to an end, and he escorted her off the floor. Felicia was waiting, watching him more closely than he cared for. He knew Felicia would be happy if he married Amanda, even if she didn't have the statuette. Whether Tina would understand his ignoring Nona's dictate was a separate matter.

Taking his leave, he headed for the door. He'd had enough for tonight, and still had work to do to catch up from his long absence. He still hadn't been by to see his grandmother yet since his return, and now Amanda had given him food for thought. He needed to plan carefully how he was going to work his way around the problem or he'd give too much away in doing so.

At precisely ten o'clock the next morning, Amanda stood in

the burgundy and cream drawing room of Barrington house, staring out over the garden at the back. For some reason she was nervous. She knew she shouldn't be. She had done this twice before. But this time there was more at stake. Her very reputation, in fact.

She was taking a huge gamble by turning Lord Thurston down. If she couldn't get Lord Wynton to come up to scratch, she might well end up a spinster. Thurston's would be the third proposal she had turned down in the past year. Soon all the eligible young men would begin to avoid her, and she would be labeled as too finicky by the dowagers.

The bell pealed and a lump rose in her throat. Rubbing her hands together, she noticed they were sweaty. What was wrong with her?

The door opened behind her and Eliza entered the room. "Lord Thurston is here. Shall I have Barrons show him in?"

Amanda turned from the window, her movements jerky. Blood pounded in her ears. Taking a deep breath to steady her nerves, she nodded. Eliza looked at her closely for a moment and started to say something. Then she seemed to decide against it and left.

She was about to let them down. Papa and Eliza. Her father liked Thurston and she knew they would have gotten along well, but she couldn't marry someone so much like him. That had been the decision-maker for her. And she couldn't forget Jon had been the one who had pointed it out.

Viscount Thurston entered the room, impeccably dressed as usual. His dark brown morning coat was immaculate over a white shirt, cravat and dark brown trousers. Taking another deep breath, she moved toward him, the skirts of her rose pink morning gown swirling around her ankles.

"Would you like some refreshment?" She was pleased to find her voice even.

He shook his head. "We need not stand on formality. You know why I am here."

For some reason, he also seemed nervous, his shoulders tensed as if expecting a blow. *What did you expect?* The thought rose unbidden. If she was honest with herself, she wondered if he didn't already know the answer and was only waiting for her to voice it.

She nodded. Seating herself on the sofa, she invited him to sit as well. Expecting him to sit beside her, she found herself unaccountably relieved when he chose a chair situated beside the sofa instead.

Once seated, he stared at her for a long minute before asking, "Well?"

A part of her was annoyed that he didn't bother to ask her again. What that would have done, she had no idea, but it firmed her resolve. If only she didn't feel so guilty about it.

She had done this before. She knew the words by rote. *I am flattered by the honor you do me, but I'm afraid I must decline.* Instead, she said, "I'm sorry, but I cannot marry you." Adequate, but not very appeasing.

"I see," was his only comment, but she noticed some of the tension left his shoulders.

The silence was deafening. She wondered what he was thinking. Whether he would ask her why and what she would say if he did.

In the end, however, he said nothing. After a few minutes, he rose to his feet. She rose as well. "I-I'm sorry." The words tumbled awkwardly from her lips.

He smiled and took her hand. "Do not be." His grey eyes were kind. "I think I knew after our discussion the other night." Raising her hand to his lips, he brushed her knuckles, then looked into her eyes. "I hope someday you find the person who can give you whatever it is you are looking for."

When he turned and left the room, Amanda collapsed back onto the sofa. Guilt ate at her over the callous way she had treated him, yet she knew that had she said yes, it would have been a terrible mistake. Feeling tears start in her eyes, she knew she had to get away. Eliza would return any minute and she did not want her stepmother to find her crying. Especially since the tears were of relief.

Jon stepped out of his coach and looked up at Number Nineteen Park Court. It looked like most of the other houses along the street, its three-story brick-fronted facade plain and unadorned. The brass knocker on the door shone, signaling the owner was in residence.

He gave his coachman instructions for when to return, then dismissed him and climbed the steps. The door opened as he reached the top step, revealing Smithers, his grandmother's butler.

"Good day, my lord."

"Morning, Smithers." He handed his hat and cane to the man. "Is my grandmother receiving?"

"In the green parlor, my lord." Jon headed toward the back of the house and the room in question.

He could hear voices as he approached the door, which sat slightly ajar, and slowed his steps. He had hoped she would be alone. It was the reason he had come in the morning. He frowned. Now what? Then the voices drifted out, and he relaxed.

"So, now what do you plan to do?" he heard his grandmother say.

"I don't know," was the reply and he recognized Amanda's voice immediately. "I haven't decided yet."

"Seems to me you're burning your bridges a bit too fast."

"I know, but I really couldn't have married him."

"If you'll recall, I told that you before."

"I know, I know. Oh well, that's over with now, and I can concentrate on more important things."

"Such as?"

"The school, of course."

His grandmother made a *tsk*ing sound. "You should not allow the school to consume you."

"I try not to, but they need so much. The new Board is horrible. We need to do something about them. We don't need the grants, so we ought to be able to teach what we feel is necessary. And Mr. Cooper is an idiot. Somehow we must get out from under the thumb of the Board."

Jon decided he'd eavesdropped enough and knocked on the open door, entering the room at his grandmother's invitation.

"Well, it's about time!" she exclaimed upon seeing him. "You've been back for days, and this is the first time I've laid eyes on you."

Jon gave her his warmest smile. "I'm afraid my secretary and solicitor are born slave drivers."

Amanda jumped to her feet as he approached, her eyes wide. It took him a moment to recognize the emotion he read there before she looked down, and he wondered what she felt guilty about.

The dowager Countess of Wynton sat in a large overstuffed chair that dwarfed her small frame. Jon was surprised by how much she had aged in the last three years and was reminded she might not have been here at all when he returned. Having lived into her seventies, he knew her health was not the best and she rarely left her home. Yet even as he looked down into eyes which mirrored his own, he could see they were still sharp and alert, although her previously blond hair was now completely white.

He bent to brush a wrinkled cheek with his lips. "How are you, madam?"

"Much better now that you're here," she replied. "Sit." Then turning to Amanda, "You too. Sit."

Jon grinned at Amanda's sudden nervousness. "Lady Amanda." He inclined his head in her direction as she resumed her seat beside his grandmother's chair.

He made himself comfortable on an overstuffed sofa and allowed his eyes to feast on the sight of her. The pink of her gown gave her skin a rosy hue and emphasized her eyes. Blue as a summer sky, he thought, and wondered when he'd become a romantic. Her hair was pulled up into a soft knot, a lone curl having escaped to trail across her shoulder, but nothing could disguise its lush brightness. He was reminded of the sun, and suddenly Nona's words came back to him.

When you tire of blue skies and sunshine abroad, you will return to find them at home. Felicia had been right. Nona had given him a description. But it didn't fit. Hadn't Amanda told him just two nights ago she'd only seen a panther in a book? Even his broad hinting about figurines hadn't elicited anything more than a polite response. Perhaps he was just being fanciful, looking for something which wasn't there.

His grandmother commanded his attention.

"Stop gawking and pay attention!" she snapped. "Amanda

and I need your help."

"Of course," he replied smoothly to cover his inattention. "How can I be of assistance?"

"You can help her find a decent headmaster or mistress for the school. Someone who doesn't think girls are idiots. And talk to Shaftesbury."

"Headmaster?" He blinked. "School?" He looked from one to the other. "What school?"

"The one in Southwark," his grandmother replied. "It's a school for girls—mostly orphans, but some merchants and tradesmen send their daughters there as well."

For the next hour and a half, Jon was introduced to Amanda's charity work. He was not pleased to discover she went into Southwark alone nearly every day to teach. Nor was he happy to learn she had to deal with an ignorant headmaster, put in place by a Board that felt learning was wasted on girls.

Amanda had been introduced to the school by her maid, Mary, who knew Mabel. Originally one of the Ragged Schools set up by Lord Shaftesbury to teach the poorest of the poor in London, it had fallen into a shambles. The teachers had been barely literate themselves, the London Board unable to cope with the magnitude of the problem of educating so many city-wide.

The situation became so bad eventually the school had been closed. Another local school took in all the boys, but refused admittance to the girls, saying it didn't have the room. It had taken Amanda nearly six months to raise the funds to reopen the school. But she had, collaborating with the orphanage for girls next door. She agreed to help raise funds for both if the girls were sent to the school. It turned out to be the perfect partnership.

There were members of the upper classes who might not care to donate funds for a school, but for an orphanage many were willing to open their sizeable purses. The London Board, however, insisted the school take more than the orphans housed next door. Grudgingly, Amanda agreed to take in those who could pay a small fee, but she insisted the school be for girls only. The Board originally balked, but when Amanda pointed out the orphanage next door was for girls only, reminded them the girls had no place else to go to learn, and threatened to take her donations elsewhere, they agreed.

Unfortunately, the Board insisted on overseeing the curriculum and appointing the headmaster. Amanda wanted a headmistress, but the Board insisted on a man. When Mr. Cooper had been appointed, he had immediately tried to reintroduce boys into the school despite Amanda's insistence that it was for girls only. It had taken Amanda's refusal to release the donations she received before he gave in.

To say Jon was amazed would be an understatement. He was flabbergasted. Amanda, at nineteen, had taken on the establishment and fought the London city bureaucracy for a group of girls who had no one else. Tina and Felicia had been her major supporters, it seemed, and it had taken Brand's influence with Shaftesbury to get her an audience with the Board, but she had done everything else.

Smithers entered the room to ask the countess where she wished to have luncheon served.

"We shall eat in here," the dowager told him.

Amanda rose. "I shall just freshen up a bit and be right back," she announced, then left the room.

Jon watched her go before turning to his grandmother, who watched him with a satisfied smile on her face. Without preamble she said, "You'd do well to marry her before someone else snaps her up."

Chapter Five

Jon winced. He shouldn't be surprised. His grandmother had never minced words with him. Why would she start now? But Amanda was not for him. As his sister's friend, he refused to subject her to the hurt he knew would follow.

"Anyone with eyes in their head could see you two are right for each other."

He wouldn't be baited. "So, tell me more about this school."

She looked at him closely for a moment, then sighed. "Not much else to tell. Now that it's doing well, it really just needs someone who can take Amanda's place. And that won't be easy. It will probably take two people to do so, although she'd probably settle for someone who might not know as much, but would be just as good with the children."

Jon's eyebrows lifted. "She does that much?"

"Yes. Besides teaching, she does most of the administrative paperwork and solicits the donations which keep the school running."

Jon said nothing, so she continued.

"There are three classes. The age groupings are, I think, four to six, seven to nine, and ten to twelve. At thirteen, the orphanage girls are apprenticed out. Amanda has taken on the ten to twelve year olds. I think the other teacher for that age group, Mabel, teaches reading and writing. Amanda is officially there to teach needlework, but works in arithmetic, French, science, philosophy, a little Greek or Latin occasionally, and who knows what else. The stupid Board seems to think all women need to know is how to keep house."

Once again, Jon was astounded. He would have never

guessed Amanda had such an extensive education. Perhaps it was because he didn't expect it of her. His own sisters were well read, knowledgeable, and fluent in French, but neither of them were versed in Latin or Greek.

"I see."

The dowager grinned, obviously enjoying herself. "Surprised you, didn't I?"

Smithers returned with two footmen and set a table for luncheon near the large windows overlooking the garden at the rear of the house. That the table was already there and they seemed to do it automatically told him his grandmother must spend many of her days in this room.

Ignoring her last comment, he changed the subject. "So, how are you feeling these days? Tina tells me you do not go out much anymore."

"These old bones are just that—old. I will admit to moving much slower these days than I used to."

Jon frowned. "Do you have pain in your joints?"

"Most days, yes. Jamison, that old quack, tells me it's just the process of getting old. He gives me laudanum for the worst of it."

"Hmmm," was his only comment as Amanda returned.

She had tidied her hair and the curl was now firmly anchored back in the top knot. She looked fresh as a flower after a summer rain and Jon felt drawn to her as a moth to a flame. He felt a little like that self-same moth—drawn to something he knew would only hurt him, but unable to resist. He wondered how badly he'd be burned if he got too close.

A sudden thought, an inspiration really, occurred to him. If she didn't have the panther, perhaps he *could* seriously consider her as countess material. According to Nona, the person with the panther was his destiny, the woman he was fated to love above all others. If it wasn't Amanda, perhaps he could have her after all. There was something to be said about your spouse having some claim on your affections—just not all. This might be something worth exploring.

After luncheon, the dowager indicated she needed to rest, and sent the two of them off. Jon's carriage had returned, so he offered to take Amanda home.

"I believe I owe you my thanks," Jon said once the coach was moving.

Amanda turned from the window, her eyes meeting his across the small space. "For what?"

"For taking the time to visit my grandmother. I know Tina makes an effort, but I'm sure she does not see her as often as she might like. My grandmother seems to think highly of you and values your friendship. It is obvious she looks forward to your visits."

"Oh."

Jon watched her for a while as the carriage made its way through the streets. He could feel her tension, but could think of no way to make her more comfortable in his presence. However, since she refused to look at him, he allowed himself the luxury of looking at her.

She had donned a pelisse in a cranberry color that buttoned all the way up to the neck. The high military-style collar emphasized the delicate slenderness of her throat and complemented the roses in her cheeks. Her golden hair was hidden beneath her bonnet, but he hadn't forgotten its color. He need only look up at the sun to be reminded.

Did the woman with the statuette know what it represented? This was the question uppermost in Jon's mind later that evening as he stood in yet another ballroom amid the same people, listening to the same superficial conversation as the night before. He had forgotten how tedious the social whirl could be.

He remembered wondering whether Nona had told the young woman the statuette represented him—and frowning at the thought. Society was famous for labeling its members and he knew the panther was a perfect representation for the way they viewed him.

What *had* Nona told her? Was it possible Nona had merely given her the statuette with no indication it represented anything or anyone? He couldn't imagine Nona doing that. She would have indicated, somehow, that the panther had a purpose. But what purpose would she have given? And if the woman knew, why hadn't she made herself known to him?

Scanning the crowded room, his gaze alighted on Amanda, standing off to the side speaking to a man he did not know. A feeling he refused to acknowledge shot through him and although his brain insisted he did not care, his feet carried him toward the couple.

As he moved through the crowd, he noticed she placed one hand on the man's sleeve, then another on his chest. A knot formed in his stomach. And when she gifted the man with a seemingly brilliant smile, he felt as if someone had just punched him in the chest. The man grabbed her wrist and placed a kiss on her knuckles before she snatched it away. Putting hands on her hips, she said something else to him, before spinning away, nearly colliding with Jon in the process.

"Oh! I beg your pardon, my lord." Her voice was breathless.

His senses kicked into high alert as he caught her softness just before she plowed into him. His hands settled on her waist and the scent of honeysuckle engulfed him. He took a deep, calming breath.

"My apologies. I did not intend to sneak up on you." Thinking fast, he added, "I wanted to ask you a question about Mr. Cooper."

The man behind her cleared his throat, and Amanda turned as if suddenly remembering they were not alone.

"Oh, Stephen, have you met Lord Wynton?"

Stephen? Perfectly styled dark hair and impeccably tailored evening attire did not impress Jon. The lines of dissipation around Stephen's golden eyes were pronounced and his smile for Amanda was just a bit too warm. A dissolute rake not fit company for any woman over the age of twelve. Jon disliked him on sight.

"I believe once, many years ago." Stephen returned the perusal Jon had just subjected him to.

"Oh, then let me introduce you again, since you've both been out of the country for a while. Lord Wynton, my cousin, Stephen, Lord Hickham. Stephen, Lord Wynton, my friend Felicia's brother."

Cousin! Jon relaxed, the tension leaving his shoulders. He and Stephen shook hands and murmured the requisite pleasantries. After a few moments, Stephen took his leave and Amanda turned to Jon.

"Thank you." There was an edge to her voice.

Jon had turned to look across the ballroom for a moment, but now his head swivelled back.

"For what?"

She smiled and his temperature shot up.

"For rescuing me."

Jon offered his arm and she laid her hand on it as the two of them began to stroll the perimeter of the dance floor. He tried to concentrate on what she was saying rather than the feel of her hand resting on his forearm.

"Stephen and I just rub each other the wrong way. I usually avoid him, but occasionally I run into him in a crush like this."

They encountered Felicia just as she was taking her leave of a knot of young women. He noted the interest that flared in her eyes as she spotted them, and could have groaned in dismay. The last thing he needed was Felicia speculating on his search. She had done enough in giving him the list. She needn't watch his every move with each woman on the list.

"Have you seen Martha this evening?" she asked Amanda.

"No."

She looked up at Jon. "Have *you* seen Miss Danvers? Or, do you see her now?"

Jon shook his head. "Not that I remember, but that hardly signifies in this crowd."

"Bother!" She shot an impatient look his way. "What good is it to be so tall if you can't find people for me in this crush?"

Jon chuckled. "If I recall your husband is even taller than I. Why don't you ask him?"

"Because he's not here yet. I came with the Westovers."

"And I haven't seen them either," he needled. "Are you sure you aren't just lost?"

She bent a disgusted look on him. "If you are not going to be of any help, I will go find Geri and see if Gerald can help me, instead."

Jon groaned. "I cannot imagine but that you and Geri together must be more trouble than society can stand in one place."

Amanda giggled at that and Jon was surprised at the pleasant feeling the sound engendered.

Felicia snorted. "This is her first full Season out of mourning. You haven't seen them before because they have been visiting Ted and Cecily in Bath for the last fortnight. They only returned today."

"Then I must be sure to find one of them to find out how Ted fares these days."

Viscount Thurston moved into view at that moment and Felicia waylaid him as he approached, commandeering his arm for an escort. Apologizing profusely, however, he explained he was Amanda's partner for the next set and had only come to find her.

Jon kept his expression neutral as he reluctantly relinquished Amanda to her erstwhile suitor. Amanda thanked him again for his assistance with her cousin before taking the viscount's arm and strolling away. Jon resisted the urge to grab her back, consoling himself with the thought that not only had she turned down the viscount's marriage proposal, he had garnered the supper dance, which happened to be a waltz.

Felicia watched them go as well, an unreadable expression on her face, before turning back to Jon.

"I suppose you'll have to do until I find Brand or Gerald," she retaliated.

"I don't know that I can stand to be relegated to second—or third—place in your affections." He chuckled. "Perhaps I ought to go home and take to my bed for the rest of the Season."

Felicia's laughter had heads turning in their direction. "Goose," she declared good-naturedly as she took his arm and they began to stroll.

Coming upon Tina conversing with Lady Rampton, they stopped. Dressed from head to toe in an unbecoming shade of purple, Lady Rampton had been among his grandmother's set of friends years ago when she refused to acknowledge him. He wondered why Tina bothered with the old harridan.

"My dear Lorraine must be delighted to have you back," the woman gushed as he bowed over her hand. Her reference to his grandmother by her given name made him instantly wary.

He smiled. "She did seem pleased to see me."

"How was Grandmama?" Tina turned to him. "I haven't been to see her yet this week."

"She is in good spirits, but a bit lonely I think. Lady Amanda was visiting when I called."

"My Sophie and I often have tea with her ladyship," Lady Rampton added. "She just adores it when my Sophie reads to her."

Jon noted the look that passed between his sisters, but was distracted a moment later by the arrival of a young woman. Lady Rampton nearly pounced on her, pushing her toward Jon as she made the introductions.

"Have you met my daughter, Sophie? Sophie, this is Lord Wynton, our dear Lorraine's grandson."

Pale blue eyes looked up at him out of a pleasantly rounded face surrounded by dark gold curls. She would have been pretty if not for the distrust he read in her expression. Nevertheless, he bowed over her hand and requested the next set.

As the couples lined up for a country dance and Sophie watched him warily, he wondered if she would say something to explain why she seemed to dislike him on sight, or whether she'd remain coy and pretend as if she didn't. They had little time to speak, and she said nothing when the dance brought them together. He resolved to wait her out.

When the dance ended and they left the floor, she stopped suddenly and turned toward him. "May I speak freely, my lord?"

He inclined his head. "Of course."

"I do not wish to appear forward, but I don't want to marry you," she stated bluntly.

Jon was taken aback by her declaration. She had asked to speak freely, but he hadn't anticipated such directness. His surprise must have been written all over his face for she smiled at his speechlessness, and he was struck by how pretty she really was.

"I should apologize," she began, "but I have gotten nowhere with Mama on this subject and I would appreciate it if you did not play into her hands."

Jon shook off his paralysis. "I see. And what would make your mother think I might be amenable to such a match?" He did not want to hurt this young woman's feelings, but she was definitely not for him.

"Because she thinks that as our families are somewhat related, a new generation ought to continue on."

Jon racked his brain for a connection and found none. Except for noting once years ago that Lady Rampton seemed a little young to be one of his grandmother's particular friends, he had given his grandmother's circle of friends little thought.

She sighed. "I don't suppose you know my mother was the previous countess's younger sister."

He shook his head. Actually, he hadn't paid much attention to the details about his father's family. He had known his father was the youngest of three boys, and that the oldest had married. It had not occurred to him to wonder about his oldest uncle's wife. They had all died before he'd ever set foot in England.

She glanced around them. "Well, I hope you aren't offended. But if you do not pay me any attention after this, Mama might leave it be."

"Very well, I will try to pretend as if you do not exist." He had to restrain himself from laughing. She was very earnest, but he knew he would not have given her a second thought anyway.

Returning her to her mother's side, he bowed and left. Heading for the refreshment table, he spied Amanda still strolling with Thurston. She was smiling and nodding at something the viscount was saying and he felt that smile like a physical blow.

Perhaps he ought to forget about the statue and just pursue Amanda instead. Knowing she didn't have it lightened his spirits. There was much to be said about having a wife who was easy on the eyes and he could watch Amanda indefinitely and not tire of the view.

She was still sometimes nervous in his presence and he wondered if there was a way to ease the strain. Perhaps if they shared another kiss. His body reacted powerfully to the thought, and he wondered if she would taste as sweet as before.

A footman went by carrying a tray of glasses filled with champagne. He snatched one from the tray as the man passed and took a large swallow. He didn't like champagne, but it gave his hands something to do. The supper dance was due to start soon, and suddenly he was nervous. Perhaps tonight would be a good time to start soothing over the hurt. If he could.

Another footman passed and he deposited his empty glass on the tray and moved toward Amanda.

Amanda was trying to come up with a way to part from Lord Thurston without hurting his feelings when she sensed someone approach them from behind. She and Thurston still conversed easily enough, but now there was a different quality to their interaction and they both seemed reluctant to walk away from each other. Unfortunately, if her senses were correct she was about to be confronted with the only other person in the room she was likely to be more awkward with.

The men exchanged greetings while she looked on. They seemed to genuinely like each other, and had interests in common. She did not consider herself one of those interests, however. When Thurston bowed to her and retreated, Jon turned to her with a smile and offered his arm. Her knees went weak at that smile and she had to forcibly remind herself he was only being polite.

Waltzing with Jon was her idea of heaven. Despite her own concerns over his attentiveness or lack thereof, her body responded to his touch and she did not protest when he pulled her closer than she knew he should. She was tempted to give herself up to the music, melt into him and see what he might do, but his reaction the last time she got so close stopped her. The last time she had been impulsive in his presence, she had been thoroughly kissed, then summarily dismissed. She would not allow that to happen again.

And, of course, there was also the possibility someone might notice and she could ill-afford to become the subject of the gossip mill. Her refusal of Lord Thurston's suit had already drawn comment, but her father and Eliza, although disappointed, were firmly in her camp. Their unwavering support went a long way to diffusing the disapproval.

When the music ended she felt flushed and a little lightheaded. Snapping open her fan as they left the floor, she waved it vigorously. Jon noticed the action.

"How about a little fresh air before supper?" he asked as they reached the terrace doors.

Unable to speak, she merely nodded. Her heart beat furiously in her breast as they slipped out the doors into the cool night air.

"We should not be out here long," he said as they stopped on the terrace. Two more couples followed them out, and another couple came up the stairs from the garden.

She looked up at him as the space around them appeared to fill with people. He seemed expectant, as if he was weighing what to say next.

"We need to talk," he murmured, glancing around the area, "but not here."

An excited shiver tripped down her spine as he led her down the stairs and into the garden. Stealing a glance at him, she was only marginally aware of where they were going.

"About what?"

He stopped and turned toward her. "About what happened in the library at the Abbey three years ago."

"Oh." She hadn't thought he'd address the problem head on.

"I won't apologize for kissing you," he told her, "but I will for what happened afterwards. I have no excuse for what I said to you. It was uncalled for."

They had moved off the path to beneath the branches of a large tree which obscured most of the light from the moon. As they were too far from the house for any of that light to reach them, they may as well have been standing in total darkness. Jon's face was hidden in shadows, his voice disembodied, although she could make out his white shirt.

"Then why did you?"

"I was being selfish."

"Selfish?"

"I knew I was leaving for an extended tour of the Continent and I did not want you to read too much into it."

"So you were having one last dalliance before you disappeared?" Had he just been toying with her?

"No, that was not it at all." Surprise colored his words.

"Then what was it?" She sounded like a harpy, but she couldn't let it go. Somehow, they had to get past that afternoon at the Abbey and since he'd brought it up, she was determined to finish the discussion.

"I was trying to answer your question."

She frowned. "What question?"

"You asked me, if I recall correctly, why I didn't like you?" She was thankful for the darkness as she felt heat blossom in her cheeks. "I was trying to show you I didn't dislike you. Only it got out of hand."

"Oh."

"You might also recall you actively pursued me all during that Season, and as I was not ready to follow Felicia and Brand down the aisle, I thought it was best you not imply too much from the kiss. My method of doing so was unfortunate."

Amanda didn't know what to think. He was right. She *had* pursued him shamelessly three years ago. She had often deliberately put herself in his way, forcing him to ask her to dance out of politeness. More than once she had sought him out in a card room until Eliza firmly forbade her to enter another one.

"I did not intend to hurt you," Jon continued, and she heard the regret in his voice. "The look in your eyes that day has haunted me for three years."

Amanda was astounded. She had spent the last three years hating him for his cavalier treatment of her, and blaming him for her inability to accept any other men in her life. It never occurred to her he might have regretted his outburst, or he might have felt guilty over his handling of the situation.

Perhaps, she acknowledged wryly, looking off over the darkness of the garden, it was time for her to accept some of the responsibility for what happened. After all, if she had only told him the truth about why she had been in the library in the first place, the rest would not have happened. But was she willing to now?

"Very well," she said, "I accept your apology." The words hung between them, then she took a deep breath of cool night air and continued, "And I apologize as well for my own behavior. I can only say, in my defense, I was too young to understand how uncomfortable I must have made you feel."

The tension she sensed in him earlier receded.

"Perhaps," he said softly, "it's time to let bygones be bygones, and start anew."

When he bent close, Amanda steeled herself not to move backward, expecting him to kiss her again, but he hesitated. Their faces were close, their breath mingling, yet he remained still. What was he waiting for? Did he expect her to do—or say—something? If so, what?

Jon was close enough to see the uncertainty she was feeling. What should she do?

"Shall we start over?" His *sotto* voice brushed over skin.

Her eyes widened. "I-I, uh, yes, I suppose we could."

His gaze bored into hers, drawing her in. When his lips curved into a smile, her heartbeat doubled. "Then kiss me."

Her mouth nearly dropped open in shock. She searched his eyes for...what? She opened her mouth to reply, then shut it when nothing came out. It was suddenly warm in the garden, yet she had been thankful for the coolness when they first emerged from the ballroom.

"I-I can't," she finally managed.

"Why not?"

Blood flooded her face, then receded. Unable to stop herself, she moistened her lips. "I don't—" she glanced around her, "—I don't know how."

She was surprised she could see the wicked glint that appeared in his eyes. It set off bells in her head.

"Would you? If you knew how?"

Amanda didn't know why he wanted her to kiss him, but her blood heated at the thought. Despite everything she'd ever been taught telling her it was improper, she wanted to kiss him. Wanted to know if it would still be as magical as the last time. She nodded, the movements jerky, then tipped her head back to look up at him.

Jon smiled, his eyes glittering in the faint light. "Then pay close attention," he murmured, and covered her lips with his.

The kiss was whisper soft. Delicate, almost fragile. Jon's lips moved gently over hers, teasing, nibbling, beckoning. Inviting her closer, yet he did not press. An arm slipped around her, the touch light and non-demanding. She knew he held back, waiting for something. Waiting for her. He lifted his head.

Raising up on her toes, she followed, not wanting to break the contact, and pressed her lips against his. His arm tightened fractionally, his lips firmed slightly, and when her lips parted beneath his, his tongue swept in.

Warmth engulfed Amanda, blood pounded in her veins with the force of a cannon. Heat slithered over her skin, igniting fires in its wake and melting everything in its path. She had expected Jon to take control, to ravish, as he had before, and when he didn't, she was lost. She was no match for his gentleness. Caught off guard, she followed blindly, straining upward when he raised his head the second time.

"We need to go back." The words hovered between them. "We have been out here too long."

Amanda was still floating. Right now, she would have agreed to anything. Lifting lids she hadn't realized she'd closed, she stared up into eyes obscured by the shadows and wished she could read his face. But for now it mattered not.

As if in a trance, she allowed him to turn her, place her hand on his arm, and lead her up the path and back into the ballroom. The room was only half full and she realized they'd missed supper. Her cheeks warmed as she thought of how long they must have been out in the garden. If anyone noticed...

She scanned the room, noting with relief the absence of his sisters and her stepmother. They would have been doomed if any of them had noticed their absence and return. Moving into the crowd, she hoped no one else had either.

Chapter Six

Amanda was sitting outside in the garden the next afternoon when voices drifted out of the salon.

"Are you sure?" Eliza's voice carried through the open window.

Another voice spoke too low for her to hear what was said, but she was sure it was her father's.

"And no one knows where?"

Her stepmother must be sitting near the window, Amanda thought, but her father was obviously further inside the room.

A light breeze wafted through the garden and the scent of lavender swirled around her.

"You have to find her, you know. You will never rest until you do." Her stepmother's voice was full of sympathy and Amanda wondered who they were talking about.

Her father must have raised his voice because she heard the words *vicar* and *cottage*, but not the whole statement.

"Nora should have known better." Her father's voice was clearer, indicating he'd moved closer to where her stepmother sat.

"She did what she thought was best," Eliza answered. "As I recall, she didn't want to..." The next sentence trailed off as Eliza obviously moved.

Then Amanda heard no more. She tried to return to the book open in her lap. Unfortunately, her concentration was non-existent and the Greek letters and words on the page were suddenly undecipherable. She closed the book and sighed. It was no use pretending. She set it down beside her panther. She hadn't read a complete paragraph in the last hour. And now her parents' mystery had completely obliterated what was left of her concentration.

The events of the prior evening played in her head. What should she do now? Now that she knew she was still in love with Jon. Last night had only served as a reminder and reawakened those feelings she thought she had buried for good. It was no use berating herself over her wayward heart now. Someday, somehow, she'd make him see that they belonged together. Even if she had to hit him over the head with her panther to make him realize it.

If his grandmother had her way, they would be spending a lot of time in each other's company over the rest of the Season— or at least for the time that they were in London. The dowager wanted him to assume oversight of the school. She had been blunt about his ability to deal with the other men involved. They would respond more readily to him than her. It was a fact of life, but Amanda disliked it all the same.

Another light breeze ruffled her curls. Looking up at the nearly cloudless sky through the tree above her head, she closed her eyes, breathed in the flowery scents of the garden around her, and was transported into the past.

Her mother had loved the outdoors and Summersea would be beautiful at this time of the year. She could see clearly the rolling countryside of the Lake District. The meadows, lakes, fields and forests. It was a wonderful place and they had spent hours walking through the gardens and fields, picnicking and picking flowers. She had known, with the insight of a child, that her parents were angry at each other. It was the reason she and her mother were at Summersea while her father was still in London. She didn't care.

Her mother was perfect in her eyes. With golden hair, sky blue eyes, perfect skin, and a musical voice, Katherine Cookeson had been everything to her young daughter. Amanda had worshiped her. She remembered clearly the day they had come upon the gypsy. Sitting beside one of the lakes, he had been fishing. Her mother asked him if he had caught anything and whatever he'd answered made her mother blush.

The next day, they had gone to the gypsy camp in the pony cart. Her mother told her to go play with the other children while she spoke to Gregor, the fisherman from the previous day. She hadn't seen any other children, so she'd stayed put, more than a little afraid of leaving the security of the pony cart on her own. It was sometime later that a little girl emerged from one of the wagons and saw her.

"Hallo," she said. "I'm Caro. What's your name?"

Feeling somewhat lonely, she was surprised when the girl spoke to her. Dressed in a loose-fitting white blouse and dark skirt, the girl was barefoot, her black hair hanging in unruly curls down her back. But she was smiling and Amanda responded to the smile.

"Katie," she replied, using her mother's name for her. It was short for her second name which was the same as her mother's, and her mother told her it brought back memories of her parents whenever she used it, for that was what they had called her as a child.

Caro coaxed her from the cart and the two had gone off together. For the next three weeks she and Caro were inseparable. The second day she came, Caro convinced her to take off her dress, stockings and shoes, so they could play in the small lake nearby. It was so hot she agreed.

Sitting on the bank of the lake, she watched Caro play in the water. Caro didn't seem to worry about being in the water. But Amanda was only willing to put in her feet.

"Katie," Caro called. "Come on in. It's not deep."

Amanda shook her head. She wasn't as fearless as her new friend. She watched as Caro played and splashed in the water, even going under the water and coming back up—and wished she could too. But she didn't know how and, at seven, was a little afraid.

One of the older boys came along on the other side of the lake. He was wet, as if he, too, had been in the lake, his pants clinging to his legs, his chest bare. He stopped when he saw Caro.

"Caro!" he shouted. "What are you doing?"

Her friend looked up from where she stood and smiled brilliantly. "JoJo! Where have you been?" she shouted back. "Come meet my new friend."

The youth dove into the water, coming up nearly beside

her. "Where?"

"Over there." Caro pointed her way. "Her name is Katie, but she won't come in the water."

"Why not?"

"I think she's afraid. But you can help. I don't think she can swim."

Caro had been right, of course. She and her mother had done many things, but playing in a lake and swimming had not been one of them.

She had been excited when she and her mother left the camp that afternoon. Her mother seemed distracted, but she had been so excited about playing in the water that she hadn't noticed. Over the next few days, JoJo and Caro taught her to swim. Because it was the middle of the summer, she and Caro had spent most of their days playing in the lake to keep cool.

She could look back on those three weeks as magical. JoJo had been wonderful to her and, at seven, she had developed a huge case of hero-worship. Even after she and her mother left for the last time, she had never forgotten him. She still remembered the conversation she had with her mother as they left the gypsy camp behind for the last time, the black panther securely wrapped and sitting in her lap.

"I'm going to marry a gypsy when I grow up," she announced.

Her mother merely glanced at her, her large blue eyes slightly saddened. "Perhaps," she replied. "But whomever you marry, you must make sure you truly love him."

"I will. I'm going to marry JoJo," she declared. "Nona said he was my very own prince."

Her mother laughed. "And how will you find him, darling Katie?"

"Nona said he would find me," she responded with all the confidence of a child. "She said my kitty would help him find me."

"That's nice," her mother said absently. "I hope someday he does."

Amanda opened her eyes and looked up at the blue sky overhead. "He's found me, Mama." She sighed. "Only I'm not sure he knows it yet."

A short time later she was again distracted, this time by the arrival of her brothers.

"Mandy!" George squealed and launched himself at her. Picking up the sturdy little boy, she returned his enthusiastic hug, then looked up for the others she knew would be with him.

Nicky followed his brother down the path, and was, in turn, followed by their governess, Miss Byrnes. Amanda looked up and smiled at Nicky, who glanced down at her book and asked, "What'cha readin'?"

"Homer's *Odyssey*. Would you like me to read you one of the stories?"

"Does it have soldiers in it?" George asked.

"Sort of. But there's lots of fighting."

"Oooooh," George exclaimed with the excitement of a four-year-old who played incessantly with his toy soldiers. "I wanna listen too."

"I will read to you both, if it is all right with Miss Byrnes."

Both boys turned to look up at their governess.

"It's all right with you, Bernie, isn't it?" Nicky asked, his dark eyes imploring.

Amanda nearly laughed out loud as she watched Miss Byrnes soften under that puppy-like stare. At seven, Nicky was already a charmer. The woman smiled and ruffled Nicky's sandy curls.

"You may stay," she said. "I'm sure you will love spending some time with your sister. I will return for you at tea time."

Amanda smiled at her. "Thank you. I will try not to excite them too much."

The woman acknowledged her words with a smile. Then she turned and headed back up the path while Nicky picked up her panther to seat himself beside her, keeping the statuette balanced on his knees. George had already made himself comfortable in her lap. Picking up the book, she translated as she read the story of Odysseus' return to his palace after many years away, his subsequent reunion with his wife, and how he and his son slew all the many suitors who had been plaguing poor Penelope.

When the governess returned to collect her charges, Amanda hugged both of them and sent them on their way.

Nicky put her panther in her lap as he left, and now she ran her hand over it as her thoughts returned to the night before.

She wished she knew what Jon was thinking...or feeling. So far, nothing in his manners or actions indicated he looked upon her as anyone other than his sister's friend. Of course, there was the explanation and kiss last night. There was more to the aftermath of the kiss three years ago than Jon had told her—of that she was certain. How important it was for her to know, she wasn't sure.

Knowing she would be spending more time with him, she wondered if she dared to ask. Perhaps later, when she felt more comfortable in his company. For now, it was enough that she could speak to him without becoming too self-conscious. Rising from the bench, she shook out her skirts, picked up her book and panther and headed for the house. Eliza would probably have tea served in the drawing room.

"Have you been matchmaking again?"

The dowager countess looked up from her teacup, a puzzled look in her eyes. "Again? And for whom?"

Jon watched her carefully. He wasn't sure she wouldn't disclaim all knowledge of Lady Rampton's machinations, but he needed to know.

"I was all but accosted by Lady Rampton last evening."

"Ah." His grandmother put a world of feeling in that one syllable, not all of it positive. "Margaret is a peagoose. Thankfully, her children take after their father and have better heads on their shoulders."

"You were fond of her sister?" He was opening old wounds, he knew, but he couldn't help himself. Despite having danced with and kissed Amanda, Sophie's words returned to haunt him later in the evening.

"Yes," she sighed.

They both knew this conversation would get them nowhere. It never did. Ignoring it was the best thing to do, but sometimes it needed to come out. He could not forget that his grandmother had refused to acknowledge his mother and tried to deny him his inheritance. They had made their peace with each other, but occasionally the past reared its ugly head.

"There is little use in denying it. We have trod this path before, and I suspect we will venture down it again before I breathe my last. There is nothing more to say that hasn't already been said."

Jon knew she was right. She had already expressed her apologies for her neglect and bitterness. And she had done everything she could to dispel the rumors of a feud within the family. In addition, she had been invaluable when it came to pulling off Felicia's wedding three years ago. So, why did he continue to punish her? It didn't say much for his character, that he couldn't forgive one frail, old woman.

Taking another sip of her tea, she put the cup down and looked directly at him. "Despite my own bias, I think young Sophie wouldn't have you at any rate."

Jon grimaced. He'd asked, but she might have softened the blow a bit. He'd told himself he didn't want her either, but that was before Felicia told him she was the same Sophie on his list. Now he had a dilemma on his hands.

He admitted to himself that his great-grandmother had been wily enough that Sophie might just be the person with the statuette. A remote connection who knew the family history. Her blue eyes and darker blonde hair didn't quite match the description he'd been given, but colors change slightly and she could have been a child when Nona gave her the statue.

Of course, he didn't know anything for sure because he hadn't asked Sophie about a panther. He'd been too amused by her forthright declaration that she didn't want to marry him to consider anything else. Unfortunately, she might just be Fate's idea of a joke.

Someone who didn't want him, but was supposed to be his destiny.

Jon joined Amanda and his grandmother later that week as they conducted interviews. Governesses all looked the same, he thought. From the top of her severely styled head to the toes of her serviceable black half-boots, Miss Addams looked no different than the three other women who had occupied the same chair during the previous two hours.

The dowager signaled the end of the interview and he heard Amanda sigh as he escorted the woman from the room. It had been his grandmother's idea to interview out-of-work governesses as possible teachers and a headmistress for the school, but so far, none seemed to be what Amanda was looking for.

When he returned, Amanda looked up at him. He knew she had not expected to see him when she arrived earlier, but he was certain her eyes had lit up for a moment at the sight of him.

For the past few days he had paid her more attention than he had ever paid anyone else. He wondered if he had finally crossed the line to courting her. So far, no one seemed notice his interest, and he hoped to keep it that way. Just two mornings ago, he'd visited the school. He'd deliberately arrived at the time he knew she would be leaving in order to escort her home. After a tour of the premises and an introduction to Mr. Cooper, he understood her feelings.

"Are there any more?" he asked his grandmother.

"Two more," she replied, consulting the sheet in her lap. "The next one is due in ten minutes."

Jon seated himself in the chair the last woman had just vacated and allowed himself the luxury of looking at Amanda as she and his grandmother discussed the last candidate. Dressed in a morning gown of periwinkle blue, her golden curls framing her face, she was a sight for sore eyes. Just watching her made his temperature rise, and reminded him of how well she fit in his arms.

"We haven't found anyone yet who would do," Amanda said. "Not one of those women could handle a whole classroom full of girls. One or two at a time, maybe, but not a whole class full."

"Perhaps," he interrupted. "But how can you tell?"

Amanda started. When she looked at him, surprise filled her eyes. "How do I know?" She cocked her head to one side, thinking. "I'm not sure. Intuition perhaps? Supposition? A feeling? I don't really know, except that I just know." She shrugged eloquently.

"I see."

Smithers interrupted with the next young woman. Jon vacated the seat to resume his position near the window, and continue his currently favorite pastime of watching Amanda.

Miss Marianne Dalrymple was the most interesting young woman to come in the door yet. Like the other applicants, her red hair was styled in a knot at the back of her head, but she had softened the effect by releasing a few curls around her face. Dark eyes, intense and alert, sparkled above a pug nose and wide mouth. She had a low, yet strong voice he had no doubt could be heard above a noisy classroom.

As the interview proceeded, he noted she was well-read and intelligent. Her references, referred to by his grandmother, were excellent. She agreed with Amanda on the breadth of an education girls should have, and made sympathetic noises when informed of the orphanage. She had been orphaned at an early age herself.

He could see she was nearly exactly what Amanda was looking for, but then she did something none of the other candidates had done. She smiled. It was not just any smile, it was a smile full of warmth and compassion. And right then he knew what Amanda was looking for. She was looking for someone who would love the girls as much as she did.

Someone who would make the effort to get to know the girls. Someone who would understand when one of them was upset or unwell. Someone who wasn't angry at the rest of society for her place in it. Someone who knew what it was like to have no one, but still make something of herself. In short, Amanda wanted someone who would encourage the girls, understanding the obstacles they would eventually face. Someone who had faced some of the same obstacles and made it past them.

Before she left, Amanda gave her a card with the address of the school on it, instructing her to show up there the next morning at ten o'clock sharp.

The last woman was also an improvement on the first four, but not in the same class as Miss Dalrymple. Amanda, however, saw something in her as well and she, too, was given a card and instructions to appear at the school in two days time.

By the time the last one left, it was time for tea. As Smithers and a maid set up the tea near the dowager's chair, Amanda approached.

"What did you think of the last two?" she asked.

"I thought the red-haired one—Miss Dalrymple, was it?— was probably the best, but the last one—Miss Gaines?—was quite good too. She won't be as optimistic, though, but she'll do well."

"Hmmm. I was thinking the same thing. At least Miss Dalrymple had a pleasant disposition. The first ones looked as if they had never smiled in their lives."

He chuckled. "Somehow, I'd guessed that the dourness of the first few had discouraged you. So, what do you plan to do when Miss Dalrymple and Miss Gaines arrive at the school?"

"I thought I'd have them observe for a while, then invite them to participate. I think Miss Dalrymple will make an excellent teacher, and Miss Gaines might be best suited as a headmistress. All I need to do now is get rid of Mr. Cooper."

"Neither of them is as well educated as you."

Amanda stilled before turning to look up at him with wide, suspicious eyes. "How do you know?"

Jon noticed the sudden reticence and wondered if he had ventured into forbidden territory. It occurred to him that he'd never seen her reading, never gotten the impression she was interested in anything other than the normal female pursuits. Had she deliberately hidden that side of herself?

The dowager called to them from across the room and he was saved from replying.

Over tea, the three discussed family. No longer moving in society, the dowager was eager to hear of the latest goings on. Jon noticed she was more alert today than she had been when he visited her two days ago. And she did not seem to be in as much pain. He wondered if her doctor had followed his suggestion and changed what she was taking for her painful joints.

"Those three scamps were everywhere," the dowager was saying to Amanda, laughter in her voice. "You should have seen them."

"I didn't have to," she replied. "I have seen them before.

And you are right."

He had only been half listening to the conversation, but now he joined in.

"To which three scamps are you referring?"

Amanda burst into laughter, her soft chuckles sending pleasant sensations throughout his body. "I take it you haven't made the acquaintance yet of your nephews and nieces?"

"I have, of course, but there are four of them, not three."

"Shana could never be classed with the other three," his grandmother said, referring to Tina's five-year-old daughter. "The other three, however..." She let the sentence hang, as if the ending were understood.

"Andrew and the twins?" he asked.

"Two-year-olds are the worst," Amanda told him, a mischievous twinkle in her eyes. "They are nearly as aggravating as full grown men. They don't take direction, they are often hard of hearing, and they never tell you what's wrong when they're out of sorts."

Jon's eyebrows rose. "I think I've been insulted. Either that or Andrew, Michael and Caroline have."

"Probably the latter." This from his grandmother, but she was laughing all the same.

Jon was tempted to agree. At two, Brand and Felicia's twins, Michael and Caroline, and Tina and Jay's son, Andrew, were perpetual motion machines. How their nannies kept up with them was a mystery to him. The last time he had been at Felicia's the twins had been loose in the garden. The gardener, she'd informed him with sparkling eyes, had already threatened to quit twice that day.

Just before taking their leave, he asked after his grandmother's health. "I am doing better these days," she told him. "This new stuff tastes horrible, doesn't make me as sleepy as the laudanum did, and seems to work better. Thank you."

He smiled in acknowledgment and bent to kiss her cheek. "You're welcome," was all he said before escorting Amanda out.

Three nights later Jon stood at the top of the stairs leading down into Lord and Lady Carmichael's ballroom, scanning the crowd. The air was thick and stuffy, stale with the scent of unwashed bodies, perfume and flowers. Lady Carmichael was apparently one of those matrons who eschewed fresh air, for none of the terrace doors or windows stood open, despite that the evening was balmy with only a slight breeze. There was no sign of Amanda. Descending the stairs, he was met at the bottom by none other than Charity Bascomb.

Manners prevented him from brushing past the red-haired beauty, but he did not want to be saddled with her when he found Amanda. He'd noted her interest over the last week, but had made his own disinterest clear. That she continued to connive for his attention had begun to make him wary. Just two nights ago she'd managed to trap him into dancing a waltz with her. Remembering that, he took the opportunity afforded by the musicians, and danced a quadrille. She had not expected him to ask her to dance so soon. He saw it in the widening of her eyes when he requested the set, but she had no choice but to accept. If she turned him down, he would not ask her again. On the other hand, if she danced with him, he would not ask her again without eyebrows raising. Even though he'd recently paid marked attention to Amanda, he made a point never to dance with her more than once in an evening.

Returning Charity to her mother's side, he bowed and made his escape. Quartering the room, he finally found Felicia speaking with one of the dowagers in a corner. She glanced up at him as he approached then excused herself to join him. She got right to the point.

"Amanda's not here."

Jon did not answer. Felicia had actually answered two questions at once. Yes, he wanted to know where Amanda was, but he wondered whether she'd noticed his interest. Now he knew, and wondered whether she'd say something about the statuette. She didn't.

He glanced around the crowded room. He still had two young women on his list he hadn't spoken to—as well as Sophie. He grimaced. He did not want to speak to her again, but if he was correct, he could continue to pay attention to Amanda without guilt. He noticed one of the young women on his list across the room. She was one he had not been formally introduced to. He wasn't sure he wanted to ask Felicia to introduce them, but it was either she or Tina, and he hadn't seen Tina yet tonight.

Felicia stared at him in surprise when he requested she introduce him. For a moment, he was sure she was about to say something, then suppressed the comment and did as he asked.

MaryAnne Lester was a dangerous combination—beautiful and devious. He wondered if Felicia's reaction to his request for an introduction had anything to do with Miss Lester's character, but he consoled himself with the thought that Felicia had put her on the list.

Her conversation was desultory, but filled with sexual innuendo he would not have expected a young woman her age to be aware of. Looking down into eyes a shade lighter than his own, he noted that she appraised him openly. It was an uncomfortable feeling. As if she was weighing his physical possibilities as well as his bank account.

"I don't suppose you've ever seen a panther?" he asked at one point.

She batted artificially darkened lashes. "That depends, my lord."

"Depends on what?"

"On why you want to know?" Then she laughed at her own apparent witticism.

Jon gritted his teeth. He'd told her the same story he had told Amanda about the non-existent menagerie in Rome.

He supposed her high-pitched laugh might have been pleasing to some, but it grated on his nerves. As the music came to a close, he escorted her from the floor and headed back in the direction of her chaperone. Her fragrance, a sickly, sweet scent, assaulted his nose.

Opening her fan, she began to wave it delicately in front of her face. "It is quite warm in here, my lord. Could we step out on to the terrace for a moment?"

Not on your life, he nearly replied. "I'm afraid I must decline," he lied smoothly. "I am engaged for the next set and my partner will soon be wondering where I am."

Stopping before her companion, he bowed over her hand. He knew from her reactions, she had no idea what a panther

Denise Patrick

was, so he was sure she did not have what he sought. Besides, he was reasonably sure Nona would not have selected someone so forward.

Striding toward the staircase, uncaring that if he was seen leaving it would expose his lie, he nearly bowled over a young woman who stepped into his path while looking the other way. He recognized Martha Danvers.

"I beg your pardon, my lord," she squeaked nervously as his hands steadied her.

"The fault is all mine, Miss Danvers. I should have been paying better attention to where I was going."

"Oh." She looked behind herself as she spoke and Jon frowned. He couldn't imagine who she might be running from.

"Might I be of assistance?"

"What? Oh, yes." She glanced back again and he noticed a young man watching them.

"Are you acquainted with that young man?"

"We have been introduced before," she answered, "but he asked me to dance, and I did not wish to."

"Then you should not."

"But I lied," she confessed nervously, blood rushing into her face. "I told him I was already engaged for this set."

Fate had saved him. He smiled broadly. "Ah. Then, if I might be allowed to assist you. I, too, am in need of a partner. Perhaps we can join this set."

Laying nervous fingers upon his arm, she nodded and allowed him to lead her out onto the floor to join the cotillion.

When the set was over, he found Felicia in the crowd and left Miss Danvers in her care. Knowing Felicia would keep an eye on the shy young woman, he collected his hat and cane, and departed before anything else delayed him.

Chapter Seven

Amanda looked over the bent heads of the girls as they worked on their embroidery. Each girl worked on a square of linen which would later be sewn together to make a quilt. The quilt would then be sold and the proceeds given back to the orphanage. It was a good project for the girls, and it helped the orphanage.

Wandering through the rows, she looked over their shoulders, giving words of encouragement, advice and help when needed. At the back of the room, she discovered Cassie staring at her still blank square of linen, tears running down her face. Lizzy, the girl next to her, looked up.

"She's real sad," she whispered in explanation. "No one can cheer her up."

Amanda nodded and knelt beside the little girl's seat. "What is amiss, Cassie?" she asked gently. "Do you want to tell me about it?"

"I miss my mama." The little girl sniffed. "I know she's in heaven, but I still miss her."

Amanda sat on a small bench nearby and drew the child into her arms. "I still miss mine too," she told her. "She went to heaven a very long time ago."

Cassie's dark eyes looked up into hers and for a moment Amanda thought she looked familiar, but the moment passed and Cassie asked. "How old were you?"

"Eight," Amanda replied. "Even younger than you."

The dark head rested against her shoulder. "Oh." Amanda held the child for a few minutes until she said, "I wish my papa would come."

This was news to Amanda and she pushed the child back to look at her. "You have a papa?"

Cassie nodded. "He didn't live with us, but he always sent us money and he came to see me. Sometimes he even brought me presents."

"Do you know his name?"

The little girl shook her head. "Mama never told me. She said we couldn't live with him, but he would always take care of us."

"What was your mama's name?"

"Eleanor."

"Just Eleanor?"

The child nodded. Amanda's frustration knew no bounds. Here was a child who apparently had a parent, but no one knew that, nor could the child provide enough information to track him down.

Amanda wasn't so naïve that she didn't understand the import of what Cassie could tell her. It was likely she was the by-blow of some member of the nobility, which was why she had her mother's nondescript last name of Smythe. He had apparently taken good care of her and her mother and even came to visit once or twice a year at the cottage where they lived. Unfortunately, her mother kept nothing which would identify him. Or, if she had left his name somewhere, it wasn't obvious. When she died, there was no place for Cassie to go, and no one to notify.

Her mother had been buried in the churchyard and Cassie had been brought to the orphanage by the vicar's wife. She had been brought to this particular one because one of the women in the village had a maid who had come from here. The maid said they would take good care of her.

Jon was waiting for her as she emerged from the building shortly after noon. Leaning against his curricle speaking to his tiger, she knew a sudden sensation in the vicinity of her heart. She would never get tired of looking at him, she decided. Spotting her, he came forward as she reached the bottom step.

"It's been four days," he said without preamble. "I hope you have recovered."

"I have, thank you," she replied, a blush tinting her cheeks.

There was no way, short of the truth, she could think of to explain her four-day absence to him. And that would never come from her.

Jon lifted her to the seat, then joined her. Accepting the ribbons from his tiger, he waited until the man had taken his seat at the rear before maneuvering the horses away from the curb.

Once they were traveling more in the open he glanced her way. "How was class today?"

"Fine." She hesitated. Could she ask for his help? Perhaps she could find Cassie's papa for her. Her heart went out to the little girl who obviously was loved by both of her parents, regardless of her birth. She wondered if the child's father searched for her.

"But...?"

"I discovered today that Cassie has a father, but she doesn't know enough about him to lead anyone to him."

Jon said nothing in reply and she felt her spirits sink. Maybe he wouldn't want to help her find Cassie's father.

"I'd like to try and find him for her, but she truly knows nothing except her mother's name."

"Would she even recognize him if she saw him?"

"I would think so. She is ten, after all."

"What all does she know?"

Amanda repeated all that Cassie had told her, then added her own conjecture to the narrative. "I would wager her mother's name wasn't originally Smythe, either."

Jon agreed with her conclusions. In all likelihood, Cassie's mother had been an actress, opera dancer, or even a demirep whose career came to an abrupt end when she got pregnant. Lapsing into silence, Amanda tried not to think of the solid body seated next to hers on the seat. Or of the broad shoulders under the expensive material of his dark blue coat, nor the large hands expertly handling the reins. She stared straight ahead so she wouldn't be tempted to notice the way the breeze ruffled his hair or his green eyes glinted in the sunlight. He was altogether too potent a force to ignore, but she did her best, pretending to notice things along the way she had paid scant attention to before.

She had spent much of the last few days thinking of him and his sudden attentiveness. She wondered if he was courting her, but beyond kissing her occasionally, he did not seem to be. Of course, in the normal course of things, kissing her might have been considered courting, but their history told her something different.

Eliza had told her yesterday he had inquired after her at one of the soirees. Upon being informed she was unwell, he'd asked if there was anything he could do. When Eliza told him no, he'd asked her to convey his wishes for a speedy recovery. She wondered now what he could have done if Eliza had given him an affirmative answer.

Pulling up in front of Barrington House, Jon tossed the reins to his tiger, then lifted her down.

"Will you be at the Devereauxs' tonight?" he asked as he escorted her up the front stairs.

"Yes." The door opened. Jon bowed and raised her hand to his lips.

"Until tonight, then."

A week later Amanda was crossing the foyer of Barrington House when voices reached her from the library.

"You should have seen the place I went to today." Amazement colored her father's voice. "It was filthy. And the children! I can't believe we allow such places to exist. I've always thought Shaftesbury a bit radical, but now I'm beginning to think he's right."

"There are many societies out there trying to help," her stepmother replied.

Her father's voice was distant and, instinctively, she moved closer to the door.

"...three more tomorrow. Mr. Darby from Bow Street will be looking at the area around Charing Cross."

"And will you go with him?"

"No, I will finish visiting the ones on the list I have. I certainly hope I don't—"

"Ouch!" Her stepmother's voice cut across her father's. "Calm down before you hurt someone."

"I'm sorry, love." Amanda smiled at the contrite tone in her father's voice. "This whole situation has turned me into a bear."

"I understand, darling. I must remember not to stand too close when you're pacing."

"I prefer it when you stand close. I must remember to watch where I step."

"Let's hope you didn't break my foot."

Her father lowered his voice, so Amanda didn't hear his reply.

"Trent!" Eliza's shocked gasp dissolved into giggles.

Amanda turned away from the door as silence descended. She could only imagine what must be going on, and didn't want to be caught eavesdropping. Smiling, she headed for the drawing room.

Carol Tinning had eloped! The story spread like wildfire and by evening it was on everyone's lips. Not only had she run off to Gretna Green, but she had done so with the second son of a minor baronet. Her parents, the Earl and Countess of Quade, were in shock. It was said the countess had taken to her bed, prostrate with grief. The earl had gone after the couple, but all the wagers in White's famous betting book were against him catching them.

"It's a good thing she didn't have your statuette," Felicia told Jon that evening. Even the spectacle taking place onstage could not keep the theater-goers from speculating on the fate of the lovers. Whether the earl caught them or not, Lady Carol was hopelessly compromised. Only marriage would salvage her reputation.

He hadn't asked, but was glad Felicia had volunteered the information. Because she had told him she would keep out of his search, he had not wanted to come out and ask her directly. In fact, he had forced himself not to ask her about Sophie.

Earlier that afternoon, while ostensibly going over the newest plans his estate manager had sent, he had reviewed the list Felicia had given him again. Picking up a quill, he crossed off the women he determined were definitely not in possession of the statue: Catherine Hargrave, Susanna Marsden, Amanda

Cookeson, Elise Harbington, Ellen Stimpingston. Crossing off Beatrice Wyndham-Smythe, he was reminded that she had also remembered seeing a figurine at Miss Ridley's Academy, but could not recall who had it. Instead, she had recommended he ask Felicia—or Amanda.

That left Theresa Winston, MaryAnne Lester, Carol Tinning and Sophie Lawrence. On principle, he had crossed off Theresa Winston. He had no interest in a woman who could not be bothered to pay attention to her partner on the dance floor. MaryAnne Lester made him feel more like the prey than the hunter. He crossed her off too. That left Carol Tinning and Sophie Lawrence. And now he knew Lady Carol did not have the figurine. Sophie Lawrence remained. Whether she had it or not mattered little. She'd already informed him she wouldn't have him. He wondered if his great-grandmother had known he might have to work for Miss Lawrence's affections, and if that had been the goal. It didn't matter. He hadn't planned on marrying the woman with it, so there was no need. He'd only wanted to know in order to decide whether he should try to acquire it somehow. Now he wondered if he ever would.

He frowned. Either Sophie had his statue, or what? Someone had lied? If so, why? Perhaps the person truly did not know what it represented? He still could not believe that was the case. It was easier to believe Sophie had it—and move on to other things.

Like deciding whether he should muster up the courage to offer for Amanda. He didn't want to feel like he was being pushed. He was only thirty and could afford to wait a few more years. But Amanda was already twenty-one. Soon she would be considered on the shelf and she might accept the next person to ask just to avoid being labeled a spinster.

Was he ready to make a trip down the aisle? He wasn't sure, but he certainly didn't want someone else to snatch up Amanda first. As long as she didn't have the statue, he could live with his attraction to her. It might even work to his advantage in the long run because he was certain her feelings for him were more than friendly. And his grandmother would be pleased.

Amanda was having difficulty concentrating on the drama unfolding on the stage before her. She could not stop her eyes from straying to the Warringham box, where Jon sat with his sisters and their husbands, and wishing she was there instead of with her parents.

She wondered to herself what it was about him that drew her. He was handsome, but so were at least a dozen or so others she knew. He was unfailingly polite and welcoming, but that was a product of breeding and upbringing. He cared deeply for his family. That set him apart from some of the young men she knew. He wasn't a rake or rogue—nor was he trying to be. He was confident of who he was without being labeled something else.

He could kiss her senseless. No one had ever been able to do that. Not Lord Thurston, not Lord Darlington, not Lord Seevers. Their kisses had been more brotherly than lover-like. Not one of them had tried to kiss her anywhere other than her knuckles or cheek. Only Jon had been able to cause her heart to beat erratically by his mere presence, and her breath to catch by a mere touch. But was the physical attraction enough? And how would she find out?

The curtain fell and she suddenly realized she had been woolgathering the night away. She looked up as the curtain behind her parted to reveal Brand and Felicia. Jon entered behind them.

"I spoke with Shaftesbury today," he said as they strolled, ostensibly toward the refreshment area.

"And...?"

"He promised to find another post for Mr. Cooper as soon as possible. He isn't quite willing to convince the Board to turn a blind eye to the school, but he agreed to allow me to run the school as I see fit."

She bristled at the implication.

"You? Why you?"

"I think you and I both know why. Certainly Shaftesbury and I understood that you and my grandmother, but mainly you, run the school. We also understand that the London Board is made up of men who are impressed by their own importance and, therefore, not about to let a woman seem more capable than they."

"It's no wonder children live on the streets," she muttered angrily, "with such idiots running the city. And it's no wonder that in this day and age a ten-year-old girl doesn't know her own father's name. If she'd been a boy, she'd know."

"Perhaps," he said placatingly. "But there's little to do about it now. And you are getting what you wanted."

"Only as long as I'm willing to hide behind you," she huffed.

"I wouldn't call it hiding."

"Then what would you call it?"

"I'm not sure. But I'm perfectly willing to tell anyone who asks that I'm definitely not in charge. Unlike the men on the Board, I'm not so enamored of myself as to think I could competently run a school for girls."

A large canvas in a wooden frame was propped against a wall. In the dim light, she could see a wash of brown, blue and green. He led her around to the other side of it, shielding them from anyone who might glance down the small hallway. She knew better than to be alone with him too often, but she couldn't help herself. She wondered if he'd missed her over the past few days. She had certainly missed him.

"Where are we?" Was that her squeaky, nervous voice?

"Does it matter?"

A golden eyebrow raised. "That depends on why we are here."

He pulled her closer and bent his head. "Has anyone ever told you, you talk too much?"

She shivered as her mind raced for an answer. It was lost moments later as his lips covered hers.

Amanda didn't protest. In fact, she lifted up on her toes and wrapped her arms around his neck. Jon's hands settled on her back, pressing her closer as she parted her lips beneath his.

Warmth engulfed her, wrapping her in a soft cocoon of safety. Never had she felt so alive or so comfortable in a man's arms as she did in Jon's. His lips softened as they moved over hers, his tongue seeking the moistness within.

Her sigh of disappointment was audible as he raised his head. He kissed first one corner of her mouth, then the other.

She attempted to draw him back into another kiss when he stiffened and raised his head, searching the gloom behind her. Reluctantly releasing his hold, he turned to scan the area in which they stood.

Sanity returned slowly and she realized she was standing in his arms, a dreamy smile on her face. Thankful for the darkness that hid her warm cheeks, her eyes locked with his momentarily, then he turned and led her back toward her box.

"She's in better spirits today," Mabel told Amanda in a low voice when she inquired about Cassie a few days later. "Unfortunately, some of the girls have been teasing her because she has been saying for the past week that her papa is coming for her."

"How does she know?" Amanda hung her cloak on the peg, keeping her voice soft.

Mabel glanced around the room, noting which girls were working and which seemed to be finished.

"She says her mother told her in a dream he was looking for her and would find her soon."

Amanda sighed. "I suppose we should be thankful it was so vague. A dream like that can keep a child going for years."

"Granny went through the things that came with her and, except for a miniature that Cassie says is her mother and a small locket she says her father gave her, there's nothing there which identifies her or her father."

Amanda frowned. Lily Grantham, "Granny" to the girls, was the woman who ran the orphanage. She was a sweet woman with a sharp mind and even sharper instincts. She would not have allowed Cassie into her orphanage if she didn't think she had possibilities—and the woman who brought her hadn't been able to pay the entrance fee.

For the first time, Amanda considered the fee. It wasn't steep, but it was enough that poorer children would never be admitted. Where had the money come from? And if, as Cassie said, her father sent them money, was there more out there waiting to be delivered?

Miss Dalrymple entered the room and Mabel clapped her

hands to get the girls' attention. Amanda had, after a thorough explanation of what she expected, hired both Marianne Dalrymple and Wilma Gaines. Mr. Cooper hadn't been happy, but Amanda told him bluntly that since this was a girls' school, they did not need a man to run it. Knowing Lord Shaftesbury had promised to find him another position, and Jon was standing behind her, she had not been worried about the dislike she read in his eyes at her announcement.

Jon, Brand and Jay had all agreed to support many of Lord Shaftesbury's social reforms in the House of Lords and recruit as many others as they could. In return, the earl had agreed to convince the Board to allow the girls' school to be run as Amanda saw fit. That included getting rid of Mr. Cooper and hiring a headmistress in his stead. He didn't need to know she had already hired Miss Gaines for that very purpose. For now, Miss Gaines was helping in the middle class of seven- to nine-year-olds.

Amanda and Marianne split up the class to begin working while Mabel went off to do paperwork. An hour and a half later they were finished. It was delightful, Amanda discovered, to share her work with someone who loved it as much as she did. In addition, she learned Marianne had gone next door and offered her services at the orphanage, too. Granny had been ecstatic.

Sitting behind the small desk in the corner, she watched as the girls trooped out under Marianne's watchful eye. Cassie approached the desk and Marianne looked at her questioningly.

"Go on," Amanda told her. "I'll walk Cassie over when we're done." Maybe she'd introduce the child to Jon if he was waiting for her.

Marianne nodded and followed the girls out, closing the door behind her.

"My papa's coming for me soon," the little girl said without preamble, "so I wanted to say goodbye."

Amanda smiled. "Is he coming today?"

"I don't know." Cassie idly toyed with one of her long dark braids. "But I was afraid you might not be here when he came. I heard you telling Miss Marianne you would be away all next week."

Amanda nodded. She was glad she'd hired Marianne and Wilma. She was committed to attend the Beldons' house party and short of dying, she had been informed by Eliza, she could not get out of it. With all the preparations needed, she would be gone the whole of the next week.

"Do you not think your papa would allow you to come back to school with the other girls?"

Cassie scuffed her small foot against the worn floorboards. "I don't know. But I don't know that I want to come back. Lizzy is nice to me, but some of the other girls are not."

"Why?"

"They say I talk too fancy for them. That I am too good for them. They don't like me."

Amanda drew the child into her lap. She knew many of the orphans felt threatened by someone they perceived to be different. Lizzy was a shoemaker's daughter and was nice to all the girls, but there were others who weren't. She couldn't solve everyone's problems, but she wished she could solve Cassie's. With all her heart, she wished Cassie was right—and her father was indeed out looking for her and would find her soon.

A noise in the hallway caused Amanda to realize they had been there for a while since the girls left. It was probably time for her to return Cassie next door and head for home herself. She could hear a heavy tread as, with a sigh, she rose to retrieve her cloak from the peg by the door.

"Come." She held her hand out to Cassie. "I'll walk you back next door."

The door swung open and a man stepped into the room.

Amanda took a step back and her heart sank. *This* was all she needed.

"I was told I would find..." the man began, but stopped abruptly as he realized who he was speaking to. "Amanda?"

Speechless, her father stared at her. She looked back at him in shock for what seemed like an eternity. The high-pitched squeal that erupted from beside them had both of them turning.

"Papa!"

If there hadn't been a bench near enough for her to sit on, Amanda would have fallen to the floor, watching in amazement as Cassie launched herself at her father. It was her father's reaction, however, which caused the tears to spring to her eyes.

"Cassie!" Joy blossomed on his face as he caught the little girl, picked her up, and twirled her around, just as he used to do with her. "I have been looking everywhere for you."

She watched the reunion in awe, her mind barely able to assimilate the activity her eyes witnessed. Papa? Cassie's papa? Her own father? How was it possible? In stunned disbelief, she watched him put the child down and drop to his knees, his face alight, and pull her into his arms.

A shadow in the doorway had her looking up to find Jon standing there. Glancing at the two other occupants in the room who were more involved in themselves for the moment, she slipped quietly out into the hall.

Stepping into Jon's arms was like reaching a safe harbor after a storm. She hadn't even realized tears had begun to slip down her cheeks until they were in Jon's coach and underway.

The day was cloudy and a light drizzle was falling. When Jon handed her a square of embroidered linen, she suddenly wondered why she was crying. Was she happy Cassie had found her father? Yes. Was she shocked he also happened to be hers? Yes.

Raising her eyes to Jon's, she found him watching her, concern clear in his eyes. "I'm sorry," she said. "I don't know what has turned me into a watering pot."

"Did something happen before I arrived?"

She nodded, the movement jerky. "Cassie's father came for her."

Chapter Eight

Jon was relieved to hear the mystery of Cassie's absent father had been solved. He hadn't really believed it would happen, but now that it had, he could concentrate on Amanda herself again, not her quests. For the past few days, he had been trying to decide first, whether to ask her to marry him, and second, if he did, how to do so without a declaration of undying affection.

Drops of rain marked the windows of the coach and pattered on the roof. The rumble of the coach over the cobblestones seemed loud in the silence, but Jon was focused on Amanda.

"That's good, isn't it?" Reaching over, he cupped her chin and ran his thumb over the tear tracks on her cheeks. "The tears were of joy, not anything else?"

She smiled sadly. "I think so." She paused. "It's just that...I never told you about the conversation I overheard almost two weeks ago. Papa and Eliza were in the salon overlooking the garden and I was outside reading. I only heard part of it, but enough to know Papa was looking for someone who had disappeared and was frantic to find them again. Eliza encouraged him to keep looking. She actually told him he would never rest until he found her."

Understanding dawned as she spoke. "I didn't realize he was looking for a child. The only name I overheard was 'Nora'." Her voice lapsed for a moment, then she continued. "Cassie told me her mother's name was Eleanor, but..." her voice trailed off, at a loss for words.

Amanda leaned against him and his arms encircled her.

She was soft and warm against him, but he sensed something wrong. The scent of honeysuckle soothed his senses and although he pushed back the hood on her cloak, he resisted the impulse to bury his face in her hair.

"I'm happy for Cassie, but I don't know what to think."

"About what?"

"I don't know." Her response was so soft he had to bend closer to hear.

"It must be a shock to discover the person you were so intent on finding was your own father."

"I suppose that's it, but what will everyone think?"

He chuckled. "Do you care?"

She sat back. "I don't know. There has been enough talk about our family over the years. But compared to this, all that gossip was inconsequential."

"Do you not want your father to bring her home?"

"I—" When she looked up at him, her eyes reflected her confusion.

"You do realize," he said softly, "that England is one of the few places in a very large world where being born on the wrong side of the blanket can affect your entire life? In many other countries a child is a child—and isn't blamed for the circumstances of its birth."

"I've never really considered it before." She sighed, leaned her head back against the cushions and closed her eyes. "But now that gives me two things to worry about."

Tenderness he'd never felt for anyone outside his family invaded his heart. The tension in her face caused his chest to tighten. At that moment he wanted nothing more than to be the one to erase all her worries and resurrect the smiling, carefree Amanda he was used to.

He couldn't solve the Cassie problem, but he wondered what other dilemma lay so heavy on her heart.

"Two?"

She nodded. He pulled her close again. It seemed comfort and a listening ear was all he could offer for now.

"My father didn't know how deeply I was involved in the school. Eliza and I kept it from him. Knowing his views about women and learning, we just never told him. I'm afraid he will forbid me to return." She shivered lightly against him. "What am I going to do? I don't want to stop.

"When I first started going, your grandmother suggested I come to her home first, and she had her coachman take me and bring me back every day. I have even spent quite a bit of time with your grandmother while Papa and Eliza were in the country. Papa never suspected. It has only been during these last few months that I have taken my own coach. It has caused some minor speculation, but now this—this just might cause more than speculation."

"I cannot vouch for the possible gossip, but today's events would have happened eventually as long as Cassie was there. Even if your father hadn't shown up when you were there, if he brought her home—and it sounds like he will do that—she would have said something eventually."

"I suppose you're right, but it still doesn't solve my dilemma. I have never disobeyed my father, but I think I would do so if he forbade me to go back."

Jon could not believe he'd been given such a perfect opening. He wanted her, that he knew. For him, that was enough. Of course, there was still his statuette to decide what to do about. But since he hadn't planned to marry the woman with it, he could marry Amanda and decide that later. And he could solve this particular problem if she'd let him.

The decision made, he leaped. "I suppose, then, you'll just have to marry me."

Amanda froze. Had she heard aright? Had he actually proposed? It was roundabout, and somewhat backward, but she knew he had actually said the words *marry me*.

Her head snapped up and she stared at him in astonishment. Her mouth worked for a few seconds as she struggled with what to say, then she blurted, "Why?"

"Why, what?"

"Why would you...?" She was unable to complete the question.

"Because I know how much the school means to you. I'd never make you stop completely, but some day it only stands to reason you will have to scale back your involvement."

He ran his knuckles down the side of her face in a caress

that heated her from the inside out. Tilting her face with his fingertips, he looked down into her eyes for the space of a heartbeat before he covered her lips with his.

Amanda responded without thought. Parting her lips beneath the pressure of his, she gave herself up to the wonder of the moment. His tongue slipped in to meet hers and she kissed him back as he had taught her. When her arms slid up and around his neck, he pulled her closer, angling his head to deepen the kiss.

No words were necessary to answer his proposal. She gave him her answer by her response. His hand rose to her neck, freeing the clasp of her cloak and it slithered into a puddle on the floor of the carriage. He never broke the kiss as his hands moved to her waist, lifted and dragged her across his lap.

She could feel the pounding of his heart as he lifted his head and stared down into her eyes. "Will you marry me, Amanda?" His voice was soft, brushing over her skin, chasing away the worries of minutes ago and enveloping her in a haze of contentment.

"Yes." Breathlessly, she stared at him in wonder, then turned her burning cheeks against his jacket. It was slightly damp and smelled of the rain, but still provided comfort.

He chuckled and the sound thrilled her to her toes. "Surely you are not suddenly shy?"

Bemused, she didn't trust her voice to answer and so shook her head. She wasn't shy, but the hand stroking her back was causing such pleasure to ripple through her that she did not want him to stop.

"Then look at me." The tenderness in his voice was nearly her undoing, and she raised her head to look up at him just as the coach slowed, then came to a stop.

She thought she heard a huge sigh escape before she scrambled off his lap and reached up to check her hair. She looked around for her cloak just as the door opened. Stepping down, Jon lifted Amanda out, retrieved her cloak from the floor, and escorted her quickly inside.

Once in the foyer, he handed the cloak to Barrons before turning to her.

"I suspect your father is not far behind us. I had my

coachman take an indirect route here. Do you wish to freshen up before meeting him again?" When she nodded, he stepped back. "I will await you in the drawing room."

Uncaring what Barrons likely thought, she flew up the stairs to her room. Ringing for Mary, she splashed water on her face to cool her heated cheeks and erase all traces of her earlier tears while she waited. Fifteen minutes later, once again composed, she descended the staircase and entered the drawing room. She'd hurried and hadn't taken the time to change her dress, hoping she would be downstairs with Jon when her father arrived. She wasn't fast enough.

Eliza sat on a sofa near one of the tall windows, Cassie beside her. Jon was nowhere to be seen. Eliza looked up from speaking to the child.

"Amanda! Come join us," she called brightly, and Amanda moved toward them.

"Where's Jon?" she blurted.

Eliza blinked at the familiar use of the earl's name, but hesitated only a moment before answering. "He and your father are in the library."

"Miss Amanda," Cassie asked, "why did you leave? I wanted you to meet my papa."

Amanda looked down into the dark eyes of her half-sister and tried to decide how to explain. Weighing and discarding a number of possibilities in the space of a few moments, she finally hit on a portion of the truth.

"A gentleman came to collect me and I saw him waiting outside. I knew I would see you later and I thought Papa would want to bring you home himself."

"Is my papa your papa too?" the child asked in tones of wonder. Outside the clouds parted and a shaft of brilliant sunlight shone through the tall window behind them. Looking down at her, Amanda realized Cassie's hair was a rich auburn color, a blending of brown, gold and red. She wondered if her mother had been a redhead.

"It would seem so."

Eliza's glance from one to the other during the short conversation was speculative, but she said nothing. The short exchange, Amanda mused, had likely given her enough information to determine where it was her father had found his lost child.

Eliza rose. "Are you hungry for luncheon?" The question was directed to Cassie. "I will take you upstairs and introduce you to your brothers and you may have luncheon with them." To Amanda she said, "I'll be back down in a few minutes."

"I have brothers too?" Cassie was clearly overwhelmed, but Amanda knew Miss Byrnes would help her to adjust. It was the wide-eyed stare which reminded Amanda she'd thought Cassie looked familiar at first. Now she realized Cassie reminded her very much of Nicky.

"And a baby sister too," she heard Eliza say, but Cassie's response was lost as they left the room.

Amanda was indecisive for only a few moments before leaving the room as well. The library beckoned. She might not be welcome, and Eliza probably expected her to remain in the drawing room, but she couldn't stay away. For all his love and doting on his children, the Earl of Barrington was still a traditionalist when it came to marriage proposals and settlements. Once she agreed, she would no longer be a necessary participant in the discussions.

The door to the library was a solid oak panel. Closed tightly this time, no sound escaped. She sighed. So much for eavesdropping. If she wanted to know what was going on, she'd have to walk in. Taking a couple of deep breaths to give her courage, she reached for the handle and twisted it slowly.

Inching the door open, she put her eye to the crack, but could see no one. She knew the library was not empty, as she could hear her father's voice.

"I hadn't realized Nora had died until the bank contacted me. By then she'd already been dead nearly two weeks. The vicar and his wife were away, and the housekeeper disclaimed all knowledge."

Jon said nothing, and her father continued. "But enough about that. I want to know what Amanda was doing there," he demanded. "And don't tell me I ought to ask her. The fact that you arrived to collect her means you can tell me just as well as she can."

Amanda entered the room then. She knew Jon wouldn't tell

her father; especially after what she had revealed in the coach. That was her responsibility.

"But you should, Papa."

She approached where they sat in two chairs before her father's desk. They were comfortable and she did not sense any tension in the air. That boded well.

"It would not be fair for you to ask his lordship to divulge a confidence."

The Earl of Barrington looked up as she advanced and grimaced. She was still wearing the heavy lavender twill gown she'd been wearing earlier and now she wished she'd changed. It looked too much like something Miss Byrnes might wear—prim and unobtrusive, rather than fashionable.

Jon rose to his feet and seated her in his chair, remaining to stand behind it, his hand resting lightly on the back. She smiled up at him as she sat. Her father watched the by-play, but said nothing. Jon's presence gave her courage and she turned to face her father.

"You originally went to the orphanage, did you not?" she asked and when he nodded, continued, "And Granny, I mean Mrs. Grantham, sent you next door to the school."

"Actually, while I was there, a group of girls came in and Mrs. Grantham indicated Cassie should be with them. When she was not, the young woman escorting them indicated she had remained to speak with the other teacher and gave me directions to find her. You know what happened next."

Amanda acknowledged the statement, still hearing Cassie's "*Papa!*" ringing in her head. She wondered if she would ever get over the shock—or learn the whole story.

"How long have you been doing this?" he asked.

Amanda sighed. Now was the moment of truth. She was positive he did not expect to hear her answer or explanation. "Almost two years," she replied, and launched into an explanation of how she came to be involved, starting at the beginning.

Jon was impressed she told the story impassively, never once laying the blame for her father's ignorance of her involvement at his feet. Instead she made it sound as if she didn't feel he'd consider it important. After all, many members of the nobility were involved in charity projects, this was just another one. She hadn't felt he would mind, especially since the dowager countess of Wynton was the major patron of the school.

Eliza entered the library at the tail end of Amanda's explanation, announcing luncheon and inviting him to dine.

Over luncheon, the discussion was of their engagement. He'd spoken to her father before her arrival in the library. The notice would appear in the next day's *Times*. The question of when was a sticky one. With only three weeks left in the Season, Eliza said it was almost impossible to plan and execute a wedding in that time.

Amanda said she did not want a large wedding or long engagement. Relieved, he agreed. Eliza's knowing look nearly made him squirm in his seat.

And what of the Beldons' house party? Now that they had Cassie, Eliza did not want to leave her alone so soon. Amanda did not bother to hide her relief when it was decided they would have to bow out, and he wondered if the school was the reason she hadn't wanted to go.

He'd already sent his regrets. He didn't tell them that a weekend at a house party with Charity Bascomb and MaryAnne Lester in attendance would have made him nervous.

It was Eliza who decided they could plan a simple, family-and-close-friends-only wedding. Unfortunately it still meant a large number of people. The Cookesons were a large family and, except for a great-aunt who had disappeared many years before, most still kept in touch with the earl as the head of the family.

But where to have it? That was the question he knew they were still mulling over as he entered the Wolverton rout with Amanda on his arm later that evening.

The significance of their entrance, followed by a beaming Earl and Countess of Barrington was not lost on those in attendance who noticed. That he never left Amanda's side throughout the whole evening, dancing two waltzes with her, and that Amanda danced with no one else was tantamount to a declaration which was confirmed in the next morning's *Times*.

Amanda stopped by to visit Jon's grandmother the next day before heading to the school.

The dowager countess had already seen the notice in the *Times* and her delight knew no bounds as she reminded Amanda it was three years late.

"Men!" the dowager said in disgust. "It was obvious at the Abbey three years ago that you two were perfect for each other. Then he ran away." Her snort of disgust conveyed exactly what she thought of Jon's actions.

When she paused, Amanda took the opportunity to change the subject. "It's fortunate I hired Miss Gaines and Miss Dalrymple. I do not think I will be available much during the next few months."

The dowager nodded. "How are they working out?"

"Wonderfully, actually. Marianne Dalrymple turned out to be the perfect replacement for me. She doesn't read Greek or Latin, but the girls don't need to know that as much as basic reading, writing, and arithmetic." She put her teacup and saucer down on the low table before her. "She has also started helping out at the orphanage and Granny is ecstatic. The girls all like her too. I couldn't have asked for a more perfect replacement."

"So, you won't worry so much about the school when you aren't about?"

"I suppose not. But I think that Miss Gaines, who I have decided will take over as headmistress when the Board finally makes arrangements for Mr. Cooper to leave, should make weekly reports to you when I'm not in town. Now that Jon has convinced Shaftesbury to allow the school to run without Board interference, someone needs to oversee."

"I think I can manage that. And with this new medicine my doctor has been giving me, I might even be able to manage the occasional visit."

"That would be wonderful. Getting out of the house occasionally will be good for you."

The dowager smiled.

"And how is Cassie doing these days? Any sign of her father

yet?"

Amanda smiled. "Oh! You'll never believe it, but he came for her. He'd been looking for her for weeks, he said."

"You don't say? And was he someone we knew—just as we speculated?"

Amanda grew silent, then she laughed. "You might not believe me if I tell you."

"Try me," the dowager said with undisguised curiosity.

"Cassie now resides at Barrington House." The dowager's eyes widened. "Her father is also mine."

A smile lit the dowager's face. "How old did you say she was?"

"Ten," Amanda replied. "She was born the year before Papa married Eliza."

The dowager nodded. "Your father is a good man. I hesitate to say this to you, but he should never have married your mother. They were both much too young, and Katherine was too spoiled. I think most everyone knew it was destined to be a failure, but even your father's friends could not talk him out of it. However, she was good to you, despite dragging the Barrington name through the muck."

"I don't remember much of her, except the summer before she died. That last summer we spent at Summersea was the most wonderful summer of my life. I have never forgotten it." Looking over at the dowager, she grinned. "It was the summer I met Felicia, Tina and Jon."

The dowager said nothing, the expression on her face eloquent, and Amanda noted the effort it took not to allow her jaw to drop.

"I've surprised you, haven't I?"

"I don't think surprised quite covers it."

"I don't think he remembers, though."

"Why would he?"

"I don't know, but I guess I always thought he would."

"Did he know your name?"

Amanda shook her head. "No. My mother always called me Katie, you see. So, when I first met Felicia and she asked me my name, I told her it was Katie. And that's the name she told him when she introduced me."

"I see." The tightness in the dowager's voice had Amanda looking at her closely. "Am I to assume that this was one of those summers he and Tina spent with the gypsies?"

Amanda nodded. The dowager's demeanor reminded Amanda that Jon's grandmother had originally refused to even recognize her grandchildren when they were young, leaving them to Felicia's father to raise. That she still had feelings concerning their gypsy background amazed her.

"Why do you think he doesn't remember?"

"I think I have always assumed that if he remembered, he would know that we belonged together. That his great-grandmother would have told him." She told the dowager countess of Nona and her panther, and promptly swore her to silence. "You mustn't tell him." She couldn't keep the wistfulness out of her voice. "I want him to remember on his own."

Tears brimmed in Amanda's eyes, but she refused to allow them to fall.

"You love him very much, do you not?" The dowager's voice had gone soft, with a hint of tears in it.

Amanda nodded again, and in a barely audible whisper, replied, "Since I was seven years old."

It was Tina who came up with the perfect location.

"Collingswood," she announced. "It's perfect."

Seated in the drawing room at Barrington House, Tina, Eliza, Felicia and Amanda were discussing possibilities over tea.

"It's only a couple of hours away and large enough to hold a house party of twenty or more families. The village church is small, but perfect. Everyone important enough to invite to the actual wedding will fit, and it's beautiful at this time of the year."

Collingswood was one of the estates belonging to the Marquis of Thanet. Situated a mere two hours away from London by coach, it was a good retreat from the city, without being too distant.

"And," Felicia joined in, catching her enthusiasm, "it would not be looked at askance because Jon is her brother."

"Our grandmother could make that short of a trip without too much trouble, either," Tina added. "We could make it a three or four-day house party with the wedding and a ball on the last day. We could also invite people to the ball who will not be invited to the wedding."

"A house party would be perfect," Eliza said with a nod. "We'll draw up a guest list and you can tell me if we'll all fit."

Amanda had not given the location much thought. She'd just assumed she'd be married in St. George's. Once she and Eliza had begun the planning, however, she realized that she didn't want a large, lavish affair after all. As expectations grew with the size of the church, a small village church not far from London would be perfect. Jon had already told her he would procure a special license.

"I already have a gown I think would be perfect to be married in," Amanda told Eliza later. "If you want we can lengthen the train, but I rather like it as it is."

"Which one is that?" They were still in the drawing room, Tina and Felicia having departed for their own homes a short time ago. It was nearly time to dress for dinner, but neither had moved.

"The white one with silver. You might remember that you said it looked like a possible wedding dress when I ordered it. Perhaps I had a premonition."

Eliza's laughter rang out in the room, her violet eyes dancing merrily. "I did, didn't I? And now that I remember, I'm right too. It will make a beautiful wedding dress. Honiton lace will create a beautiful veil, and if we lengthen the train using the same lace, it will be quite lovely."

"This is turning into an easy wedding to plan. I'm afraid Lady Thanet is going to do all the work."

Eliza's eyes twinkled. "I think that's exactly what she wants to do. As I understand it, the duchess planned her wedding, then the duchess's wedding was taken care of by Lord Wynton, so now I think she feels it's her turn."

Amanda giggled. "If I remember correctly you, the dowager countess, and the Duchess of Westover did all the work for Felicia's wedding—not Lord Wynton."

Eliza chuckled in agreement, then continued, "You might

think the Cookesons are a close-knit clan, but it's nothing compared to those three. It's good you, Her Grace, and Lady Thanet are friends because I suspect the three of you will be living in each other's pockets for the rest of your lives."

"I hadn't quite thought of it that way."

They sat in silence for a while, each deep in their own thoughts until laughter reached them from the garden. Amanda immediately recognized Cassie's voice. Looking over at Eliza, who had turned as if to look out the windows into the garden, she wondered about her stepmother's reaction to Cassie's presence.

"So, what do you think of Cassie?"

Eliza turned to look at her. "She is delightful. I have already told your father she will have to go off to school in a few years, and I suspect she will have all the young swains at her feet when she finally comes out too."

"You intend to keep her?" Amanda couldn't hide her surprise.

"Of course." Eliza's response was automatic. "Is there any reason we should not?"

Amanda colored. "I don't know. I didn't know if you'd let Papa keep her. Society can be cruel to people in her circumstances, and their families too."

"I know, but we have always known that. And accepted it."

Amanda looked at her in surprise. "Always known...?"

Eliza smiled. "Yes, always known. I have always known of her existence. I even met her mother once. I insisted on it once I realized Trent intended to continue to support her and eventually acknowledge her."

"Why?"

"Why what? Why would I insist on meeting her mother?"

"That, and why would he acknowledge her? He didn't have to. In fact, many wouldn't."

"Because, unlike many of our class, your father takes his responsibilities seriously. For him, a child is a responsibility, no matter what side of the blanket it is born on. He told me about Nora and Cassie early on and knowing I might have her under my roof eventually, I wanted to see for myself what kind of woman her mother was."

Denise Patrick

"And what kind of woman was she?"

"She was an opera dancer, but not your typical one. She was a sweet young woman, forced by circumstances into a profession to support her and an ailing parent. While many in that line of work are little more than professional courtesans, she was not one of them. She was actually quite talented, but once Cassie was born she wanted to settle down and be a mother. She was lucky the child's father was your father, and not someone else who might have just turned his back on her. Life is hard for a young woman in her position, but she did the best she could."

Nicky's laughter joined Cassie's as Eliza continued.

"Your father was not the first man in her life, but he was the last. Although he offered to buy her a house in town, she wanted the quiet of the country. All she asked for was enough for her and Cassie to live on. She could have asked for much more and your father would have given it, but she even refused his offer to buy the cottage she rented."

"I would never have guessed."

"I don't think many would," Eliza confirmed. "Your father is an amazing man." Laughing at the indulgent look Amanda sent her way, she continued. "Yes, I know I'm biased, but it's one of the reasons I fell in love with him. He is fiercely loyal and protective."

"I suppose that protective streak is where his ideas on women came from?"

Eliza's laughter died abruptly. The violet depths clouded over and a shadow passed over her face. She regarded Amanda seriously for a long time before she spoke again.

"No, your mother taught him that." The sadness in Eliza's voice caught Amanda off guard.

Amanda did not understand the uncomfortable silence that descended. Eliza had always been warm and loving toward her. Never had she spoken badly of her mother—in fact, she had never spoken of her mother at all. Even during her first Season, when the rumors had surfaced concerning her mother, Eliza had sent her to her father for explanations. "It is not my place to discuss your mother with you," Eliza had told her once. "I never met her." And Eliza had kept true to her word—always

120

leaving her father to explain awkward comments away. Yet Amanda sensed Eliza would not shy away this time.

"How?"

"Do you really want to know?" Eliza asked. "You know I have made it a practice not to speak of your mother to you. I have always felt it would be wrong for me to do so."

"I know. Papa always said you never wanted me to forget her. And he always said my memories of my mother should be good ones. But lately, I have begun to realize I need to know the bad as well as the good. For instance, why is it the old tabbies think I'm like her just because I turned down three proposals? And how did she instill such medieval ideas into Papa about women and education?"

"To answer your last question first—it was because he gave her so much freedom. After her death, he felt he had given her too much freedom to do as she pleased, to read what she wanted to read, to attend lectures, and to be the person she wanted to be. That much freedom, he decided, was unhealthy for a woman, who couldn't understand the ramifications, or act responsibly. It would have been simpler if he had just relegated her to the category of most bored wives who stray after the marriage bed is no longer new and exciting, but he didn't. Instead he attributed her wildness to her reading materials, the crowd she associated with, and the general freedom he gave her."

"So he decided women were ill-equipped to deal with too much knowledge, lest they act on it without understanding?"

"Precisely."

"And the other?"

"Your mother's affairs were well-known. I think what made them so scandalous was that she didn't wait until giving your father an heir before they began. There was never any question but that you were your father's child, but after you any children were suspect. What the old tartars think they see in your refusals is her inability to settle on just one man. But it is just an excuse for gossip, and they don't know you."

Amanda thought back to the summer they spent at Summersea and her mother's subsequent death in childbirth. She now understood the child could not possibly have been her father's. Would her father have accepted it had it lived? It was a moot point, but she thought she understood a little better how her mother's actions might have hurt him deeply and firmed his resolve.

Chapter Nine

"I'm so happy for you," Felicia said, giving Amanda a warm hug. "I always thought you and Jon were almost the perfect couple."

"Almost...?"

Seated on the floor of the nursery in Waring House, Amanda and Felicia were watching the two raven-haired toddlers as they alternately stacked and knocked over blocks, all the while squealing with glee.

"Well," Felicia smiled impishly, "Brand and I *are* the perfect couple, but you and Jon come close."

Amanda giggled at her friend. "I remember telling Nona that when I married JoJo you would become my big sister. I think she thought it was funny."

"I think we all three have at one time or another thought Nona was a little...well...daft. But after Tina and Jay, then me and Brand, I think Jon knew his days were numbered."

Caroline approached Amanda with a block. "Your turn." She indicated the half-finished tower. Amanda dutifully added the block to the top.

Michael, not to be outdone, grabbed one from the many scattered across the floor and ran to Felicia. "Mama's turn, Mama's turn!"

As Amanda watched Felicia add her block to the tower to the delight of her children, she wondered what it would be like to have Jon's child. Would he have dark hair and green eyes, like his father? Or would he be fair, like her? Felicia's children had inherited their mother's hair coloring, but their father's eyes.

"So, have you and Jon discussed the statuette?"

Felicia's question drew her from her thoughts, and a blush covered her face.

"No," she confessed sheepishly.

"No?" Felicia's disbelief was tangible. "Then wh—"

"You're the only one who knows about my panther and that Nona gave him to me. I know he doesn't remember me yet, but I want him to remember on his own. So, I haven't said anything."

A calculating look entered Felicia's blue eyes. Confusion chased across her face, then disappeared, to be replaced by a mischievous grin.

"Very well. Never let it be said I couldn't keep a secret."

The twins' nurse entered the room carrying a tray. As she put it down on the table and turned to survey the disarray, both children ran to her.

Felicia rose from the floor, shaking out her dress of green muslin. "I'm afraid we have made quite a mess," she told the woman.

"Nothing worse than usual, Your Grace," she replied. "Isn't that right, loveys?" Both children giggled.

Amanda watched Felicia hug and kiss both children, then followed her out the door and down the stairs.

"Have you and Jon discussed anything beyond the date?"

Amanda shook her head. "No. Since Tina and Eliza have everything well in hand, I have let them do the planning. Eliza has already picked out flowers and such. I already have a dress. The only thing I've been asked is whether I want a bridesmaid. And I'm not sure I do."

"Why not?" They reached the second floor and turned toward the drawing room.

"Because my Aunt Barbara will insist it be one of her girls and I don't want to fight about it."

"And you don't want either of your cousins?"

"Not really. We have never been close and I'm not sure I trust either of them not to do something horrid and ruin the day."

"Oh."

"I'm sorry," Amanda told Jon three days later as they returned from the school. With the decision made not to go to the Beldons', Amanda felt free to attend to her class for the rest of the week.

"Sorry for what?" he asked, momentarily taking his eyes off the horses to glance over at her.

"For the invitation you received," she answered. When she noticed a frown appear between his eyes, she added, "Or maybe you haven't seen it yet."

"I must confess to be unaware of any particular invitation for which you might be apologetic."

Amanda sighed. He hadn't received it yet, but she knew it was coming.

"Eliza will have sent you an invitation for tea today. I'm surprised you didn't get it yesterday."

"And this makes you sorry?" he teased.

"No. It's just that all my relatives currently in London, as well as those close enough to make the trip, will have also been invited."

"Ahhh." There was a wealth of understanding in that one syllable, but Amanda knew he didn't completely understand her reservations.

Normally, only Cookesons and their various relations would be invited to this particular gathering. At a stretch, that might have included Felicia and Brand, but not Tina and Jay nor the dowager countess, who she also knew had received an invitation. However, Eliza had invited Tina and Felicia for Jon's sake and an invitation had also been sent to the dowager countess, though Amanda did not expect her.

Her father's sister, Lady Althorpe, was pretentious and controlling. The reigning matron in her corner of the world near Bath, she was known to have an excessive sense of her own consequence, managing to find fault with everything and everyone around her. Eliza had once been one of her favorite targets until the earl bluntly informed her that if she couldn't be civil to his wife, she would no longer be welcome in his home. She was just as likely as not to say something about Jon's background and make everyone else uncomfortable. Amanda knew Eliza hoped the presence of Jon's family might check Lady Althorpe's acerbic tongue.

"And who would that be?" he asked, interrupting her thoughts.

"I'm not sure of everyone, but I'm sure my Aunt Barbara, Papa's sister, will be there. She is Lady Althorpe. I hope she will leave her daughters, Sonya and Cynthia, at home, but she probably won't. She is not very nice sometimes," was all she would say about her aunt. "My cousin, Jeremy, is her son and the current Lord Althorpe. Papa is still his guardian." What she didn't say about him was that he was spoiled, self-centered and already on the road to dissolution. Eliza often said she hoped her father could influence him into turning off that particular path.

"My Scottish cousins wouldn't have received word to come yet, so I don't expect to see them before we leave for Collingswood." She was actually looking forward to seeing them when they arrived. "My father's aunt, Marian, may be there. She has never married, but that hasn't stopped her from being the favorite of most of the nieces and nephews. Her favorite topic of conversation however is her sister, Constance, who disappeared many years ago and was subsequently disowned by my great-grandfather." Jon's brows rose at that statement, but he said nothing.

"My cousin, Lord Hickham, may be there, but I hope not. Cousin Doyle is actually Papa's cousin, and a barrister. I suppose it depends on his time commitments. His sister, Catherine, I'm not sure, but if she comes, her husband won't come with her. I doubt we will see his other sister, Letitia."

"How is Lord Hickham related?"

"He is my mother's nephew. Her brother, my Uncle Thaddeus, died only a few years after she did. He was much older than she."

Jon nodded as she related the information, but did not add anything more to the conversation as they drew up in front of Barrington House. She could guess his thoughts. He probably thought of the coming afternoon as an obligatory duty necessitated by a marriage. He would suffer through it, as he must all other social duties, but would not let it bother him unduly. She hoped he wouldn't suffer too much.

"I will pick you up at five," he said as he escorted her inside.

Amanda's spirits lifted instantly as she remembered their promised outing.

"Of course," she smiled. "I'll be ready."

Slipping up to her room to change for luncheon, she could already feel the anticipation building. Spending an hour alone with Jon beforehand would make tea with her relatives much more palatable.

Lunch passed uneventfully. Nicky and Cassie were allowed to dine with the family simply because it was just the five of them. Although her father had said nothing about her "charity work" as she termed her teaching, she knew it still bothered him, as evidenced by his slight frown every time Cassie slipped and called her "Miss Amanda".

After lunch, Eliza went to confer with Cook about the number of people invited for tea and Amanda slipped into the garden with a book. The book, however, was never opened as Amanda found her thoughts wandering.

It still amazed her that Jon had asked her to marry him. Why? His response, she realized, had only been part of the truth. He knew the school meant a lot to her, so his answer made sense in the circumstances. But now she'd had a couple of days to think on it, she wondered if there wasn't some other reason why he had decided upon her.

The most obvious reason to her was that he knew about her panther. It was only logical Jon would not tempt fate by not marrying the person Nona had selected for him. Knowing she was that person should have encouraged her, but it didn't. She wanted him to marry her because he wanted to, not because he had been told to.

Suppose he doesn't know about the panther? You might recall telling him you hadn't seen a panther figurine, a voice reminded her. *What if he really does just want to help you and marrying you is the best way he can do that?*

She grimaced. Maybe she shouldn't have lied to him about her panther. She wasn't sure she wanted him just because he wanted to help her with the school, either.

So, what do you want? the voice mocked her.

She sighed, but knew where this was leading. She might have thought she could live without love, but continuing to deceive herself was useless. She wanted him to love her. And she wanted him to love her because he felt something for her. It was too painful to think that he might only care for her because he knew she had JoJo.

He desired her. She understood this from their embraces. His touch never failed to cause a spreading tingling and warmth throughout her body. His glance alone caused her skin to prickle with awareness and her heartbeat to double—no, triple. And his kisses... Dear God, what his kisses did to her wits was unconscionable. The world should not be allowed to stop whenever he chose to lay his lips against hers.

So how did she find out what she wanted to know? Short of coming right out and asking him, how was she to find out if he knew about her panther? And how was she to find out if he remembered their meeting fourteen years ago?

Amanda was waiting in the front hall when Jon arrived to pick her up for their drive. She didn't want to seem impatient, but she needed to leave the house. As soon as Barrons reported that Jon's curricle had arrived, she tied her bonnet ribbons and pulled on her gloves. Jon was just stepping down from the conveyance when she hurried through the front door and down the steps.

Surprised at her actions, Jon said nothing beyond a greeting, then lifted her to the seat. Comforting warmth enveloped her at his touch. Once he was seated beside her and the curricle was underway, he glanced over at her, a question in the emerald depths. When she didn't respond, he turned to concentrate on guiding his horses through the afternoon traffic. She would explain later. For now, she allowed herself to relax and enjoy being in Jon's company as they turned into the gates to Hyde Park.

As they proceeded along the circumscribed route, she occasionally felt Jon's eyes on her and knew he still puzzled over her actions. Even though they were stopped frequently by acquaintances wishing to tender their congratulations, it seemed like mere minutes later and they left it all behind. Her spirits plunged with the thought that they were returning to Barrington House so soon and she nearly asked Jon not to take her back. She was, therefore, pleasantly surprised when they headed in a slightly different direction, eventually pulling up in front of his grandmother's house on Park Court.

Ushering her inside, she heard him tell Smithers not to inform his grandmother of their presence for at least fifteen minutes, then escorted her into the small library which overlooked the front of the house. She removed her bonnet and gloves, setting them on a small table just inside the door, then moved further into the room, scanning the bookshelves as she heard the door close behind her.

"Amanda." Jon's voice was impatient. She didn't blame him for being annoyed. She'd not been very communicative since she'd left her home. She moved toward him, seeking, needing his comfort.

When she reached him, he slipped his arm around her waist and led her over to a small sofa covered in blue damask situated before the empty fireplace. Once seated, he slid his arm around her shoulders, holding her securely.

"Now, what has happened, and why do I feel as if we somehow escaped from Barrington House?"

Amanda giggled. She knew he was trying to lighten the mood and she appreciated it. Knowing she could not explain the entire situation in a few minutes, she opted for superficiality.

"My Aunt Barbara and her family arrived not long before you did." She sighed. "We have never really gotten along and my cousins just put me out of sorts. I wish we didn't have to go back, but I know Eliza and Papa would never forgive me if we didn't appear."

"I would say you have the right of it there since today's gathering is in our honor. But we will muddle through."

"I suppose so." She wasn't convinced, but wasn't willing to spoil his afternoon. He would soon see for himself how difficult her aunt and cousins could be.

Jon rose and picked up a small box from the mantel above the fireplace, then returned to sit beside her again.

"This is for you," he said, opening the small box to reveal an exquisite, square cut diamond in a delicate gold setting. Lifting it from the bed of velvet, he slipped it on her finger.

For a moment, she merely stared at it. There was little light in the room, only that which streamed through tall windows on the other side of the room. But even with such meager light, the diamond had a brilliance which threw light all on its own.

Raising her eyes to his, she cast about for something other than "thank you" to say and found nothing more appropriate.

"Thank you," she said softly.

He smiled and her blood heated. "You're welcome."

Amanda reached up and slipped her arms around his neck as his head descended toward hers. When his lips settled over hers, she sank into the kiss. Angling his head and pressing her into the cushions against the back of the sofa, she was only barely aware of his arms sliding around her waist, pulling her close. She melted against him, wanting nothing more than to remain here and ignore the outside world. She sighed when he lifted his head fractionally, kissing first one corner, then the other of her mouth before settling back on her lips again.

Time stood still. Lost in each other, the kiss could have lasted minutes—or hours—and neither would have noticed. The mantel clock ticked, outside carriages rumbled past, and from beyond the library door a familiar *tap-tap-tapping* intruded into Jon's consciousness.

Raising his head, he smiled as another soft sigh escaped Amanda and she settled herself against his chest, eyes closed contentedly, her hand resting over his heart, and the diamond winking in the limited light.

"Now is not the time for a nap," he chuckled, glancing at the clock. "It is time for us to leave."

Amanda groaned as she opened her eyes to look up into his amused face. "No," she said. "I don't want to go." Closing her eyes again, she settled back against him. "Let's just stay here."

Jon's low laughter covered the door to the library opening, but both clearly heard, "Well? Are we going or not?"

Amanda's head snapped up and whipped around to find his grandmother standing there leaning heavily on her cane watching them, a look of gleeful speculation in her eyes. She turned to look back at him. He merely shrugged, rose to his feet, then helped her to hers. He supposed he should have warned her, but she looked so deliciously flustered when his grandmother had spoken, that all he could think of was soothing her some more. Unfortunately, he couldn't do that at the moment.

It wasn't until they were in his coach and nearly at Barrington House that Amanda found her voice.

"I didn't think you would be able to come," she said in wonder. "But I'm so glad you could make it."

The dowager made a sound which sounded suspiciously like a snort. "Knowing your aunt, Lady Althorpe, would be there, I felt it was necessary." Waving her hand toward him, she continued, "Not that the boy can't take care of himself with the likes of her, and Tina and Felicia will make sure all goes smoothly, but I couldn't resist the possibility I might miss some fireworks." She chortled. "Not enough excitement these days—got to take it where one can find it."

He tried, vainly, to smother his amusement, but Amanda looked up at him at that moment. Her eyes narrowed as she looked into his, and he knew she'd been worried about his reaction to her various relations. She did not find it as amusing as he did, but he was still touched by her obvious worry over her relations' reactions. It made him curious.

They were only a little tardy, and by no means the last to arrive. Eliza was both surprised and delighted to see his grandmother, as was Tina, who was already there, perched on a burgundy-and-cream striped sofa with Jay beside her. He helped his grandmother into a straight-backed, yet comfortably padded chair, then perched on the arm of the sofa Amanda occupied.

Amanda's father performed the introductions, Eliza poured tea, and Jon studied the varied relatives as he was presented.

Lady Althorpe looked nothing like her brother. Large boned with dark brown hair and eyes, her face might still have been pleasant except for the disapproving scowl that seemed to be permanently etched upon it, and deepened when she looked at Amanda or Eliza. She might have been a handsome woman at one time, but now her preference for a hairstyle more suited to a debutante than a matron, and a heavy hand with cosmetics combined to make her look more like a fish out of water.

Her daughters, seated on either side of her, might have been two identical bookends, but he would later learn that Miss Sonya was three years senior to Miss Cynthia. The two girls wore nearly identical blue-and-white dresses and their sandy hair was pulled back into a soft style in an attempt to make them look older. Their brother, Lord Althorpe, looked much like most of the typical young bucks who graced the balls, parties and soirees of the elite and he wondered why he hadn't seen him before since the young viscount didn't look much older than Amanda.

Mrs. Catherine Farnsworth was a sweet, young woman. Although she was obviously related to Trent, possessing the same grey eyes and light brown hair, Lady Althorpe ignored her. He would ask Amanda why later. Her brother, Doyle, she informed him, sent his regrets.

Great Aunt Marian sat beside Catherine and he instantly categorized her with his grandmother. Her hair was completely white, her face lined and wrinkled, but the twinkle in her dark eyes was nothing short of mischievous. She was delighted to see his grandmother, the two having been friends years ago, and they immediately fell to discussing bygone days.

Catherine's sister, Letitia, sat on the other side of Marian. Letty, as she was called, was acting as Marian's companion today as Marian's regular companion was down with the sniffles.

Because this was a family gathering, Cassie, Nicky, and George were also present with Miss Byrnes seated discreetly in a corner keeping a careful eye on her charges. He noted Tina had already engaged Cassie in a conversation, putting the little girl at ease. George had run to Amanda as they entered, and she now held him in her arms, while Nicky shadowed his father.

The conversation was somewhat stilted until Felicia and Brand arrived. With profuse apologies, Felicia explained Brand had to break up a melee of two-year-olds before they left. Tina inquired whether her son, Andrew, had been part of the group and was informed that of course he had.

"But," Felicia said gaily to the assembled company,

"Caroline won this one. She was the only one still standing and not crying by the time we managed to separate them." Accepting a cup of tea from Eliza, she finished by saying to Tina, "Mama would have been proud of the way she got the better of the boys, but I'm not sure we should encourage those tendencies. She'll be a terror by the time she's ten."

Felicia's entrance and story seemed to loosen some of the tension in the room and people began to talk among themselves. Amanda took the time to approach and speak to Catherine, inquiring as to her own little ones. Felicia and Tina, upon learning Catherine also had a two-year-old, joined the conversation and soon the three were comparing notes. Surprisingly, Letty had been drawn into conversation with the dowager and Great Aunt Marian.

Amanda put her brother down and turned to scan the room. Cassie joined her as she crossed the room to speak to her cousin, Jeremy, while George clambered up beside his mother. Her father asked Jon a question about horses, and the two fell into conversation about Trent's newest acquisition.

Although she knew he could be selfish, vain, spoiled and a host of other things, Amanda often felt sorry for Jeremy. Living with his mother and sisters could not be easy. And she knew he resented the fact that her father was his guardian.

"How are you, Jeremy?" she asked.

"Fine," he replied sullenly.

"I haven't seen you this Season," she said conversationally. "Where have you been?"

"I have been at Althorpe most of the time. I have responsibilities now." Amanda frowned lightly at his tone. He sounded as if he was trying to convince himself, yet his father had died over two years ago.

"I see."

"Don't believe him," Sonya said, joining them. "He goes to Bath all the time."

"Man's got to have some fun," he snapped at his sister.

Sonya merely rolled her grey eyes at him and made a very unladylike sound. Jeremy turned and stalked off. Amanda watched her cousin go and wondered if her father had any influence on him at all. It was obvious he needed a man's guidance—or his mother and sisters would drive him around the bend, if they hadn't already.

Amanda turned back to find Sonya watching her and Cassie through narrowed eyes. A chill washed over her. She did not want to cross words with Sonya today.

"How have you been, Sonya?" she asked.

Sonya ignored her. "Who's she?" She indicated Cassie. "Aunt Eliza shouldn't allow the help's brats to mix with family. Mama would never have employed someone with a brat."

Amanda was taken aback by the sudden attack on Cassie, although she should have expected it. Obviously, no mention of Cassie had been made before she and Jon arrived. She wondered if it had been done intentionally.

"I beg your pardon." Amanda could not keep the shock out of her voice. "This is my sister, Cassie. And you are being unforgivably rude."

"Your sister! You don't have a sister that old. We've never seen her before."

Amanda shrugged. It didn't take long for her patience to wear thin around her cousins.

"You're not very nice." Cassie spoke for the first time, drawing Sonya's gaze back to her. "I should tell Papa."

"And what will he do?"

Amanda smiled. "You probably don't want to know," she told her. "Cassie just came to live with us and he's very protective of her right now."

It was the tone of Amanda's voice which made Sonya glance at Trent, standing across the room, then back to Cassie. With their own townhouse being let for the Season, they were staying at Barrington House. However, she knew her father would not hesitate to put them all out if Cassie was hurt in any way.

Taking Cassie's hand, they turned and walked away, leaving Sonya staring after them.

"Why is she so mean?" Cassie asked her.

"I don't know," Amanda answered. "She has always been that way. Maybe some people are just born mean."

Cassie giggled. "Maybe her shoes hurt." Amanda looked down into laughing dark eyes. "That's what my mama would have said."

Cassie's laugh was infectious and Amanda chuckled along with her. Letty approached, having left Aunt Marian and the dowager to their reminisces.

"What's so funny?" she asked in greeting.

"Cassie says the reason Sonya is so mean is because her shoes hurt."

"She might be right," Letty said with a grin. Rich auburn hair, threaded with gold, reds and browns, was pulled back and severely contained in a bun at Letty's nape. Her grey silk dress reflected the silver in her eyes below a smooth wide brow and dark eyebrows. There was a quiet gentleness to her that often caused people to overlook her, but which complemented her chosen profession, that of a paid companion.

"How are you these days?" Amanda asked her.

"I'm doing well," she answered. "Congratulations."

"Thank you."

"I knew someday you'd make a splendid match. Is he truly as dangerous as he looks?"

Amanda glanced over at Jon. "Dangerous? Jon? You must be joking."

Letty laughed and, looking down at Cassie, winked. "I was right. I win."

"Win what?" Cassie asked.

Letty looked at Amanda. "I wagered Doyle that you were in love. You know what men are like. He scoffed. But anyone who can't see that Lord Wynton looks as if he could eat young misses for breakfast is obviously in love."

Amanda's blush had Letty grinning in triumph.

"Aren't you supposed to be in love when you get married?" Cassie asked.

Letty and Amanda exchanged glances. *Not in our class.* "Of course you are," Letty answered her. "But boys are silly about love and my brother is no different."

"Oh."

"So Doyle hasn't found anyone to capture his fancy yet?"

"No one who will put up with him, you mean?"

Amanda grinned. "Well, that too."

"Know any martyrs?"

"What's a martyr?" Cassie interrupted.

"It's a person who suffers for something they really believe in," Amanda answered. She looked up as Aunt Marian motioned to her, looking at Cassie as she did so. "Come and meet Great Aunt Marian."

"Will *she* like me?"

"Of course she will," Letty answered. "Aunt Marian likes everyone, but especially little girls." Amanda agreed.

"...never heard from her again," Great Aunt Marian's words reached her as they approached.

"Poor Connie," the dowager clucked.

"From the letters we found, she might have been poor, but she was very happy. Papa just never understood."

Introductions were performed and Cassie executed an admirable curtsy for both the ladies, charming them immediately. A few minutes later, Cassie was sitting between the elderly women with small plate of biscuits, and Amanda and Letty were sent on their way.

"At least we know Aunt Marian won't let Sonya or Cynthia near her," Letty observed as that lady shooed the two of them away.

"I was so glad to see you today," Amanda said without preamble as the two headed toward the double glass doors leading to the garden. "I wasn't sure if you were back in London."

"Actually I have only been back for a few days. Catherine insisted I come with her today, then Aunt Marian sent word that Stella was ill and asked me to fill in. I would have preferred to start looking for another position as soon as possible."

"Perhaps you need a break," Amanda suggested. "And I could use a friend."

"Do I get to put Sonya or Cynthia over my knee? Preferably both?" she asked as they stepped through the open glass doors.

Outside, Amanda giggled. "That would be a wonderful sight to see. I suspect neither of them has ever had any discipline."

Letty smiled. "You are probably right."

They walked among the roses for a bit before Amanda spoke again. "How is Aunt Marian doing these days? I'm ashamed to admit I never see her anymore."

Letty chuckled. "She is fit as a fiddle, but likes the rest of us to think she's helpless. She doesn't need a companion, but she and Stella get along so well I think it's good for both of them."

"And you?"

Letty sighed. "I know most of the family thinks I should replace Stella, but I cannot do it. Aunt Marian would never want to cause discord, and I can see that if I don't find another position soon, Doyle and Catherine will begin making noises."

"Families can be such a trial, can't they?" Amanda voice was light, but Letty understood her problem with her cousins.

As they headed back toward the drawing room a short time later, Letty gave her one last bit of advice. "It's your wedding, Amanda. You should be able to have it however you wish. And if you don't want either of those spoiled brats as a bridesmaid, you should not have to have them. Cassie would be a better choice anyway."

"Thank you, Letty. I will remember that."

They entered a room full of only women. Tina was explaining the preparations for the wedding being made at Collingswood. As she and Letty joined the group, Eliza told her the men had gone off to the stables to look at a new stallion her father had recently purchased. They would return soon.

"I suspect listening to wedding plans would not be high on their list of things to do," Amanda commented.

When the men returned, the gathering began to break up. Lord Althorpe had been enlisted to escort Catherine, Letty, and Aunt Marian home. Felicia, Brand, Tina, and Jay left soon after, Jon's grandmother traveling with Tina and Jay. Soon only the Althorpe ladies were left, as they were staying at Barrington House.

Amanda walked into the front foyer with Jon.

"I think Eliza and I will be at the Mathesons' tonight. Will you be there?"

He lifted her hand to his lips, lingering over the smooth skin of her knuckles. "I will plan on it," he replied, and collecting his hat from the butler, he left her standing in the doorway.

Chapter Ten

Amanda sat at her dressing table allowing Mary to put the last touches on her hair. In her mirror she could see Cassie, sprawled on her bed, chin propped in her hands, feet waving in the air—watching her intently.

"When I'm bigger, will I get to go to balls too?"

"Of course, Miss Cassie," Mary answered before Amanda could. "And you'll be the belle of the ball too. Your papa will have to shoo all the young dandies away."

Amanda chuckled as she watched Cassie's eyes grow wide. "Truly?"

"Of course," Amanda confirmed, picking up a strand of pearls from her jewel case. Mary clasped the warm baubles about her neck and stepped back as Amanda rose. "What do you think? Will I pass?" she asked Cassie.

Sitting up, Cassie studied her intently for a few moments. Amanda had chosen a blush pink silk overdress trimmed along the scalloped edge with a darker shade of the same color over a white lace underdress. A large white bow with trailing ends adorned the back at her waist. "You look very pretty," Cassie finally said solemnly.

A knock on the door forestalled Amanda's response. Mary opened it to admit Eliza. Amanda frowned, as it was obvious Eliza was not dressed for the evening.

"Lord Wynton is here," she announced. "I'm afraid I won't be accompanying you tonight, so I sent round a message and asked him to escort you." At Amanda's questioning glance, she replied, "Barbara is being difficult."

Amanda said nothing more. Turning toward the bed, she

noticed Cassie had picked up her panther and was now holding it. For a moment, she panicked. What if Cassie dropped it?

Keeping her voice steady, she said, "Be careful with that."

Cassie looked up. "Will it break?"

"I suppose it could."

"It's pretty. I like black cats, even though Mrs. Harper said they were bad luck."

"It's a special kind of cat," Amanda said, picking up her shawl. "It's a panther."

Cassie cocked her head to one side, studying Amanda for a moment. "What kind of cat is a panther?"

"Perhaps you should ask Miss Byrnes if she knows," Eliza answered. "If she doesn't, perhaps your papa has a book in his library about them."

Amanda's giggle caused both to look at her. With a mischievous twinkle, she said, "For shame, Eliza. Encouraging yet another girl to raid Papa's library. Now if it were Nicky, or George..."

Cassie put the statuette back and joined the two women who were now laughing.

"What's so funny?"

Eliza bent and gave the little girl a squeeze. "Nothing really, love. It's just that your papa gets annoyed when he finds Amanda reading books in his library."

"Then I shan't ever go in there," she announced.

This statement caused the women to laugh again and the three of them left Amanda's room in high spirits.

On the way down, Cassie skipped on ahead, giving Eliza a chance to speak privately to Amanda.

"Are you sure about Cassie?"

Turning to look at her stepmother, Amanda had no difficulty understanding her question. Earlier, she had told Eliza she thought Cassie would make a beautiful flower girl. They both understood this would cause some problems. After all, few people were yet aware of Cassie's existence. And she could probably predict Aunt Barbara's reaction.

"Yes." Amanda stopped, causing Eliza to do the same, and turned toward Eliza. "Is Aunt Barbara going to be dreadfully put out?"

"Probably," was the answer. "She is already outraged over Cassie's very existence. Needless to say it is the reason I am staying home."

"I see. What do you think I should do?"

Eliza was the family peacemaker, so Amanda was sure she wasn't going to like her idea. But she had asked, and was not surprised at the response.

"Cassie could be your flower girl, and Sonya, Cynthia, or both could be bridesmaids. I know it would make the wedding larger than you wanted, but..."

Amanda frowned, but her tone was one of resignation. "Do we have the time to have all the dresses made?"

"We could," was all Eliza said.

They continued the rest of the descent and joined an impatient Cassie at the bottom.

"Cousin Letty is right," she said to Amanda as the two ladies reached her.

"About what?"

"He does look dangerous."

"And how would you know?"

Cassie's smile lit up her small features. "I peeked," she replied, sending Eliza into a fit of laughter.

Jon turned from his perusal of a small painting as Amanda entered the salon. His mouth went dry as he took in the sight she presented. The deep pink of her gown put that same color in her cheeks. Her blue eyes sparkled with amusement and he wondered what caused it, until he noticed Cassie's dark head poke around the door momentarily before it disappeared again. No doubt the two had been conversing as she came downstairs. His eyes settled on her lips and he was suddenly warm. Full and soft, he could hardly focus for remembering what they felt like beneath his own.

"I'm sorry to have kept you waiting, my lord," she began. "Eliza only just told me you were here."

He smiled and raised her hand to his lips. "I have not been waiting long."

Once in his carriage, he said, "I hope all is well. Eliza's note only said she could not accompany you this evening and asked that I escort you instead."

"I'm afraid my Aunt Barbara is being a little difficult over Cassie's presence."

Jon relaxed back against the luxurious squabs. 'A little difficult' was probably a weak explanation for Lady Althorpe's reaction to the presence of a child born on the wrong side of the blanket in her brother's household. More likely she was bemoaning the possibility her precious daughters would be sullied by contact with Cassie. There was nothing he could do about that, so he did not pursue the conversation.

Felicia must have been haunting the door because she appeared almost immediately as they entered. Smiling gaily, her eyes dancing with excitement, she nearly pounced on Amanda. "I did it!"

"Did what?"

"Thurston and Martha Danvers are engaged," she announced. "I knew they were perfect for each other. Martha is beaming so brightly, she looks beautiful."

"Did I miss an announcement?" Amanda asked. "I haven't heard or read anything."

"It will be in tomorrow's paper. I know because Martha told me, and Lord Thurston confirmed it."

"Then I must find and congratulate them both."

Jon cleared his throat. "I suggest we go in and not clutter up the Mathesons' foyer."

The two women threw him identical disparaging looks, then turned and headed for the ballroom. Biting back a grin, he followed.

Jon stood gazing out over the assembly while Lord Cornaby droned on and on about why it was unhealthy to allow the masses to be educated. A fervent opponent of Lord Shaftesbury's reforms, he was known to buttonhole any unsuspecting member of the House of Lords and pour out his views for hours on end. Tonight, Jon was his victim.

Listening with but half an ear, Jon made appropriate noises in all the right places while he scanned the floor, looking for one person in particular. Unfortunately, he couldn't seem to locate Sophie Lawrence tonight.

He told himself he was sure Sophie had his figurine, but

even though he had taken the plunge and pledged himself to Amanda, he still wanted to ask her about it. He needed confirmation that he was right, and asking Felicia was out of the question.

"Your pardon, my lord, but I am engaged for this next set," he interrupted Lord Cornaby's monologue.

"Then don't let me hold you up, my boy," the aging peer replied. "I think we understand each other on this issue."

Jon did not respond. Inclining his head in acknowledgment, he turned to seek out Amanda. The next dance was the supper dance, a waltz, and he had waited all evening for it. He was looking forward to holding Amanda in his arms.

He found her in a group with Felicia, Tina, Geri and Martha. Martha blushed as he offered his congratulations, and the other three merely shooed them off as he apologized for relieving them of Amanda's company.

"I don't think I have ever seen Martha looking quite so pretty," she commented as they took their place on the floor.

"You didn't hear it from me, but perhaps Felicia was right."

Her giggle was infectious and he felt his lips stretching in response. As they twirled around the floor, Jon was conscious of the scent of honeysuckle she wore. It wafted around him and teased his senses. He was aware of the brush of her skirts against his legs and the softness of her skin through the layers of clothing she wore. Soon, he told himself. Soon, he would have the right to uncover every inch of her luscious body and explore it to his heart's content. But for now, he had to keep himself under control, so he searched for another topic of conversation to keep him from imagining what it would be like to undress her.

They danced in silence until she said, "It was good to see Great Aunt Marian, and Catherine and Letty. I even spoke to Jeremy for a short time."

"My grandmother seemed to enjoy your great aunt's company, although they spent most of their time discussing your missing great aunt, Connie."

Amanda nodded. "That is Great Aunt Marian's favorite topic of conversation. Aunt Constance was the youngest of my great-grandfather's five children. She and Aunt Marian were very close, I understand. When she fell in love with a vicar and their father refused his suit, she ran off with him anyway, but to shield him from her father's wrath, she staged her own death. According to Aunt Marian, their mother knew all along and kept in contact with her and even occasionally sent her money until great-grandmama died. When my great-grandfather learned of it after her death, he burned all the letters, so contact was lost completely. He might have gone after her even then, but my great-grandmother had anticipated he might and left nothing with an address on it, so he didn't know where to look."

"I see. And your cousin, Letitia?"

"Letty? What of her?"

"I noticed the two of you slipped away for a short while."

"Oh. I just wanted to talk. She is closest to me in age, although actually a year younger than Eliza, and I have always found her easy to talk to. She is a lady's companion, so I hadn't expected to see her. I had heard she was with her employer in France recently, but as it turned out, that lady died only a few weeks ago, so Letty returned. She has only been in the city for a few days."

"Is it too much to hope her employer left her something?"

"I suspect it is, but it doesn't matter. Letty is not destitute, but she enjoys what she does. Catherine and Doyle both would never turn their backs on her and neither would Papa. I think they would all prefer that she marry, but she has no interest in that direction. Their next preference would be that she displace Aunt Marian's companion, but she is reluctant to do so."

"To keep everything in the family?"

"I suppose. She did tell me she would begin looking for another position as soon as possible, but agreed to come to Collingswood for the wedding."

The dance came to a close and they joined his sisters, their spouses, and the Duke and Duchess of Westover for supper. Much of the conversation centered around the antics of their children and Amanda found herself wondering again what her and Jon's children would be like. If Felicia's and Tina's children were any indication, they would be high-spirited and mischievous handfuls all around.

Jon would be a good father, she thought. During tea, he had spoken to all three of her siblings and despite Cassie's declaration that he was dangerous, she knew Cassie liked him. Nicky and George had both told her that they were glad she was marrying someone who was a great goer. She wasn't sure what they meant by that, but she knew they approved of him and that was enough.

"He doesn't know," Felicia said to Tina as the two of them strolled the perimeter of the ballroom.

"Doesn't know?" Tina said in astonishment.

Felicia shook her head.

"Then why ask Amanda to marry him?"

"I don't know. That's what I'm trying to figure out."

"Should we ask?"

"No. I hate to say it, but I think that he might have asked her because he thought she didn't have it."

"Didn't have it? But why?"

"I think he doesn't want to fall in love."

Tina finished the contents of the glass in her hand. "He's probably being a typically obtuse male." Motioning to a footman, she deposited the empty glass on his tray before turning back to Felicia. "I know he's our brother, but he can be as unreasonable as the rest of the male population when it comes to love."

Felicia groaned. "I never thought he'd be that stupid, but that scientifically inclined brain of his probably considers love folderol or some such."

Tina glanced over at her as they skirted a knot of young women. "When I was fourteen, I asked Mama whether Aaron would ever love me." Felicia grimaced at the reminder that Tina had once been betrothed to her oldest brother. Tina would have been miserable had the marriage come to pass. "Papa overheard me and said he would, but he'd never admit it. He said men were silly that way. They refuse to fall in love. Then, when they do, they refuse to admit it."

"You would think Jon would know better."

"It was Mira who told me men don't think with their heads most of the time."

Felicia's laughter had heads around her turning.

"So, if you don't think he knows Amanda has his statuette, who do you think he thinks has it?" Tina asked.

"I'm beginning to think it's Sophie."

"Sophie Lawrence? You're sure?"

Felicia nodded. "He's been acting strangely around her—and I've seen him watching her with an odd look in his eyes. Of course, she's not here tonight, so I haven't been able to observe."

"Hmmm. Why would he think that?"

"It might have to do with her slight connection to him."

"Ahhh. I hadn't thought of that. Considering Jay was Aaron's younger brother, he might think Nona would have selected someone somewhat connected."

"That, and he doesn't remember Amanda from the Lake District."

"So, should we say something?"

Felicia shook her head. "I promised to stay out of his search, and except for telling him Lady Carol didn't have it after she eloped, I have kept my promise."

"Hmmm. Good point."

The two stopped near an open window. A light breeze stirred the drapes pulled back to let in the warm night air.

"He and Sophie would have made a good match, but if he wants Amanda, who am I to quibble?"

Tina laughed. "You and Amanda have been thick as thieves since you met at that Young Ladies' Academy. I didn't imagine you'd object, regardless of Nona's promises."

"I think I should be insulted that you think I would actively encourage Jon to go against Nona's wishes. If Nona promised him that statuette, but he's marrying Amanda without definite knowledge of who has it, maybe he's given up on it."

Tina nodded. "Maybe he's decided Amanda's more important. Nona would have approved if that's the case."

"I would wager Nona told him to follow his heart and if it's led him to Amanda, she wouldn't have objected—even if it meant he wouldn't get his figurine."

"What are you two plotting now? And can I help?"

Felicia and Tina spun around, discovering Geri had snuck up on them.

The sisters laughed. "Nothing, right now," Tina answered. "But now you mention it, perhaps you can help us plan some of the activities for the house party before Jon's wedding."

As the ladies began discussing various activities, none of them noticed a shadow detach itself from the wall outside the window and slip from the terrace into the garden below.

Amanda was tired. It had been a long day, and she wanted nothing more than to return home and curl up in bed. But she had to find Jon first and she hadn't seen him since supper. Where could he have gotten to?

She glanced in the direction of the card rooms. Dare she go into one? During her first Season as a naïve debutante, she had entered one or two in search of him until Eliza firmly forbade her to enter another one.

She was about to head in that direction when she found him. Standing near the terrace doors, he was speaking to Lady Denbury. Her hand was on his sleeve and she was waving her fan flirtatiously. Moreover, it looked as if the two of them had just entered the ballroom from the darkened garden. Amanda saw red and it had little to do with the rubies that graced Lady Denbury's swanlike neck.

She told herself she wasn't jealous. Lady Denbury and Jon had been friends three years ago. Felicia had hinted they had been more than just friends, but she hadn't understood then. Now she did, and it did nothing for her peace of mind.

As if he realized he was being watched, Jon suddenly looked up and their eyes met across the room. He gave her a slow, bone-melting smile then turned back and disengaged himself from his companion.

"My goodness!" Heart in her throat, Amanda whirled to face Felicia. "If Brand looked at me like that in public, the maids would be mopping up the puddle for days!"

"Felicia!" Amanda gasped. "You startled me."

"I should say so," she replied. "An elephant could have passed by and you wouldn't have noticed unless it stepped on you."

Amanda could not stop the flames that rose in her cheeks, growing hotter under her friend's amused gaze.

"I'll not tease, though," Felicia continued, "because I'm so happy for you. I forgot to ask earlier, but where's Eliza?"

Grateful for the reprieve, Amanda relaxed. "She decided to stay home with Cassie."

"Lady Althorpe, or your cousins?"

"Both, I think. In fact, Eliza and I are letting her stay with me until they leave. Unfortunately, to keep the peace, Eliza has suggested I allow one or both of my cousins to be my bridesmaids if Cassie is the flower girl."

"I'm sorry," Felicia commiserated. "Maybe you and Jon should have gone with Lady Carol."

Amanda was still laughing when Jon joined them.

A short time later they were in his coach headed for Barrington House.

"Lady Thanet asked me to remind you that you are expected at Thane House for breakfast. She said she was sure you wouldn't want to forget."

Jon turned to look down at her in the meager light of the coach. Her golden curls seemed to glow in the dimness. Turning toward her, he slid an arm around her shoulders and pulled her close.

"I had not forgotten," he replied, "but perhaps you ought to join us."

He was afraid Tina was going to take him to task about the statuette, but knew she wouldn't if he brought Amanda along. So far he had avoided her, but soon he just might have to come up with a suitable explanation for marrying Amanda instead of Sophie.

Amanda shook her head, her hair brushing against his cheek. "No. She made it quite clear that this was a discussion between you and her alone. I received the distinct impression that even Lord Thanet would not be present."

Jon was thankful for the darkness of the carriage that shadowed his face for he knew Amanda would have wondered at the grimace that crossed it at her words. He could only hope it would indeed just be he and Tina tomorrow morning. If Felicia joined them, he could be in for a thorough cross-examination. He loved his sisters dearly, but he refused to be nagged by them.

"All the same, I might need you to save me then."

He sensed her grin. "I'm sure you are quite capable of handling your sister, my lord," she retorted, but her voice was a bit breathless.

"You think so?"

She raised her eyes to where his should be in the shadows and opened her mouth to answer him, but no sound came out as he decided she had presented him with too perfect an opportunity, and kissed her.

He felt the small shiver that went through her before she surrendered. He kissed her thoroughly, delighting in the taste of her and the feel of her softness pressed against him. His hand came up to stroke a smooth cheek as he raised his head, aware that her hand had climbed to his shoulder.

The coach came to a stop and he released her reluctantly. When the door opened, he exited, then turned to lift her down, escorting her to the now open front door of her home.

"Until tomorrow," he promised, bowing and lifting her hand to his lips.

She nodded and smiled, then slipped inside, and the door closed firmly behind her.

As the butler took her cloak, she asked after the rest of the family and was told they had all retired. Climbing the stairs slowly, sliding her hand along the smooth, polished banister, gave her time to relive Jon's kiss. Could he tell how she felt from their kisses? Did he know already how much she loved him? She stopped and closed her eyes momentarily as she reached the top. In a very short time, she might be climbing the stairs in Kent House with Jon at her side. She hugged herself at the thought, unable to stop the joy flooding her entire body as she continued down the hall.

Entering her room, she found Mary asleep on the chaise, and Cassie asleep in the bed. Waking the maid, she allowed Mary to help her out of her dress and into a nightgown, then take down her hair. When Mary approached with the brush, Amanda waved her away, sending her off to seek her own bed. She only took a few minutes to brush and plait her hair, then crawled into bed beside Cassie. As she did so, she encountered something hard. Searching, she discovered Cassie had JoJo cuddled in her arms as she slept. She gently disengaged the figure from the sleeping child and held it to her breast for a moment. It was warm from Cassie's body, and she smiled as she put it on the bedside table.

"I have been meaning to speak to you."

Amanda looked up from the invitation she was addressing as Lady Althorpe entered the small parlor she and Eliza had turned into a planning room for the wedding. One look at her aunt's face and Amanda knew this was not going to be pleasant.

"About what, Aunt?"

Capping the inkwell and putting the quill back in its stand, she turned in her chair as her aunt seated herself on a nearby sofa.

"I thought to provide you some guidance in the matter of this wedding. Have you already consulted with the bishop and secured St. George's?"

"No, Aunt. I am not—"

"What? Whyever not?"

"Because I am not being married there. Surely you heard all of this yesterday?"

Lady Althorpe turned red. "I did, but I thought surely there must be some mistake."

"No. No mistake. His lordship and I do not want the fuss of a large, elaborate affair."

Lady Althorpe's eyebrows shot up. "Fuss? Is there a reason for the rush?" Her dark eyes narrowed at Amanda, pointedly staring at her waist.

Amanda stiffened. "I beg your pardon, Aunt. What exactly are you implying?"

"Nothing," was the sharp reply. "I was merely wondering aloud what everyone else will be thinking."

Amanda kept her temper with difficulty as her aunt continued.

"People will wonder at the rush," she stated. "Are you trying to cause a scandal?"

Amanda grit her teeth and counted to five. "No, Aunt. And I do not think anyone will consider a house party and wedding a scandal. Except, of course, those who are looking to find one."

Lady Althorpe drew herself up. "No one should be married by special license unless there is a necessity for it."

"We are being married by special license because it is what we want. Waiting six months or so does not appeal to either of us."

"I see."

The sound of laughter and squealing echoed from the garden beyond the windows, drawing their attention. A high-pitched indignant voice was heard. "Nicky, you give that back!"

Amanda smiled. Nicky and George had welcomed Cassie into the nursery with open arms and, as a typical boy, Nicky couldn't resist teasing her. She wondered what he'd stolen this time.

Her aunt's disapproving voice dampened her humor.

"And what is that child doing in this house? Your father's selfishness will cause a scandal on its own."

"Selfishness, Aunt? Surely you are not speaking of Papa."

"But of course. It is unseemly for your father to have foisted his by-blow on the rest of you. It is a wonder Eliza hasn't objected."

"But of course I didn't object, Barbara." Eliza spoke from the doorway, surprising them both.

Relief poured through Amanda as her stepmother entered the room.

"But...but you cannot possibly wish to have such a child under your roof. People will be scandalized," was the protested reply.

Eliza seated herself in a chair. "Oh, pooh on anyone who is scandalized. Cassie is a child and neither Trent nor I will countenance anyone who speaks ill of her."

"I should have known you would indulge Trent's whims." Lady Althorpe sat up straighter and looked down her nose at

Eliza.

Amanda always found herself amazed at her aunt's audacity in thinking that she, the daughter of an earl, was somehow superior to Eliza, the daughter of a duke.

"I suppose many will applaud your charitable nature, but don't think that they won't pity you for having to take her in."

Amanda had to bite her tongue to keep from saying something rude, but Eliza refused to be baited and merely looked at Lady Althorpe for an extended moment, then turned to Amanda.

"Cassie's first fitting for her dress is this afternoon. She would love it if you came along."

"I do not think I have any plans," Amanda replied.

"Good. Now, Barbara—" Eliza turned back to Lady Althorpe, "—we must have an answer today regarding the girls as bridesmaids. With Cassie being fitted today, we will need to have—"

"Certainly not!" Lady Althorpe screeched. "I will not have my daughters consorting with that...that..." She turned to Amanda. "And you should not even consider tainting your wedding with her presence."

Amanda gasped. "Tainting my—"

"Very well," Eliza interrupted. "You will, of course, receive an invitation. It is your choice whether you attend."

Eliza's voice was clipped and Amanda realized she was holding on to her composure with difficulty. It was unfortunate her aunt didn't.

Lady Althorpe sputtered. "You would choose her over your own family?" she asked Amanda in a shocked voice.

"Cassie is my sister, Aunt. If you cannot understand that, I see no reason to continue this discussion."

"And what of his lordship? Does he, or his family, not object to her presence?"

Amanda knew she shouldn't have laughed at her aunt, but she couldn't help it. "Of course not. Lady Thanet pronounced her a perfect angel and can't wait for Cassie to meet her own daughter."

"Hmmph. I should have known. What else should one expect from gypsies?"

Amanda stood abruptly and stared daggers down at her aunt. "This conversation is at an end. I will not continue to listen to you malign my betrothed's family. I am sorry you cannot see past your petty prejudices, but I am not sorry not to have either Sonya or Cynthia in my wedding." She turned to go, but looked back at Eliza. "Please excuse me." Then hurried from the room before Eliza answered.

As she reached the front hall, she realized she didn't know where she was headed. She hadn't thought about what she was doing when she left; she'd just needed to put some distance between herself and her aunt's hateful presence.

Barrons looked at her quizzically as she stood in the spacious foyer and she felt her cheeks warm under the butler's scrutiny.

Glancing down at her attire, she made a quick decision and hurried up the stairs.

Chapter Eleven

Jon arrived at Thane House that same morning promptly at ten and was shown into the small green and yellow breakfast parlor where Tina sat, a plate of eggs and toast in front of her. Hiding his relief at not finding Felicia also in attendance, he took a seat beside his sister and let the footman pour him a cup of coffee before Tina directed the man to leave the pot, and the room.

He had spent most of the night going over in his head what he would say to his sister about choosing to marry Amanda. Short of declaring his undying love for her, he had come up blank. So it was with carefully concealed pleasure he realized she did not want to talk about his statuette at all.

"Since you have only recently returned from the Continent, would I be wrong to assume you are not planning to take Amanda back there on a honeymoon?"

"I hadn't thought that far ahead yet," he admitted. "But the truth is I would prefer we spend the summer at the Abbey."

"I see."

Jon watched her pour herself a cup of tea. He studied her as she sipped the fragrant brew, careful to keep his expression neutral as she studied him in return.

"I thought I might make a suggestion of where to spend a short honeymoon before you repaired to the Abbey for the summer."

"You don't think I ought to just take Amanda to the Abbey? Hopefully the neighbors would not disturb us."

"I think the Abbey a wonderful place to spend the summer, or fall, or any other time of the year. But, Jon, it will be your home. At least for some period of time, the two of you ought to go somewhere alone where you can spend time with each other without the demands of responsibilities."

"And where would you suggest that be? You do have such an idyllic place in mind?"

She laughed. "Of course I do. I wouldn't have started the conversation if I didn't have someplace in mind."

"And are you going to tell me where?"

"You could just remove to the Dower House at Collingswood when you are ready to leave the ball. I do not think you want to stay in the house with all the guests, but you would not want to travel all the way to London at that time of night, either. Besides, you would not have any time together if you returned to London right away. The Dower House is perfect."

He should not have been surprised his ever-practical sister had taken on not only planning his wedding, but his honeymoon as well.

"It is not far from the main house," she continued, "but far enough that we would not bother you. It can be separately staffed and has recently been completely aired and cleaned. There would be plenty of room for just the two of you. And those gossips who seem to make it a habit to pop up where they are not wanted would never find you."

Jon leaned back in his chair, staring past her at nothing in particular. She had a good point, he conceded. These past few weeks had been little more than a whirlwind courtship. Although he knew Amanda better now than he had before, a few weeks alone after their marriage was a very good idea.

They would be alone at the Abbey, but there they would be lord and lady and other things would command their attention. It *would* be better for them to get to know each other on neutral ground, so to speak.

Jon left Thane House in good spirits. In typical male fashion, he had not thought about anything past the wedding night. It occurred to him once that Amanda would like to travel, but having just returned to England he did not feel it prudent to leave again. Perhaps next summer they could take a trip to Paris. Or maybe he'd borrow Jay's yacht and take her to the Mediterranean. He had the feeling she'd love Italy and Greece.

Amanda caught her breath at her first sight of Collingswood. Set in a wooded valley bisected by a wide river, the area was lush and fertile. The woods consisted of trees of every kind, elm, oak, birch, beech and teemed with life. Birds flew overhead and the occasional small animal scampered across the perfectly manicured lawns and well-kept drive.

As the house came into view, she studied it. Built of golden cotswold stone, it stood three stories, plus attics, and was built in the Elizabethan style in the shape of the letter "E". The late afternoon sun reflected off rows of windows in ornately carved frames and she could see the pennant flying from the corner of one of the end sections below which, she would later learn, was the master suite. It looked warm, welcoming and inviting.

"It's a lovely little place, isn't it?" The dowager spoke to her.

Turning to look at Jon's grandmother, she agreed. "It's beautiful."

"Although I am partial to the Abbey myself."

"Then you must come to visit often," she offered.

The dowager chortled. "I think I will content myself in the city for at least the next few months."

Amanda blushed, but managed to say in a calm voice, "Then perhaps for Christmas?"

"Perhaps," was all the dowager would say as the coach came to a stop.

Jon was waiting as the door opened. Fitting his hands around her waist, he lifted her down, then turned to help out his grandmother and Letty.

Letty had been a pleasant surprise. It transpired that, after her discussion with Jon at the Mathesons', he suggested to his grandmother a companion might be a good idea and Letty would make an excellent one. His grandmother had, to his surprise, agreed. Letty had been sent for, interviewed, and hired within the day. In addition, after Aunt Barbara's ultimatum concerning Cassie's participation in the wedding, Amanda asked her to be her bridesmaid, to which Letty also agreed.

Catherine and Doyle were delighted. Catherine's husband even agreed to come for the wedding. Her cousin, Lord

Hickham, sent his regrets along with a gift. Now, if Aunt Barbara would only... No, she wouldn't think it. She wouldn't wish Aunt Barbara and her two cousins would just decide not to come, but she knew she did. It was highly unlikely to happen, so she kept those thoughts to herself. Aunt Barbara might not want her girls in the same wedding party as Cassie, but she would not invite speculation by not appearing at all. Those same girls would eventually have to make their own debuts and memories were long among the gossips.

As Jon escorted the ladies into the front hall, Tina hurried to meet them. While she greeted her grandmother, Jon took the opportunity to invite Amanda to go riding with him as soon as she had a chance to change.

Shown by the housekeeper to a pretty room decorated in turquoise and white while Tina took care of her grandmother, Amanda found her maid, Mary, already there.

"'Tis a lovely place, m'lady," she said as she helped Amanda out of her traveling dress of dark green cambric.

"It is, isn't it?"

She washed the travel dust from her face and hands, then changed into a dark blue habit trimmed with light blue frogging before hurrying back downstairs to meet Jon.

A short time later, mounted on a frisky grey mare, Jon led her away from the house and stables.

The afternoon was warm, the sun shining brightly in a nearly cloudless blue sky.

The scent of wildflowers, grass, and earth mingled in the air. Birds and other small animals were present in abundance as they entered a small forest. Riding along a sun-dappled path, Amanda watched one squirrel chase another from one tree to another until they were lost from view.

"It's lovely," she told him, eyes alight at the activity all around her. "I don't know why Tina bothers with London."

Jon chuckled. "There are times when she doesn't know either. She insists she's a country girl at heart, but she also loves the theatre, museums and other sights to be found in the city."

Amanda allowed him to move slightly ahead of her as the path narrowed, giving her the chance to admire the way he sat on his horse. The dark brown riding jacket fit across broad shoulders with nary a wrinkle, and the muscles of his thighs were clearly visible as he controlled his horse with an easy grace. He wore no hat and the midnight dark silk of his hair invited her to touch it. If she had been closer, she might have given in to the impulse to reach out and do so.

She allowed her thoughts to drift for a moment, smiling giddily as she reminded herself of why she was here. Four days. In four days she would finally achieve her destiny. She would marry her prince. Nona's promise had come true. She wasn't sure how it happened without Jon knowing about JoJo, but she would not decry the fates who saw fit to ensure it had.

Eventually she would have to tell him about JoJo. How would he react? What would he say? She closed her eyes momentarily and tried to picture his reaction when she presented the statuette to him. It would be easier to guess at his reaction if she knew what Nona had told him regarding it. But she didn't. She could only hope he'd be happy to have it.

Three years ago she would not have believed it could happen. After the scene in the library at the Abbey, she had thought her dreams lost forever; her heart broken beyond repair. Yet she had persevered, moving on with her life while waiting for him to return.

The path widened and she moved up beside him as they emerged from the wood into a meadow. Climbing a steep path to the top of a rise, they drew to a halt near a lone oak tree and she caught her breath at the vista before her. Undulating fields in a checkerboard of brown, green and gold spread out as far as the eye could see. Occasionally a hut or cottage sat on the edge of a field, and here and there she could make out a road or fence dividing the parcels. A broad river meandered through the area, the sun glinting on the surface.

Looking back in the direction they had come, she could see the house in the distance. The formal gardens were extensive and dotted with at least three small pavilions. A grassy area beyond them sloped down to a small lake.

Jon dismounted and moved to her side. Leaning forward, she put her hands on his shoulders as he lifted her down, acutely aware of the tensile strength in his arms. Once on the ground, however, he didn't seem inclined to let her go, so she remained still, unsure of what to do.

"This is my favorite spot at Collingswood." Jon spoke above her head. "There have been times when I have spent hours up here just sitting and looking out over that small valley."

She turned to look at the view. "It's quite beautiful."

Jon moved behind her and slid his arms around her waist, anchoring her against him. For a moment he allowed in the sense of satisfaction at having achieved a goal.

You'll never be one of us. He could still hear the sneer in Aaron's voice as he made it clear what he thought of Jon. *Just a gypsy brat trying to get above himself.* The first time he'd heard those words, he hadn't even understood them. At six, he hadn't understood that having a great-grandmother who was a gypsy was a bad thing; hadn't realized that many would consider him tainted. *Go back to your own kind.* Aaron's words had hurt. But more than that, they'd spurred him to prove that he could be one of them.

And when he began to understand what it was about him that caused Aaron's disdain, he vowed he would fit in. That, regardless of his gypsy heritage, he was still English, and a Peer of the Realm, and no one would take that from him.

He wondered if that was the reason he was attracted to Amanda. If deep down he wasn't still trying to prove that he could have something that Aaron would have denied him? That, despite his dark hair and slightly swarthy complexion, he could be desirable to someone as perfect and beautiful as Amanda. Was his attraction to her based on the lure of forbidden fruit?

Amanda's honeysuckle scent reached him and he closed his eyes as he breathed it in. It soothed him in a way few things did. He'd been restless and unsettled for so long, he hadn't realized until now that in Amanda's presence he did not feel on edge or wary. When had she become a safe haven for him without him being aware of it?

Apprehension wormed its way into his heart. He would not rely on Amanda for comfort. Reliance would lead to dependence, and dependence might lead to love. He could not love her. They were just friends. They enjoyed each other's company. What more did he need?

She didn't have his statuette, so he knew whatever feelings he might have for her could only be friendship or respect. He was only supposed to love the person with the statuette. He had no worries that that person might be Amanda.

The Duke and Duchess of Westover were the first guests to arrive at midmorning the next day, followed by a steady stream of family and a select circle of friends. Jon, who had not been privy to the guest list, except to be asked if there were any particular friends he wanted added, was surprised to see Charity Bascomb and her parents among the guests.

"It's because Felicia wanted to invite Martha and David," Amanda explained. "Besides, she's harmless."

Jon wasn't sure, but merely replied, "If you say so."

Amanda laughed outright at him then. "Felicia said you'd be skeptical, but she assures me she will keep Charity in line."

Jon grinned. "It is hard to believe that my hoyden of a little sister is now such a *grand dame* that she can keep anyone in line."

"Being a duchess has its privileges."

"Obviously."

The next three days were filled with activity. Tina had planned a variety of entertainments to fill the days prior to the wedding which included a picnic, archery, croquet, boating on the river, horse racing for the men and sedate rides about the countryside for the ladies. With near perfect weather every day, everyone enjoyed the various outdoor offerings. Evening entertainments included cards, billiards and a musicale in which she and Felicia entertained the assembled company, inviting some of the men to provide voices. Jon and Amanda provided a duet as well.

The arrival of the Earl of Kirkton, his wife and sons, was noted chiefly by Trent and Amanda, pleased to see that their Scottish cousins were able to make the journey. Arriving the day before the wedding with apologies for his brother, whose wife was expecting and too close to her time to travel, the earl and his wife greeted the rest of the family warmly, especially Aunt Marian.

All in all, it was a delightful three days, and soon Amanda found herself soaking in a tub of water delicately scented with honeysuckle in her room the morning of her wedding. It was as she sat before the fire, brushing her golden tresses dry that she realized that she knew nothing of what was to happen this evening.

Tina had planned an early afternoon wedding so an informal luncheon and reception could take place between it and dinner, giving time for guests from London who had not been invited to the wedding to arrive. After an early dinner, the grand ball was scheduled to begin around eight. Once she and Jon opened the ball with the first waltz, the evening was theirs. Of course, she expected to dance at least once with her father and other assorted relations before she would truly be free.

Eliza had already spoken to her about what to expect on her wedding night, but it was Felicia who had told her that, no matter what Eliza said, the reality would be indescribable. It was the way Felicia had said it, while looking at her own husband across the room, which had Amanda looking forward to the evening, despite that Eliza's description had sounded uncomfortable and embarrassing.

Rising from the stool, her hair now dry, she crossed the room to stand before the window. Sunlight spilled into the room through the open portal, enveloping her in its warmth. Hugging herself, she savored her anticipation of the afternoon and evening to come.

Nona would have told her she had attained her destiny. She would have said she was marrying her one true love. That he was also her best friend's brother was a bonus. Remembering that long ago conversation with Jon and Felicia's great-grandmother, she chuckled at the other statement she had made. Felicia was, indeed, about to become her big sister.

She often wondered why she loved Jon so much. That he was handsome, titled, and rich was important to society, but not necessarily to her. One of her earlier suitors had been a marquess, handsome in his own way, as well as rich. Yet he had not possessed Jon's strength of character, or his gentleness. He had not seen her as a person—an educated person with whom it was possible to carry on a conversation. Jon, however, seemed not only to enjoy that about her, but also encouraged her intellectual pursuits. It was that knowledge which now caused her to reevaluate the encounter at the Abbey in a different light—and place blame for it squarely in her own lap. If she had been truthful with Jon about the reason for her presence in the library, none of it would have happened.

She still felt a twinge of guilt regarding JoJo. Maybe she'd tell him once they settled in at the Abbey.

Mary entered and began laying out her wedding clothes. In the end she had declined to lengthen the train on her dress, feeling comfortable with the short train that was already part of it. Having seen the church, she now knew she had made the right decision.

Eliza entered with Cassie as Mary was putting the finishing touches on her hair. Drawn up with a silver ribbon to her crown, the curls were allowed to spill freely down over her shoulders and back.

"Stand up, and let me see," Eliza said and Amanda did so.

The bodice of white satin embroidered around the square neckline with a flower pattern in silver thread emphasized her ample bust and narrow waist. The short cap sleeves were edged with silver trim. The skirt, also of heavy white satin, fell from the tightly cinched waist over the cone-shaped crinoline, and was overlaid with white lace shot with silver threading. When she had ordered the gown, she had specifically not wanted the customary rows of flounces and was glad for it now. The skirt fell straight to the floor, with only one ruffle at the bottom of the lace. The resulting effect was simple, yet sophisticated.

Cassie's dress had been made to match hers and Letty's. White satin with a blue sash, and flowers embroidered across the full skirt in silver thread looked particularly fetching on the little girl. Her dark hair was pulled back and tied with a large blue bow. Dark eyes looked up at Amanda, sparkling with excitement.

"Ooooh, how pretty you look."

Amanda smiled brightly at the little girl. "And so do you."

"Beautiful," was Eliza's pronouncement. She held out a flat rectangular case. "This is for you. It's from his lordship. I think he expects you to wear it."

Amanda resumed her seat in front of her dressing table

and opened the case. Eliza, looking over her shoulder, drew in a breath. On a bed of black velvet lay a necklace of alternating diamonds and pearls, a large square cut diamond hanging from the center, and a pair of pearl and diamond earbobs.

"Perfect," Eliza said, motioning Mary forward to clasp the necklace around Amanda's neck.

The diamond lay directly above her cleavage, drawing attention to the delectable swelling above the top of her gown. She often wished she wasn't so well-endowed as it sometimes made her feel top heavy. Today, however, she tried to see herself through Jon's eyes and came away with a favorable impression.

Letty arrived just as Mary was anchoring the veil made of the same silver-shot lace and decorated with orange blossoms and violets in Amanda's hair. Eliza was needed downstairs, she said, because it was time to leave. Rising from the dressing table, Amanda gave Eliza a quick hug, then Eliza hurried from the room, leaving Cassie with Amanda and Letty.

"You look beautiful," Letty said with a smile. "Nervous?"

"A little," she admitted, eyeing Letty critically.

The blue of Letty's dress matched Amanda's eyes perfectly, and created a lovely frame for Letty as well. The white lace in the flounces at the hem and falling from the elbow-length sleeves had silver thread running through it, tying it nicely together with Amanda's own dress. With her auburn hair dressed in a softer style than usual, Amanda saw Letty in a different light, and wondered, as she had before, why she was not interested in marriage.

"Your dress is the same color as my sash," Cassie said to Letty. "We all match."

"I think that's what Amanda wanted." Letty smiled down at her. "Do you think she did a good job?"

Cassie nodded as she looked over the three of them.

"We should go," Letty said to Amanda. "Everyone was leaving as I came up. Your father will be waiting for us downstairs in the hall."

Cassie skipped ahead, and Amanda was conscious of her father's gaze as she descended the stairs, pride and joy clearly written on his face.

"I will be the envy of everyone present for having such

beautiful girls," he remarked and Cassie giggled.

They rode in an open carriage to the church in the village. Many of the villagers turned out along the road and along the village street to see them go by. The sun shone brightly with not a cloud in the sky. Since it was early afternoon, it was very warm and Amanda was glad she'd chosen not to embellish the gown with longer sleeves or extra layers. The church bell was ringing as they approached the small stone edifice and the crowd outside erupted in cheers as the carriage came to a stop.

He helped Letty down first, then Cassie, who gave him a hug before he set her on the ground to follow Letty inside. When her father escorted her into the small entry, Cassie was holding a small basket filled with rose petals and listening intently to Letty's instructions. Handing Amanda a bouquet consisting of white roses, orange blossoms and violets tied with white and silver ribbon, Letty then picked up her own bouquet consisting only of the same roses and orange blossoms and tied with the same white and silver ribbon.

Cassie moved into position and Letty turned to Amanda. "Ready?"

Amanda looked up at her father, who smiled reassuringly, glanced down the aisle to where Jon and his friend, Ted Hartwell, stood before the altar, then back at Letty, adjusted her veil, and nodded. Letty moved into place in the doorway, the signal to the person at the organ to begin playing.

Cassie started down the aisle.

From where she stood, Amanda could see the church was decorated all over with flowers and ribbon. Splashes of color adorned the pews, the large windows, the altar, and even some of the wall niches. At the front, directly ahead of her, was a large stained-glass window depicting Christ kneeling at prayer. The sunlight from the outside streamed through the colored panes, showering the front of the church with a rainbow of color and light. As she waited with her father, she relaxed and allowed the peace of the small church to steal over her. Today was the day she'd waited fourteen years for. Closing her eyes briefly, Nona's face came to mind. Jon's great-grandmother was smiling at her and in that moment Amanda knew all would be well.

Letty started down the aisle and she and her father moved into place.

"I hope you will be happy, poppet," her father whispered to her.

She looked up at him and smiled. "I will, Papa."

Her father squeezed her hand one last time for reassurance as Letty reached the front of the church, and they started down the aisle.

Jon stood at the front of the church watching first Cassie, then Letty, come down the aisle. His glance drifted over the front pews where the respective families sat. On the side directly in front of him sat Jay and Tina, their daughter, Shana, between them while Jay held Andrew on his lap. Next to Tina sat his grandmother, and next to her sat Felicia and Brand, each holding one of their twins. In the pew behind them sat the Duke and Duchess of Westover, and the dowager duchess.

On the other side of the aisle, Eliza sat with Nicky and George, with space left open for Trent and Cassie to join them once Amanda was safely delivered down the aisle. Beside Eliza sat Great Aunt Marian. In the pew behind sat Lord Althorpe, his mother and sisters, the Earl and Countess of Kirkton and their two sons. The next pew held Catherine, her husband, Henry, and her brother, Doyle. Jon had found himself enjoying the company of the Farnsworths and Doyle Cookeson over the last three days, which was more than he could say for the company of Lady Althorpe.

Letty reached the front and took her allotted place. Jon's eyes snapped back to the aisle as the organ player increased the volume of the music, and the assembly rose to their feet as Amanda and Trent began to advance down the aisle.

Chapter Twelve

"Might I beg a favor of you, cousin?"

Amanda looked up into the startling blue eyes beneath the golden brows of her cousin, Angus, Viscount McQuarrie. "Of course," she replied as the music for the country dance ended and they strolled toward the edge of the floor.

"Would you introduce me to the angel over yonder in blue?" he asked, nodding in the direction of a group of young people.

Glancing in the direction he indicated, she scanned the group, noting only one young lady in blue. Her eyes widened. Angel?

"Truly?" she asked, trying to keep the disbelief out of her voice.

Angus nodded as a slow flush reddened his cheeks.

Amanda turned to glance back at the group to make sure she had determined the right woman. Had Angus lost his mind? At five years older than she, he was a striking young man, and probably her favorite male cousin. Tall and broad shouldered, with mesmerizing blue eyes and guinea gold hair liberally streaked with red, he was a gentle giant of a man. As far as she could tell there was nothing wrong with his eyesight or his mind.

Arriving as late as they had, he, his parents, the Earl and Countess of Kirkton, and younger brother, Dougal, had not much of a chance to meet many of the other guests. After the wedding had been the earliest real opportunity they had to mingle, but she noted his family spent most of it with other members of the family catching up. Living in Scotland meant contact was sparse, with weddings, funerals, and the occasional baby christening bringing them together.

Reaching the knot of young people, she introduced him into the group. Chatting amicably for a few minutes and accepting the group's congratulations, she eventually wandered away, leaving Angus standing beside his angel. She was smiling to herself not much later when she noticed the two of them dancing. She wondered if he would still think she was an angel by the end of the evening.

"What's so amusing?"

Her husband's deep voice drew her from her reverie and she turned to find Jon behind her. Looking up into eyes regarding her with barely controlled hunger she felt a small shiver go through her.

"My cousin, Angus, asked me to introduce him to Charity Bascomb," she replied. A dark eyebrow raised in query. "He called her an angel."

"Perhaps to him she is," he mused.

She was not convinced, but did not pursue the subject. Angus and Charity no longer interested her at all and she knew it had everything to do with the arm resting possessively at her waist as they moved through the crowd, and the dark head tilted attentively toward hers.

Earlier, they had stood for what seemed like hours while the cream of Society streamed past to tender their good wishes. Amanda had noted many envious glances cast in her direction, as well as the flirtatious invitations cast at Jon, and found a possessive streak in herself she hadn't realized she had.

When the musicians began another waltz, Jon drew her out onto the floor for their second dance of the evening. Looking up at him, she was reminded of what she had learned this afternoon. Her husband's name was Jonathan. Felicia and Tina always called him Jon, and his great-grandmother had called him JoJo. It never occurred to her it was short for anything else.

"Why does no one call you Jonathan?"

"That was my father's name," he replied. "I have always just been Jon."

"Oh." She was silent while they reached the end of the floor, negotiated the turn, and began the return trip. "I like it."

"You may use it if you wish," he allowed, "but it may take me some time to get used to it."

"And Richard?"

He frowned momentarily. "That was my great-grandfather's name. He was Lord Milden of Mildenwood Hall."

This was the first she'd heard of any relatives other than Tina and Felicia, but the music was ending and she had no more time to question him. As they left the floor, they were met by Ted Hartwell, the Duke of Westover's younger brother, and Jon's friend from his days at Oxford. Tina and Felicia joined them shortly, and asked Amanda to accompany them to say goodnight to their children.

Having done so for the last three nights, Amanda agreed, although she did think it was a bit late. The children were all asleep already, but Felicia and Tina both kissed smooth cheeks and straightened blankets and she looked in on her own siblings before they left. As they headed back down the stairs, Amanda paid little attention to where they were going, listening to Tina and Felicia talk of the children instead. It wasn't until they reached the front hall and found Jon and Ted waiting for them that she realized it had all been planned.

Minutes later, she and Jon were in a carriage heading away from the house. The moon was nearly full in a cloudless sky and its light spilled into the carriage lit only by one small lamp. The heat of the day had given way to a cool night, and she was reminded that she had no cloak and was still wearing her wedding dress. One hand absently rubbed her arm where goosebumps had risen.

Jon noticed the action.

"Cold?" he asked, wondering at the same time how she could be. They could be traveling through a blizzard right now and the last thing he would be was cold. Not with her sitting beside him.

"A little," she answered. He slid an arm around her, drawing her close against his side.

"We are not going far." He answered the question in her eyes. And it was a good thing too, he thought. Temptation had never been this hard to resist and he wondered if he would survive it. He would not be responsible for his actions if he even

167

so much as kissed her before they reached their destination, he told himself sternly. Touching her was a big enough risk. Tamping down his rising passion, he watched her rest her head against his shoulder in much the same way his nieces did. The innate trust in that small action touched a part of him he'd thought long buried.

He had escaped Nona's prophecy. But despite that, he knew his feelings for Amanda went beyond mere liking or even the mutual respect he'd convinced himself he wanted. She might not be his destiny, but she could still tug on the door inside himself that was kept firmly locked. If he wasn't careful, she'd pull it open.

Amanda was no longer cold. The moment he put his arm around her, one large hand curled around her bare arm, the coolness of the night vanished. Resting her head against his shoulder, she allowed herself to relax. In truth, it did not matter to her where they were going.

That they were going alone, beginning their honeymoon, however, generated a different set of feelings, the foremost being the return of the anticipation she felt earlier in the day. Eliza's and Felicia's words came back to her, and she could already feel her skin becoming heated. What would the night bring? Would it truly be as indescribable as Felicia said? And would she feel any different in the morning?

The carriage rocked to a stop and Jon moved to help her out. Once her feet touched the ground, she looked up and couldn't suppress the exclamation of wonder that escaped.

Before them stood a miniature palace. There were three rows of windows across the front with fanciful scroll and plasterwork around each window and the door. The carvings and what looked to be parapets on the roof matched the elaborately worked iron fence and gate, the posts of which were topped with brightly lit lamps. The darkness made the color of the stone difficult to discern as the light from the lamps created a warm, golden glow about everything within its reach. It reminded her of somewhere, but the impression was fleeting, and lost altogether moments later.

Jon escorted her through the gate and up the steps. The

door opened as they reached it and they entered a foyer which was as simple and elegant as the outside was ornate. A large chandelier hung from the high ceiling, casting light over simply painted cream-colored walls with oak door lintels. Two small paintings adorned a wall to her left, and a large staircase dominated the area to her right in the same wood.

"Thank you, Keyes," Jon said to the butler standing beside the door. "That will be all for tonight."

"Very good, my lord. And congratulations to you both."

They both thanked the butler, then Jon led her up the staircase and down a short hallway. She wanted to ask where they were, but words failed her and soon were superfluous as Jon ushered her into a dimly lit room, kicked the door shut and backed up against it, pulling her with him. Breathless, she braced her palms against his chest and looked up at him.

His gaze scorched her as it roved over her form, lingering on the swell of her breasts and the pulse beating at the base of her throat. She could feel her skin flushing and the hands at her waist burned her skin through the material of her dress. Had she really been cold before?

"It's been too long," he said softly, pulling her closer as his head descended toward hers. "Much too long."

Amanda met him halfway, lifting up on her toes, and sliding her hands up over his shoulders. Jon tightened his arms around her as their mouths met, and nearly groaned out loud at the feel of her soft curves pressed against his. Her lips parted beneath his and his tongue surged inside, seeking, tasting, possessing. *Mine!* he wanted to shout. *Mine! All mine!*

She was soft, sweet, tasting slightly of the champagne that had been flowing freely for most of the evening, and he drank greedily from her lips. His hands speared into her hair, destroying her maid's work in moments as the curls came loose, tumbling down over her shoulders and back. Sinking into the kiss, he felt his control slipping. He had been waiting all day for this, and it had been an excruciatingly long day. He hadn't laid eyes on Amanda until she arrived at the church, but all morning the anticipation had been building. Even the time spent catching up with Ted had not made the time pass fast enough.

If patience was a virtue, after today he was a candidate for sainthood. Yet he knew he had to slow down. A little voice in the back of his head reminded him she was an innocent and he did not want to frighten her.

Dragging his mouth from hers, he buried his face in her neck, inhaling the scent of honeysuckle lingering on her skin. His nimble fingers made quick work of the buttons marching down her back as he brushed his lips across her neck and on to her shoulder. When a moan escaped her, he raised his head to look down at her.

Amanda lifted heavy eyelids to look up at eyes which glittered in the lamplight. The shadows in the room almost made him look sinister. She could feel his rapidly beating heart as he unleashed a smile so hot, she thought she would melt. Blood rushed to her head and she swayed on her feet. As she caught her breath, she felt his hands on her back and noticed her dress seemed to sag. Slowly his hands released the top of her dress.

Lowering her arms, she allowed the top to slide free, and was momentarily disconcerted when not only the dress, but also her corset, slid into a puddle at her feet, leaving her standing before him clad only in her chemise and drawers, shoes and stockings. She had to fight the urge to raise her hands to cover her breasts as his heated gaze touched them.

Reaching up, her eyes never left his face as she began to loosen his cravat, unwinding it slowly, then letting it fall to the floor. The fire in his eyes flared at her boldness, yet encouraged her. Sliding her hands inside his coat, she pushed it off his shoulders and he let go of her long enough to allow it to drop as well.

She kicked off her slippers just before he reached down and lifted her into his arms to carry her to the bed she knew must be somewhere behind her.

The only lamp lit in the room was on the small table beside the bed, and it was turned down very low. That explained why the room was so dim. Yet the drapes stood open, allowing moonlight to stream through the two large windows situated on either side of the bed.

Depositing her on the sheets, he took a moment to remove

his own footwear before turning back to her. Her chemise, drawers and stockings soon went the way of the rest of her clothing, as did his shirt. Then his mouth was plundering hers again and she lost all sense of time and place.

His hands were everywhere, stroking, teasing, caressing, and she could feel the fire he was slowly building to a fever pitch. His mouth moved from hers down the side of her neck, to her shoulder, then to her breasts, and she gasped when his tongue laved a hardened peak. His touch was like putting a spark to very dry tinder and she felt the heat sizzle along her skin in the wake of his experienced fingers.

Felicia was right. The thought flashed through her head, then was lost as Jon's hand slid across her belly and she caught her breath as the hand slid lower.

"Look at me, Amanda." Jon's voice was hoarse, his breathing labored. And when she opened her eyes to look up at him, she noticed a fine sheen of moisture on his forehead, tendrils of dark hair clinging damply.

He was holding on to his control by a mere thread, she realized. Hot, hungry eyes moved over her and she trembled in response.

Heat blossomed beneath his hand and she could feel liquid pooling in that place between her legs where, even now, one long finger probed.

She did not expect, and could not have imagined, the sensations running riot through her body. Her skin seemed extra sensitive, responding to Jon's nearness alone, and when he touched her, the heat was intense. She could not make sense of the need that gripped her, that drove her to touch him, to pull him closer, and to whimper with want when he shifted away from her long enough to remove his last item of clothing.

She was beyond thinking, beyond trying to understand the yearning that drove her. She only knew that she wanted more. And she wanted it now.

The pain she was told to expect did not even register. The feeling of being lifted higher, of soaring directly into the sun, experiencing its searing heat, only to explode upon reaching its core—that registered. The sensation of floating, of being suspended in mid-air, that, too, registered.

She did not remember crying out his name at that final moment, nor did she know that the intensity of his own release shook Jon deeply. She only knew that she'd been granted a glimpse of heaven in her husband's arms and at that moment, whether or not he loved her didn't matter at all.

Amanda awoke to the feeling of being surrounded by warmth. A heavy weight lay across her waist and a solid male chest rose and fell directly against her back. Having never awakened with another adult in her bed before, she found the experience a bit unnerving. They were both naked, so rising was out of the question. Now what?

The arm draped over her waist moved suddenly, its hand splaying against her stomach, then moving upwards, the fingers brushing lightly over her skin. At the same time, she felt Jon lever up behind her and plant a kiss on her bare shoulder. She shivered. The hand cupped her breast, the thumb teasing one dusky nipple, and she had to stifle a gasp as tendrils of heat snaked their way through her body.

It was a lovely way to wake up, she would decide later. Much later, when she lay sated and boneless in her husband's arms, the rhythmic beating of his heart beneath her ear. Fleetingly she reminded herself that Felicia had been right. Nothing Eliza said could have prepared her for last night and this morning.

Jon shifted beneath her and she lifted her head to look into his face. Her stomach rumbled as she did so and he chuckled at her blush.

"Hungry?" he asked. "So am I, but probably not for the same thing." He grinned as her eyes widened.

Amanda thought she would expire on the spot, or at the very least, burst into flame, so hot were her cheeks. Ducking her head, she hid her face against his chest and tried to steady her breathing. Jon shifted again and a moment later, she found herself flat on her back, his face above hers.

"I shouldn't tease you so, but I'm afraid that after growing up with my sisters, it's what I do best." His eyes twinkled with amusement, but were tender at the same time. "I'll see what I can do about finding us some food." A quick kiss then he slipped out of the bed and stood.

Amanda turned her face into the pillow and pulled up the covers to her neck. A few minutes later she was sure she heard soft laughter as the door to the room opened, then closed. Minutes later it opened again to admit Mary.

She only had a chance to glance around what turned out to be an enormous room before Mary ushered her out of the bed and through a door in the wall into a bathing chamber. The tub was full of steaming water, the scent of honeysuckle in the air.

"His lordship said to tell you luncheon would be served as soon as you were ready," was all Mary said before she left her soaking in the tub.

Amanda was tempted to hurry but despite her hunger, the warm water was doing wonders for the aching muscles she hadn't known she possessed. Resting her head back against the edge of the tub, she closed her eyes and let out a long sigh. Yesterday, at nearly this same time, she had been doing the same thing. So much had happened since then.

The anticipation she had felt then had been replaced with a satisfied contentment. As far as she was concerned, Nona's promise of fourteen years ago had been fulfilled. Her prince had come. Her dilemma was that she wasn't sure Jon shared her sentiments.

Would he ever love her? Felicia had told her she was sure Jon would try his best not to fall in love with her, while still giving her anything and everything she could want. He would please her and make her happy as best he could—as long as he didn't fall in love. It was up to her, Amanda, to make him fall in love—and admit it. The problem was that she wasn't sure how to go about making someone fall in love with her.

Love, it seemed to her, either happened or it didn't. There didn't seem to be any way to make someone fall in love with someone else. But at least now she had a lifetime ahead of her to figure it out.

Mary returned as she was rising from the water. Toweling herself dry, she allowed herself to be directed back into the room and helped into a day dress of periwinkle muslin. She took the opportunity while Mary was brushing out her hair to glance around the room.

Her first impression had been correct. The room was enormous. It was obviously at the corner on the floor for it went completely around it. The bed was covered with a royal blue counterpane which matched the drapes at all the windows, with the carpet a lighter shade of the same color. White furniture and white walls with sky blue upholstery on the chairs and sofas scattered about the room created a beautiful setting.

She could hear sounds coming from around the corner on the other side of the room and, having Mary tie her hair back with a ribbon instead of creating an elaborate hairstyle she was sure Jon would only demolish, went to investigate.

Two sets of french doors stood on opposite sides of the corner, both leading out onto a balcony wrapped around the end of the building. Rounding the corner, she found Jon speaking to Keyes. Looking up as she approached, Jon nodded to the butler and came toward her.

He had bathed, shaved, and dressed simply in dark trousers and an open-necked shirt. She had never seen him looking so casual, or so appealing. He exuded a raw masculinity that drew female admirers wherever he went and she was no exception. She was just exceedingly thankful he was hers.

Over luncheon she asked him where they were.

"In the Dower House at Collingswood."

"The Dower House?" she asked in amazement, remembering what she had seen of the outside of the house before they entered the night before. Recalling that it had briefly seemed familiar reminded her that her impression had been of a miniature version of Versailles. Having only seen sketches of the French court, however, she could only consider her impression vague at best.

Jon chuckled. "A bit overdone, one might say, but nice all the same. The wife of one of the early Viscount Collings had it built. She spared no expense building it either, reasoning that if she ever had to live here, she should be as comfortable as possible. The whole family lived here while the new residence was built during the late-seventeenth century. Shortly after the new residence was finished, however, they received the Marquisate of Thanet and so moved to Thane Park."

"Was she French?" she asked and when he nodded in response, replied, "I thought so. It looks a bit like some of the drawings I've seen of châteaux."

She didn't ask how long they were to stay. That truly did not matter to her. She was looking forward to spending time with him.

After luncheon, Jon showed her around the house. In addition to the large suite they occupied which was the main suite, there were another six or so bedchambers, three parlors, two dining rooms, a library and a music room.

As Jon watched her wander around the library, eyes alight with interest, he was reminded again that he'd never seen her reading. Yet his grandmother had led him to believe that she was very well educated.

Perusing the titles on the shelves, he pulled out a compilation of Greek plays, opening it just as she joined him. Glancing at the book, she asked, "Do you like tragedies?"

"Not particularly," he answered. "I never understood the fascination with dying when most people want to live."

She laughed. "I suppose it's because the people in the plays aren't real—or at least don't seem real. But somehow we supposedly learn lessons from their tragic faults."

"And you?" he inquired. "Do you like tragedies?"

"Not much more than you," she replied. "But some more than others."

"Such as?"

She took the book from him, flipped through it until she found a particular page, then handed it back to him. "This is one I like."

"*Antigone?*" He was surprised. Not only was the book written in Greek, but it would not have been one he would have picked. "Why?"

"Because she held true to her beliefs and principles. She refused to allow something as inconsequential as a king's pride to stand in the way of what she believed to be right. Her brother's immortal soul was more important."

"Some would say she lost in the end though."

"True, but she wouldn't have. And the king lost far more." She reached over and turned a page, scanning the lines. "For

175

me, however, the person who lost the most was her sister. Not only was she left behind, but she was left behind with the knowledge that she had compromised her principles to stay safe."

"And you think she should have joined Antigone and, perhaps, shared her fate?"

She sighed. "I don't know. There was a time when I would have said families should stand behind each other, no matter what. But my own family is such a perfect example of fidelity I feel a bit like a hypocrite whenever I think it."

Jon smiled at the droll tone in her voice. Replacing the book on the shelf, he said, "All families have their problems. In a perfect world we'd all support each other, but then we'd all be blissfully happy with no difficulties in our lives. Most often support comes—or at least is most welcome and needed—during those difficult times. In a perfect world, there would be no difficult times."

"I'm not sure I'd want a perfect world, but not having my Aunt Barbara turning her nose up at me or Cassie would be welcome."

"Is that why neither of your cousins took part in the festivities yesterday?"

She looked up at him. He'd noticed? "Yes. Aunt Barbara essentially said it was them or Cassie." She smiled mischievously. "I don't know why she was outraged when I chose Cassie. One of my teachers often said difficult times prove to us what kind of person we really are. I suppose I'm a coward, then, because I left Eliza to deal with my aunt."

His laughter warmed her thoroughly. "My stepfather was fond of saying that how a person responds to adversity reveals much about their character."

"Oh?"

Jon chuckled. "It usually was thrown in with more practical sentiments in response to my own railing at the world in general after something didn't go my way. So, let's just say he used it often to show me that complaining about something I had made no effort to change or was unwilling to accept if I couldn't change it, did not improve my character one whit."

Amanda did not miss the affection in his voice at the

mention of his stepfather. Jay's father had raised him—and, according to his grandmother, raised him well. If some of the rumors she had heard were true, his stepfather had done a better job with him than with his own sons.

Leaving the library behind, they strolled into the garden behind the house. Wandering the paths, they continued to discuss families and their vagaries, and soon Jon was telling her outrageous stories about growing up with Tina and Felicia.

For Amanda, the afternoon had a magical quality to it. The barriers were slowly falling but she knew they still had a ways to go.

The next two weeks were the most blissful of her life. She and Jon spent hours walking, riding and exploring the countryside around Collingswood. With nothing to do other than be in each other's company, they discovered a great many common interests.

Jon was amazed at the extent and breadth of her knowledge. That he had never seen her reading was less of a surprise to him than realizing she never let on in conversations that she was so learned. Except now that he knew it, he could look back on situations and know when she had bitten her tongue in order not to draw attention to her intelligence. Why? Even her father had seemed unaware—or was he?

It was remembering the incident in the library at the Abbey that opened the subject one afternoon towards the end of their first week.

Clouds had been building all morning as they walked through the woods to a small pond hidden in its depths, so neither were surprised when it began to rain during luncheon, continuing throughout the afternoon. Seated on one of the chintz-covered sofas in front of the fireplace in the library, her head resting against his shoulder, they had been discussing one of Shakespeare's plays when he abruptly changed the subject.

"You weren't really looking for me that day at the Abbey, were you?"

Amanda went still. *That day.* It did not take a keen mind to know what *that day* meant. Talking about it still made her a little uncomfortable.

"No," she said now. "I thought everyone was out, so I was looking for something to keep me occupied for the afternoon."

Jon was silent for a moment, then asked, "Why didn't you just say so?"

Here was the opening she needed, but could she take it? He already knew she could read Greek. If that didn't classify her as a bluestocking, she didn't know what did. She was encouraged he had not reacted negatively the day after their wedding when they had been discussing Sophocles. Perhaps she was the one who needed to let go this time.

"Because of my father."

She could feel Jon's puzzled frown above her head, but she didn't dare look up into his face. It was easier to make confessions when you weren't looking at the person.

"My father has always told me no one wanted an intelligent woman for a wife. That if it got out that I could read Greek and Latin, and I enjoyed reading more than the popular gothic novels, fashion magazines and scandal sheets, I would be labeled, and ruin any chance of a good marriage." She smiled a bit in memory. "We had words often on the subject."

Jon remained silent.

"I didn't understand why he would become so agitated when he found me reading—I spent almost as much time in the library as he did. Then Eliza explained about my mother."

"Your mother?" Jon's surprise was not unexpected.

"Eliza said my father was so infatuated with her he never questioned what she read, the salons and lectures she attended, or the friends she kept. After her death, however, he blamed her wildness on the fact that she was so enlightened. In short, he decided she was incapable of using the knowledge she gained wisely and so her education was to blame."

"I'm not sure it would have ever occurred to me to assume a person's education was to blame for their inability to conform to the norms of society. One might wonder why he bothered to allow you to be educated at all."

She laughed. "He didn't object to anything my governess taught me, but Eliza was the one who insisted that I be sent to school," she said as if she had read his thoughts. "I was so uncommunicative and withdrawn she thought that if I had a chance to be around other girls my age and be befriended, it would help."

"And did it?"

"You know what Felicia is like. I tried to stay to myself, but she wouldn't let me. I don't know if she saw me as a challenge, but she poked and prodded, and talked and became my friend in spite of myself. The other girls were content to let me be, but not Felicia."

He chuckled, the vibration in his chest tickling her ear.

"When your great-grandmother died, she was so sad, I told her about my mother's death and how much I missed her. It was Felicia who helped me realize that family isn't necessarily just those related to you by blood. The way she spoke of some of the people at Thane Park helped me to realize that ignoring others around you made your life less complete. She was the first person I discussed the school with and she encouraged me to pursue my plans. It was Felicia, not Tina, who convinced your grandmother to help. She decided your grandmother needed a project in her life to keep her going."

Jon laughed. "I think it might be Felicia who needs a project to keep herself occupied—meddling being an ongoing one. But I'm not surprised. She and my grandmother have developed a special relationship. I think it began at the Abbey during the planning of her own wedding."

"She doesn't meddle all that much." Amanda raised her head as she defended her new sister-in-law.

"She meddles enough," he said as their eyes met, his voice suddenly dropping.

Amanda recognized the new depth in his tone. He suddenly had something else on his mind other than whether or not his sister was trying to save the world, and she felt her body begin to heat in response. When he lowered his head, she didn't hesitate.

Jon took her mouth in a soul-stirring kiss that curled her toes. Languor seeped through her body, followed by heat so intense she felt as if her very bones were melting. A delicious shiver snaked along her spine.

She was convinced she would never get used to the effect Jon had on her. She would enjoy it, even revel in it, but each time it would throw her completely off balance. Was it because she loved him? Or was it just mutual attraction? Whatever it was, she would never tire of being in his arms.

Jon raised his head to look down at her. Dragging her across his lap, she registered the proof of his desire through the plain twill skirt she wore. The older matrons would be scandalized to know she occasionally left off her corset. Wriggling her derriere, she watched his eyes darken to a deep emerald and felt his arms tighten around her.

"Temptress," he murmured, sliding his hand up the blouse she wore. Within moments he had slipped the buttons free and a hand inside. His fingers skimmed over warm skin made warmer by his touch and teased a dusky nipple. When he bent his head and sucked it into his mouth, she moaned.

Her hands slid through the ebony silk of his hair, holding him close as he ravished her breast. It wasn't enough. The flames racing along her veins gathered low in her belly, liquid pooled between her legs.

Lifting her against his chest, he stood and carried her over to the chaise and lowered her to her feet beside it. Her legs barely held her as he stripped her clothes from her, all the while planting tiny kisses on nearly every inch of her skin as it was revealed. Her hands were not idle and by the time she was completely naked and he pressed her back onto the chaise, he nearly was too.

The late afternoon thunderstorm, complete with lightning, could not compete with the emotions unleashed in the library. They held nothing back, each wanting the other with near desperation, their release explosive when it finally came. And in the calm after the storm, as Jon held Amanda's sweat-drenched body, he began to question his great-grandmother's previously unassailable judgment.

Chapter Thirteen

"We have been invited to dinner," Jon told her three days before they were to leave for London. Handing her a folded piece of paper, she opened it to find a note from Tina.

"Felicia is still there?" She raised surprised eyes to his as he sat across the table from her and picked up his napkin.

"Yes," he answered as Keyes served the soup. "She and Tina often spend the first part of the summer together while Jay and Brand finalize decisions regarding their shipping business. Then Felicia and Brand head for The Downs, stopping in London long enough for Brand to deliver instructions to their manager before continuing on."

"Oh."

"I had not thought to wait and travel back with them, but we can if you wish."

"It's not necessary," she replied. "Will we stay long in London?"

"Probably not," he replied. "I would guess that you would like to look in on the school, and I need to finish up some business with my solicitor. We could both visit my grandmother, but I would like to spend most of the summer at the Abbey. I have not been there in three years."

"Yes, of course." She'd forgotten he'd been on the Continent for the past three years, only returning to London two months ago. Had it truly only been two months since he returned from his travels? It seemed like a lifetime ago that Eliza casually noted over tea that he was back in town.

Conversation over luncheon was general out of deference to the servants. They talked of mutual acquaintances and their families. It was after luncheon was over and Jon had gone off to answer a letter he received from his solicitor that disaster struck.

Curling up with a book to read, Amanda settled on a settee in front of one of the open sets of double doors in the corner of the room. A short while later she felt a sudden, sharp cramp in the vicinity of her stomach. Her eyes widened as she quickly counted days.

"Oh, no!" she groaned as the pain began to build. Getting to her feet, she crossed the room and gave the bellpull a sharp yank. Mary arrived shortly afterwards to find her mistress already curled up on the bed clutching her midsection in pain. Understanding instantly, she rummaged in the dressing table and came up with the small bottle of laudanum kept handy for just this purpose.

Amanda could not ever remember having her monthly cycle without debilitating pain. The doctor told Eliza once it was possible that once she had children the pain would lessen, but otherwise, there was little he could do other than give her laudanum for it. Unfortunately, the drug rendered her senseless. Short of living with the pain, there was nothing else that helped.

Mary hurried out and returned with a glass of water. She quickly added a number of drops to it, then helped her mistress to drink it. Once the glass was empty, Mary helped her to undress and get into bed. Taking the time to put away Amanda's clothes, she checked on her before she left.

"I will inform his lordship you are indisposed," Mary said as she headed for the door.

Amanda looked at Mary's retreating back and tried to say "No!" but nothing came out. The drug was already beginning to take effect, and by the time Mary left the room, Amanda was nearly asleep. She was deeply asleep when Jon entered the room a short time later, Mary on his heels.

Jon laid his hand against her forehead, not expecting a fever, but still relieved to find it cool to the touch. Her breathing was deep and even, but even so, he could not rouse her. Checking the pulse at the base of her neck and finding it very faint, he turned to the maid.

"What did you give her?" The maid's eyes widened at the sharpness of his tone.

"Just the laudanum like always, m'lord," she responded nervously. "Dr. Kennard gave instructions for how much and said she could have as much as she needed." She indicated what Jon thought was too much of the drug and too small an amount of water. It was nearly an overdose considering its potency.

He shook his head. "Do not give her any more—even if she awakens," he said. "Is that understood?"

"But...but...m'lord, she'll be in ever so much pain when she wakes up," Mary protested.

"For how long will she be in pain?"

"Usually three days," she replied. "Then it takes almost another whole day for the rest of the medicine to wear off."

Three days! Jon wanted to hit something, so keen was his frustration. At least now he knew how and why she had been indisposed before when he had not seen her for four days. But three days of being drugged was unacceptable.

Turning on his heel, he headed for the door, but paused to look back at the maid before he left. "No more. Is that clear?" He pinned her with a hard stare.

She bobbed her head. "Yes, m'lord."

"Inform me when she awakens," he commanded, and went out, not waiting for the maid's reply.

Going downstairs, he went into the library. Pulling the cord to summon a servant, he crossed to the desk and pulled out a sheet of paper. He was writing a note when the door opened to admit Keyes.

"I need someone to take a message to London, retrieve something and return as fast as possible."

"Of course, my lord. I will have one of the lads ready himself immediately."

"Good." Jon finished his missive, signed and sanded it, then folded it and sealed it. By the time he emerged from the library with the letter in his hand, one of the footmen was ready to leave. Giving the young man specific instructions and directions, he finished with, "Make sure you do exactly what Dr. Reynolds tells you, and return as soon as possible—today. This is of the utmost urgency."

"I will ride as fast as I can, m'lord," the footman replied and left.

Jon turned and went back into the library. Dropping into the chair behind the desk he planted his elbows on the polished surface and put his head in his hands.

He should have gone himself, but he wanted to stay close to Amanda. It was not the maid's fault. She was only following orders. What did she say? *She'll be in ever so much pain when she wakes up.* He had not missed the concern in her voice. She would not have harmed Amanda deliberately, and she had no way of knowing she'd given her mistress a near-lethal dose.

Sighing, he rose from the desk and headed upstairs to check on his wife. It would be at least three hours, possibly more, before the lad returned from London. Collingswood was only two hours away from London by coach, less on horseback, but he would have to track down Dr. Reynolds first, and Jon knew that wasn't easy. As personal physician to the Queen, Dr. Reynolds was in demand, but always on call should Her Majesty require his services.

Mary looked up at him nervously when he entered the room.

"She's not moved, m'lord."

Jon didn't think she had, but he acknowledged Mary's statement with a nod. Moving to stand beside the bed so he could look down at Amanda, he asked, "Does she have pain like this every month?"

"Every month, m'lord," Mary affirmed. "Some months is worse than others."

"And this time?" he asked. "Is this worse than last month?"

"I think so. She was already hurtin' by the time she rung for me."

Jon dismissed the maid and moved to stand at the window. Staring out over the immaculate front lawn and drive, he fleetingly thought of sending for Tina or Felicia. But what would be the use? They could offer female companionship for a female malady, but little else. No, he'd better wait to see what the footman brought back with him.

He had written to Dr. Reynolds because he was a friend

and Jon knew he was conducting trials and experiments with a somewhat new drug made from the Indian hemp plant. The last time he spoke with the doctor, he had suggested it for his grandmother's painful joints, and revealed that it showed promise in treating the pain which sometimes accompanied a woman's monthly cycle. In addition, it did so without the drugging effects of laudanum. So far, his grandmother was enjoying it much better than the laudanum her doctor previously prescribed.

As a painkiller, Dr. Reynolds told him, it showed great promise—and it didn't seem addictive. Laudanum, distilled from the same plant as opium, often was. If Amanda had this type of pain regularly, the last thing he wanted was for her to become addicted to the medicine she took for it. And spending three days unconscious and another day each month recovering didn't seem like a satisfactory solution, either.

Turning away from the window, he moved back to the bedside. Pulling the chair the maid had occupied up next to the bed, he sat. Smoothing back a lock of golden hair that fell over her cheek, he allowed his hand to linger against her skin. Still cool to the touch, it was soft and smooth, and he brushed his fingers over it, savoring the feel beneath his fingertips. He moved his hand to her neck and checked her pulse again. It was stronger this time and he sighed. There was nothing for him to do except wait. Sitting back in the chair, he picked up the book he'd brought with him and opened it.

Dusk was falling by the time the footman returned, but Amanda still slept. She was no longer deeply unconscious as she shifted occasionally as if tossing and turning, but she still had not awakened. Her maid told him she would soon and when she did, she would need another dose. The pain, she said, would *be awful.* After reading Dr. Reynolds' return letter, Jon did not doubt it, but he would do what he could, short of giving her more laudanum, to lessen it.

Amanda surfaced through layers of sleep to the sound of someone calling her name. Jon stood over her, his hand on her abdomen, talking to her. The coverlet was gone, and she could feel the cool air in the room on her feet.

"Amanda." Jon's voice tugged at her. For a moment she felt like she was floating, then a shaft of pain in the region around her stomach pierced her and she moaned.

"Amanda, wake up." Jon's voice was insistent.

"No," she whimpered. "Hurts."

"I know, love," Jon responded, "but I can't make it stop unless you wake up."

Jon watched her carefully as she slowly awakened. He'd turned her onto her back, checking her abdominal area for resistance or hardness as Dr. Reynolds' note instructed, relieved when he found none. Now, however, he could feel the muscles clenching and unclenching under his hand, and her hand moved to push his away. Her eyes were squeezed tightly shut, her breathing heavy as she gasped in pain. A tear escaped and ran down into her hair.

Picking up a glass from the bedside table, he lifted her and held the glass to her lips. "Drink."

She did as she was told, grimacing at the unfamiliar taste. Once back against the pillows, she tried to turn onto her side, but he stopped her. Mary brought him one of the towels he'd instructed her to warm and he laid it across Amanda's stomach. Her breath hitched and she whimpered again.

A short time later, she was no longer writhing in pain, and as he removed the towel and replaced it with another, he noted she seemed more relaxed. A good sign, but he wanted her to open her eyes.

"Amanda." He leaned over her and his breath feathered her cheek. "Amanda, look at me."

He knew her eyelids were still heavy. The laudanum would not have quite worn off yet. Her eyes were unfocused as she stared up at him.

"Jonathan?" she whispered in confusion. "Mary. Need Mary."

"She's right here." He hadn't expected her to want him close at this time, but he was disappointed nevertheless. Turning, he beckoned the maid to her side, then went to retrieve another warm towel.

An hour later, Amanda was resting comfortably. There was

some discomfort still, but she was awake and clearheaded. What had happened? What happened to the pain? What had Jon done?

Mary was singing his praises as if he had raised her from the dead. He might not have literally, but he had come close. Drugged oblivion was not the way she preferred to spend three to four days every month, but it had been the only way she could cope with the physical pain of her cycle. Ancient people called a woman's monthly cycle *the curse*. It might not be for some, but for her that's exactly what it was, with no relief except through unconsciousness. But now Jon had apparently solved that. How?

The object of her thoughts entered the room at that moment, followed by two footmen carrying trays of food. On cue, her stomach rumbled. Jon heard it and smiled.

Approaching the bed, he looked down at her. "How is the pain now?"

"Not as bad." She could feel the blood rushing into her face and had to stop herself from turning away.

"That's not saying much," he said wryly. "I've seen dying men in less pain than you were in earlier."

"Oh." Her stomach rumbled again and she wished she could hide her face, but Jon's eyes held hers captive.

Jon beckoned Mary to her side. "Do you want to get up, or would you prefer a tray?"

"I will get up," she responded as the maid came forward.

Jon turned away and crossed the room while Mary helped her up and into a robe of light blue silk. When he returned, after the footmen left, she was sitting on the edge of the bed brushing the tangles from her hair.

Tying her hair back with the ribbon Mary left her, she allowed Jon to pull her to her feet. She was a little unsteady, swaying slightly once standing. He steadied her, then lifted her in his arms. Dropping the brush on the bed, she put her arms around his neck and buried her face in his shoulder.

His solid warmth surrounded her, the arms that held her effortlessly bands of padded steel. The steady rhythm of his heart soothed her, coaxing her into a sense of security. The room, Mary leaving and closing the door, the rest of the world, all faded away as Jon became her whole world in that moment. She would be content to have him hold her like this forever.

Her stomach rumbled again and she heard Jon chuckle. "I'd best feed you, or you will swoon from hunger." There was laughter in his voice as he crossed to the table and set her down in a chair.

Although dying of curiosity, she could not bring herself to ask him what he'd done to alleviate her pain or how. Instead, she asked him about his other relations, the Mildens of Mildenwood Hall.

"As I understand the story, Lord Milden and my great-grandmother were lovers when she was just sixteen. My grandmother, Shana, was the result. Tina knows more of the story than I, but apparently after our great-grandfather died when Shana was nineteen, her half-brother cast her out."

Amanda shook her head. "Families can be so difficult, can't they? I suppose her father left her something and her brother didn't want her to have it?"

"Sort of. Actually, he left something to her descendants."

She looked up from her plate in surprise. "Not her?"

It was Jon's turn to shake his head, then continue. "He left a piece of property and a sizeable amount of funds for its management and upkeep to her oldest unmarried female descendant alive as of a certain date. Jay and I assume he thought she would eventually marry and he was leaving something to his granddaughter. A dowry, perhaps. Unfortunately, when the appointed date arrived, it was Tina who fit the description. It would have been my mother if he had just omitted the word "unmarried" from the requirement, but she was not only already married, but Tina, Felicia and I were already born."

"Oh. So, do you stay in contact with them?"

Jon's lips twisted. "Not really. We are not exactly on bad terms, but we don't interact much."

"I assume you are not considered the head of that particular family?"

"No. Merrick is the current Lord Milden."

The rest of the meal was finished in silence, but Amanda noticed he watched closely what she ate. Almost as if he read her thoughts, he said, "It's good you have an appetite. Eating will help."

"Eating?"

"I don't suppose you normally eat much for the three or so days you take the laudanum."

She shook her head, even as she blushed to the roots of her hair. It just didn't seem right to talk about such intimate things with a man. Even if he was her husband and knew her body almost as intimately as she did. Some things should be left to women and their doctors.

He seemed to know when she was finished. Jon rose from the table and, coming around behind her, pulled her chair back for her to rise. They repaired to the sofa she had vacated earlier, and she noticed her book was still there on the light blue cushions. Jon picked it up and set it aside as she sat, then sat beside her, sliding his arm around her shoulders while stretching his long legs out before him and crossing them at the ankles.

"You must tell me if the pain returns." He glanced back at the clock on the mantel and said, "I suspect you will need some more of the medicine in about an hour."

"Not the laudanum?" she asked, resting her head against his shoulder.

Jon shook his head slowly, but his words vibrated with suppressed fury. "No. I have told Mary never to give that to you again."

Raising her head, she was perplexed. "But Dr. Kennard said..."

"When was the last time this Dr. Kennard spoke to you concerning the pain?"

"I don't know. It has been a long time. Once he said the laudanum was all he could give me to help, Eliza and I just followed his instructions."

"And did he tell you to take so much?"

"So much?"

"The amount your maid gave you was too much. Another drop and you might never have awakened." His voice was grim and it took her a few moments to realize what he was saying.

"He—he didn't exactly say to take so much. At first he said

it should be a little less, but if it didn't seem to help we could increase the amount."

"I see."

But she didn't. And she didn't understand the fierceness she could hear in his voice. Returning her head to his shoulder, she sighed. Had they really been giving her too much? How did he know? After all, he wasn't the one in pain. He hadn't felt as if someone had been stomping on his stomach until the pain was intolerable. He hadn't felt the inability to move, nor had he shed tears of pain and prayed for oblivion.

Tonight, she thought, he must be reading her mind, for his next words dispelled the rising indignation she was feeling.

"I don't doubt the pain was severe and nearly unbearable, but that this Dr. Kennard was not overseeing how much laudanum you were taking is unconscionable. At the very least, he should have inquired every few months as to how you were doing. There was too much risk in what you were doing for him not to."

She looked up at him again. "I—I don't understand."

Jon ran his free hand through his hair in a gesture of frustration as the arm around her shoulders tightened.

"Laudanum is an extract of the same plant opium comes from. It is highly addictive and fatal in large doses. Many of our soldiers return from war addicted to opium because they were given it for pain when wounded. Once the wound heals, however, it is often too late to break the addiction. It is the reason opium dens abound."

"But if laudanum isn't good to take, then what...?"

"It's not that it isn't good," he replied. "It's just that it needs to be monitored by a doctor. One should not attempt to dose too often on your own. But there are other, less deadly, plants which are good for pain. Feverfew, willow bark, and valerian, to name a few. Although nearly everything can be deadly in very high dosages, I don't know that I've ever heard or read of anyone dying from them."

Amanda leaned her head against his shoulder again. "Is that what you gave me?"

"No. While you were sleeping—" his emphasis on *sleeping* was full of sarcasm, "—I sent one of the footmen to London to track down a friend, Dr. John Reynolds. He has been experimenting with a new drug—an extract from the Indian hemp plant. It's not really new, my Culpeper Herbal discusses its properties, but only recently has anyone really looked at it. He recommended my grandmother try it for her joints and she has found it much better than laudanum."

"And he recommended the same thing for my prob—uh, me?"

"Actually, he has been using it for your particular problem, with reasonably good results, so he sent the footman back with some and instructions for its use."

"Oh." Amanda wasn't sure whether she was chagrined he'd shared her problem with a stranger or warmed by the fact Jon cared enough to send all the way to London for help. And she wondered why he hadn't bothered sending for either of his sisters. She would have thought he might have asked them for help. But perhaps being friends with this Dr. Reynolds, he felt his opinion was a better choice.

Whatever he had decided, she would not argue with it, she thought as she snuggled closer. Being awake and not in excruciating pain was worth living with the minor discomfort she still felt. She would not dwell on her embarrassment over discussing such an intimate problem with him. Instead she accepted that she was grateful for his intervention.

Chapter Fourteen

"I'm so glad you came."

Tina was waiting for Amanda and Jon as they entered the marble-tiled foyer. "I probably shouldn't have interrupted your time together, but I didn't want you to leave without saying goodbye."

Jon bent and kissed his sister's cheek. "We would not have left without letting you know," he told her. "And you had only to ask if you wanted to know how we fared."

Tina looked at him dubiously for a moment and he deliberately kept his features neutral.

Jon was determined not to let his sisters know how things stood. He and Amanda were leaving tomorrow and he would sort out his feelings then. For now, he was content to watch over her and ensure she enjoyed her evening pain-free. Both she and Mary assured him the pain usually only lasted for three days, then she would be fine. He would see for himself tomorrow.

"Jay and Brand are in the library, if you want to join them," Tina told him. "I'll send Keyes to find you when dinner is ready." Turning to Amanda, she said, "We are very informal in the country when there is just family," then turned toward the drawing room.

Before he headed for the library, he leaned down to Amanda and said in a low voice, "You will let me know if you experience any pain?"

She blushed, but nodded. Even after three days of constant attention, she still had difficulty discussing her female problem with Jon. She knew he tried to treat her as if she were a patient—in a detached manner so as to put her at ease—but she was the one who could not forget he was not a doctor, but her husband. Something that, for some reason she could not explain, still made her uncomfortable.

Felicia entered the drawing room nearly on Amanda's heels.

"It's good to see you," she told Amanda, giving her a hug. "And you are looking happy too. Good."

"Should I not?" she asked impishly.

"Of course you should," Felicia said, grinning back at her. "If you didn't look happy, I'd be wondering if Jon was really my brother."

"Felicia!" Tina exclaimed. "You will embarrass her. She's still newly married after all."

Felicia laughed. "I think Amanda knows I would never deliberately cause her discomfort."

"No, I know you would not," Amanda agreed, suddenly serious. "But there are times when you do all the same. Although tonight I think the likelihood is that you will embarrass Jonathan if you do not watch your words."

"Jonathan?" Both ladies looked at their new sister-in-law in astonishment.

"It's his name, is it not?"

Tina recovered first. "Yes, but..."

"No one has *ever* called him that," Felicia finished.

"I know. He warned me it would take some getting used to on his part, but he has given me leave to use it—and I like it."

Neither lady had a response to that statement, and Keyes arrived to announce dinner.

Over dinner, the conversation drifted over various topics.

"The assembly was not surprised to discover you had escaped," Felicia told them. "There were a few who grumbled that you didn't get a proper send off, but we told them you were anxious to be gone."

"Most assumed you had actually left for London, so no one was prepared to follow," Tina added as she served herself a small helping of potatoes.

Jon shrugged eloquently. "Then it's good no one knew where we were headed."

"Oh, and then there was Charity and your cousin," Felicia told Amanda. "After everything that silly girl has done, I think you will now end up related. Ironies abound."

Amanda grinned as she looked across the table at Felicia and picked up her wine glass. "I introduced them."

"You? Why?"

"Because Angus asked." She took a sip of the ruby liquid. "He actually asked me to introduce him to the 'angel in blue'. I couldn't believe he really meant Charity, but he did."

"Then you have no one but yourself to blame," Felicia admonished her good-naturedly.

"Angus will be good for her," Amanda laughed. "He's gentle and kind. And he probably fell in love with her red hair—she'll fit right in at his home in Scotland."

"Considering that's the feature she dislikes most about herself, that will be a good thing, I think," was all Felicia said.

"There were no disasters before everyone finally left?" Amanda asked Tina at one point.

"Not that I'm aware of."

"Well, there was a small incident," Felicia began. "But you were too busy seeing your guests off, so I took care of it."

Tina turned to her sister, eyebrows raised in query.

"I suspect your father and his sister might have had words before they left," she told Amanda.

"Over what?" Amanda asked. "I can't imagine what else they would have had to argue about after that ultimatum concerning Cassie."

"And how would you have known?" This question came from Brand.

"I was in the nursery when Lady Althorpe came up—to see her nephews and niece, she said. She was deliberately rude to Cassie, so I asked her to leave. Unfortunately, Cassie was shaken by the time she left."

"So, what happened?" Tina asked.

"Lord Barrington came up not much later. I could tell he expected the worst." What she did not, could not, convey to the assembled group was the emotional impact of what happened next.

"I don't know why she doesn't like you, Cassie," Felicia had been telling the child. "But I wouldn't pay her any mind."

"But she's Papa's sister. If she doesn't like me, then what will he think?"

The door of the nursery opened and Felicia looked up, expecting to see Miss Byrnes and Osborne returning, but it was the Earl of Barrington instead.

"Perhaps you should ask him," Felicia had answered her, nodding toward a space behind her.

Cassie turned. "Papa!" She had run into his arms and Felicia had watched him pick her up and say something to her. Cassie nodded, then laid her head against his shoulder. Then the two of them had left, but not before he had looked over his daughter's head and into her eyes, conveying his silent thanks. She had only been able to nod in acknowledgment due to the lump in her throat.

"When he returned her nearly an hour later, she was laughing as if she hadn't a care in the world," she now told Amanda. "I was glad to see he was the one who came and not Eliza. Not that I don't think Eliza couldn't have dealt with it, but I think your father understands he will have to be the one to shield Cassie and eventually force her acceptance."

Tina nodded. "Now I understand why she seemed to leave in a huff. I didn't personally see her off, but Geri told me she left in high dudgeon."

"I'm not surprised, but I don't expect to see much of her in the near future, so I refuse to worry about it. How long did the rest of the family stay?" Amanda asked Tina.

"Just a few days after everyone left. The boys were having such a good time, I invited them to stay. Grandmama wanted to stay a few extra days anyway, and since she was going back with them, it was convenient. And Shana just adored Cassie. I think she thought it might be fun to have a big sister."

"The nursery is very quiet without them," Jay commented.

After dinner, they repaired to the drawing room, where Felicia sat at the piano and played. Eventually, Tina and Jon were convinced to add their talents and the three entertained their spouses with music and anecdotes about their mother, who had taught them to play.

"Most often I had to be bribed," Jon confessed. "No fishing, or walks in the woods until I had spent an hour at the piano. Then the exchange was two-to-one. If I spent an hour practicing, I could have two hours doing whatever I wanted."

As the evening wore on, Amanda began to understand why the three of them were so close. It wasn't just that they shared a mother—they shared each other. From an early age they had watched over each other, shared with each other, taught each other, and even fought with each other, as Jon and Tina explained when they revealed a particularly bitter fight they had once over who was to hold Felicia.

"Jon insisted I was too small," Tina explained with a laugh, "but Mama told him two years and a title didn't make him any more grown up."

"She and your father were the perfect combination for keeping me under control," Jon said to Jay. "I just never let them see it."

"There were times when he was just another child in the house too," Tina said. "I remember once overhearing Mama telling the housekeeper it was difficult raising four children alone. I didn't understand what she meant then, but lately I'm beginning to comprehend her frustration."

Jay threw a fond, but dark, glance at his wife. "It was only a short ride," he said defensively.

"True," she agreed, "but at midnight!"

"At least Shana returned healthy," he countered, to which his wife merely looked chagrined.

As they walked back to the Dower House later, Jon explained to Amanda that Jay had taken his daughter, Shana, out for a ride at midnight, and Tina had taken him to task over it.

"Midnight?" she asked in amazement. "But why?"

"He apparently wanted to show her some local site he said was best seen under the moon. Tina was not amused, but there was no harm done."

"And what did he mean 'she returned healthy'?"

"I think Tina was five—perhaps six—when she tagged along with Jay's father and I on a fishing outing. She fell in the river and caught a chill. Mama was furious."

Amanda giggled, then commented more soberly. "Jay

doesn't seem to resent it that people think his father did a better job raising his stepchildren than his own."

Jon was surprised at her reading of Jay. "Not anymore," he responded. "But he did once."

"What changed his mind?"

"Nothing, really. It was difficult for him to discuss his father with Tina when they first met. He confided in me once that there were times when he wasn't sure they were talking about the same person, so different were their opinions and impressions. But he has just come to accept that he cannot change his memories of his father any more than Tina can change hers. His father was the only one Tina ever knew. Ours died when she was just four."

"And you?"

He glanced down at her in the darkness. Her bright hair shone in the meager light of the moon, but the dark cloak she wore obscured the rest of her.

"What about me?"

"Do you have any memories of your father?"

"A few," he admitted, "but they are hazy. They are more of an impression woven through the things my mother told me about him. And the stories my grandmother has told me of him as a child. She won't admit it, but I can tell by the way she speaks of him that he was her favorite. That, I'm convinced, is the reason she took his marriage to my mother so hard."

"Yet you forgave her neglecting you and Tina."

Jon's sigh had her turning to look up at him as they emerged from the woods in front of their destination.

"There was little point in prolonging the hurt, but that's not to say I didn't resent her for many years. Even three years ago, I was not completely comfortable with her at the Abbey."

"Why?"

"Because, to the servants, she is still the Abbey's mistress. Even though she no longer resides there, and only comes for short visits, whenever she is there, the servants look to her for instructions." He paused while he opened the gate and she passed through. "But now, all that will change."

"How so?"

The glance he sent her way had her suddenly realizing

what he meant. As his wife, she was now the Abbey's mistress. Flustered, she stumbled over the first step on the stairs. Jon caught her before she fell and lifted her in his arms.

"There's no need to carry me," she told him. "I just didn't realize the step was so close."

Jon grinned down at her as he climbed the stairs. "I rather like holding you like this. Since we must deny ourselves other enjoyable activities for now, you must allow me my pleasure where I can find it."

Mortification seeped through her, and she hid her face against his shoulder. She had never blushed so much in her life as she had since she married Jon. Would he always be able to fluster her so easily?

The door opened as they reached the top of the stairs.

"A missive arrived for you while you were out, my lord," the butler said as they entered the house. "I put it on the desk in the library."

"Thank you, Keyes," Jon responded as he put her down on her feet. She followed him into the library.

"Is there a reason that the butlers have the same name?" she asked.

Jon smiled as he picked up the envelope sitting in the middle of the desk.

"Not really," he answered, "except they are all brothers."

"All? How many are there?"

"Four in all, I think," he said absently. "The oldest took his father's place in the London house when he died two years ago. The next oldest is at Thane Park, and the next here, at Collingswood. The youngest is in training and helps wherever he is needed."

Jon was frowning as he read the missive.

"And which one do we have?"

He looked up. "What? Oh, the youngest, I think."

Amanda could see he was preoccupied with his letter, so she slipped out of the room and went upstairs. Mary responded quickly to her summons and soon she was ready for bed in a burgundy silk gown and peignoir.

Mayfair was quiet. With many knockers removed, Amanda could see there were few families still in residence as they pulled up in front of Kent House. It didn't matter. She and Jon would only be in residence for about a week, then, they, too, would leave the capital for Yorkshire.

She was thankful there were so few people in residence and the street was deserted when they arrived. Especially since Jon insisted on carrying her into the house.

"You'll have to take Felicia to task for that," he teased her as he put her down in the front hall in plain view of all the servants assembled there.

Introducing her to Mrs. Barrett, the housekeeper, and Higgins, the butler, he then stood back while Mrs. Barrett introduced her to the rest of the household. Once finished, Mrs. Barrett sent the rest of the servants back to their duties and informed them luncheon would be ready when they were. Then she bustled away, while Jon ushered Amanda up the staircase.

The master suite was situated at the end of the hall on the second floor, fronted by double carved oak doors. Entering the sitting room, Amanda found herself in a garden. Flowers sprouted from vases all around the room. Roses, lilacs, honeysuckle, violets, and more, their scents permeating the air. Sofas, chairs, and a chaise, all in the style made popular in France during the reign of Louis XIV, were scattered about the room, upholstered in a floral print pattern, as was the wallcovering. The heavy drapes at the windows were of a light blue velvet and even the thick Aubusson carpet under her feet boasted a flowery motif of lilacs and violets.

She didn't have to ask. She knew Jon had had the room decorated for her. It wasn't just that much of the furniture and fabrics were obviously new, but she couldn't imagine the dowager countess, who she knew was the last countess to occupy this suite, in such a light and airy room. Hearing the door close behind her, she knew Jon stood there, waiting for her reaction.

"It's lovely," she said, leaning back against him and feeling his arms slide around her waist. For a few moments, they stood there as she took in the beauty before her, then she turned in his arms, lifted up on her toes, and kissed him.

It was the first time she had ever taken the initiative, and it completely caught him off-guard. Not far enough, however, that he didn't enjoy the experience and want more when she broke it off. But he had his limits—and she was still off limits. To prolong the kiss would only leave him in severe discomfort.

"I'm glad you like it," he said huskily.

The bedchamber was just as pretty, decorated in pastel shades of blue and green, with touches of yellow. It was wholly feminine, yet the scrolling lines of the oak furniture kept it from looking too much like a young girl's room.

"I guessed what colors you might like based on your wardrobe," he admitted when she asked how he had known what colors to use. Her laughter surprised him, but her sparkling eyes told him how much his thoughtfulness and attention to detail touched her.

Over luncheon, he told her he had to see his solicitor during the afternoon, but would be home in time for tea.

After he left, Amanda spent the afternoon with Mrs. Barrett, touring the house and getting to know it better. There were a number of rooms needing refurbishing, but she decided to wait to speak to Jon about them. Mrs. Barrett was sure he would not mind. Having been in a bachelor residence for so long, she was looking forward to having a mistress. Amanda smiled at the small, round, dark-haired woman who didn't look to be above forty. She was certain Jon would not care about such things as when the silver was polished, or whether it was a good day to air out the upstairs rooms, but an inedible meal would probably have gotten his attention.

"Have you been here long?" she asked the woman.

"Nearly all my life," the housekeeper responded, "but I didn't become housekeeper until Mrs. Leeds retired about six years ago."

Amanda nodded. She knew Jon had only been actually living in Kent House for about six years. Before that, he'd spent most of his time at Oxford or at Thane Park.

Entering a back hallway, Amanda noted a door at the end near the stairs. When she tried the door, it was locked.

"That's his lordship's workroom," the housekeeper told her. "He's the only one allowed in."

"Do you have a key?"

"Yes, but only because his lordship expects it to be cleaned regularly."

"What does he do in there?"

Mrs. Barrett hesitated. "Perhaps you'd best ask him, my lady."

It was obvious the housekeeper knew more than she was willing to divulge, but Amanda admired her loyalty and said nothing more as they turned to climb the stairs.

They emerged on the second floor in the gallery. Toward the end of the formidable parade of family portraits, her gaze was caught by a large picture of a young man. Brilliant green eyes peered out from under midnight dark brows, over a straight patrician nose and a full-lipped mouth. Except that the cheekbones weren't quite so high, the painting might have been of Jon. And if the young man hadn't been wearing a uniform.

"Such sadness, so much tragedy," the housekeeper interrupted her thoughts. "Her ladyship was nearly inconsolable for months after learning her baby was dead. He was her favorite, you know. Even though the family was not happy with his choice of bride, they missed him something fierce."

"What happened to them all?"

The housekeeper moved to stand in front of another painting, this one obviously of the family. The old earl, Jon's grandfather, stood straight and proud behind a sofa on which perched a much younger, smiling dowager. Flanked by two boys, and holding one in her lap, they looked the perfect family.

"Henry, the second son, was killed when a curricle he was racing overturned.

"Allan, his wife, and son were in France when it happened. Wasn't long after they returned that the earl took sick and died." The housekeeper indicated the last picture, showing a family of three.

"'Twas only two months later young William tumbled down the stairs at the Abbey. Master Allan, his lordship, was never the same. I heard he would go out and sit beside his son's grave for hours at a time. He was caught in a terrible storm. When they finally got him back to the Abbey, he was deathly ill, but refused to see the doctor." She shook her head sadly. "Such a terrible waste."

"What happened to his countess?"

"Lady Amelia? She was increasing, so she and the dowager held out the hope that she would have another son to carry on the line. But it wasn't to be."

"She had a girl?"

"No. It was a boy—but born dead. Mrs. Haskell's still at the Abbey. She's getting on in years, but I'm sure she could tell you more of the story."

As they left the gallery, Amanda wondered whether the dowager had ever thought about her grandchildren and what they were like. Jon had met her for the first time as a man of twenty-one, even though he'd arrived in England as a boy of six, yet she had still considered his mother unsuitable and, by association, him.

It must have been a blow to Jon to learn his own grandmother would not accept him because of the blood running through his veins. That she insisted on focusing on his gypsy background and refused to see him for the person he was must have hurt deeply. No wonder he refused to discuss his antecedents in company. His grandmother's rejection had to have been bitter tonic, indeed.

Thinking of the dowager reminded Amanda she was probably in the city. Knowing she rarely ventured far from home, but had left Collingswood in company with her father and Eliza, Amanda decided to send a note around to see if she would like some company. It would also be good to see Letty again, and find out how the school fared.

Chapter Fifteen

The country seat of the Earls of Wynton was a large sprawling mansion built on the grounds of a former Cistercian Abbey. Once a thriving concern, it had crumbled into ruin after the dissolution of the monasteries by Henry VIII and sat undisturbed for over fifty years before the Kentons had been given the property by James I. Using stones from the original Abbey, the newly titled Earl of Wynton built a veritable palace on the grounds and christened it Wynton Abbey.

The grey stone facade was stark against the verdant countryside as they bowled up the drive in the late afternoon. Amanda had only been here once before—three years ago at Felicia's wedding, and she had never forgotten the beauty of the place. That it was now her home filled her with so much happiness she could barely contain herself. She glanced her husband's way before turning back to the window of the coach.

"It's beautiful," she said. "Simply beautiful."

Jon would have agreed, except he wasn't looking at his home. Amanda's enthusiasm and eagerness was heart-warming. Three years ago he knew she had aspired to this very position, but his own stubbornness and fear had kept them apart. And he had escaped the country as soon as he could, fleeing her memory. He wondered at the twist of fate which had brought him back—to her. It hadn't been Nona. Of that he was certain.

Although he hadn't asked, the conversation he had overheard between his sisters at the Mathesons' had confirmed his suspicions about Sophie. Now that he was married and had all but given up on the statuette his knowledge caused him to question his newly awakening feelings for Amanda. In the space of two months, the statuette's importance had diminished considerably and his feelings for Amanda had grown respectively.

The coach came to a stop and he stepped down, turning to lift Amanda from the coach. The entire staff was lined up on the front steps, and once again, Amanda was introduced to each one, then taken by the housekeeper up to the countess's apartments.

Jon turned down the hall leading to the library and study. He would glance over whatever his steward had left for him while Amanda settled in.

Amanda stood in the middle of her bedchamber. She had to be dreaming. She closed her eyes, counted to ten and opened them again. No, it was all still there. She was standing in a room completely done over in white. Walls, curtains, furniture, bedding, the carpet on the floor—it was all white.

The door the housekeeper had pointed out to her earlier as leading to Jon's room opened and he stepped inside.

"Did you do this?" she asked.

She noted the surprise in his eyes. Had he known?

"No," he replied, then shocked her by adding, "I've never been in this room before."

"Never?"

Crossing the room to his side, she looked up into his face.

He shook his head. "Never. It just never seemed important."

"Then who...?"

"I suspect that's a question for my grandmother. I will take responsibility for your room at Kent House, but I thought you might like to decorate this one yourself, so I only sent instructions to Mrs. Haskell to have it thoroughly cleaned and aired."

She turned and surveyed the room again. Why would anyone decorate a room completely in white?

"Her ladyship thought it might be restful when Lady Amelia's time came. The doctor said white was a calming influence—and Lady Amelia needed that more than black at the time," Mrs. Haskell explained when Amanda asked as the tea tray was delivered. "After she died, the room was scrubbed thoroughly, then closed up. Her ladyship couldn't bear to go into it again."

Later that evening Jon and Amanda walked through the Abbey's extensive gardens. Stars twinkled brightly overhead, glittering in the dark night sky. The garden was in full bloom and the flowery fragrances were strong. In the distance, crumbling silhouettes could be seen. Jon had told her that there were still ruins on the property and promised her a tour the next afternoon.

Her gown of blush pink swirled around her feet, Jon's hand, holding hers in a strong, yet gentle grip, was warm. The shoulder beside her solid and strong.

Life could only get better from here, she thought. Maybe by next year they would have started their family. She closed her eyes momentarily, envisioning a dark-haired child with vivid green eyes. A soft sigh escaped, garnering her husband's attention.

"Are you tired?"

"No."

Letting go of her hand, he put his arm around her shoulders, pulling her closer. She leaned her head against his arm.

"Then why the heavy sigh?"

"I was just thinking of how beautiful this all is—how perfect."

"And...?"

They had turned and were making their way back to the house, the lights in the garden salon beckoning.

"And speculating on what would make it even more perfect."

They reached the terrace steps and ascended. Jon stopped and turned to look down at her.

"And did you come up with an answer?"

His face was in shadow, but she could almost feel the heat in his eyes as they took in her bare shoulders and skimmed over the tops of her breasts.

"Mmmmhmmm." Her hands crept up the front of his jacket, looping behind his neck as she rose up on her toes. "I

205

Denise Patrick

think the only thing we could add would be a little one of our own."

She saw his teeth in the darkness as he smiled and pulled her closer.

"Is that a suggestion? Or an invitation?"

Her fingers threaded through the thick, dark hair at his nape, as he bent his head closer.

"Both," she responded against his lips, then promptly forgot everything else as his mouth slanted over hers with possessive intent.

He kissed her deeply, his tongue dueling with hers in the warm moist cavern of her mouth. His hands on her back pressed her against his hard, muscled frame and she registered proof of his desire against her belly. When he raised his head, she strained to keep the contact, brushing her lips over his jaw and down the column of his throat.

A hand slid up her back and speared into her hair, destroying her coiffure and causing the golden curls to spill down over her shoulders and back. She barely registered the pinging of the pins as they fell on the flagstones. Jon lifted her in his arms as she tugged at his tie, loosening and removing the neckwear as he carried her inside and up the stairs.

In his room he put her down on her feet beside the massive bed, quickly and efficiently stripping her of every stitch of clothing. No longer a complacent partner in their lovemaking, she returned the favor, running her hands over the muscled planes of his chest as she did so.

He was a magnificent specimen—and he was hers. Hers to have and to hold. Hers in sickness and health. Hers to grow old with. Hers, and only hers, to love.

She gasped as he pressed her back onto the silken sheets of the bed, coming down beside her. One hand stroked across her collarbone, down to her breasts, tweaking each nipple as it went, then lower over her flat stomach to the juncture of her thighs. She moaned as his mouth teased a pink nipple and his hand continued its gentle exploration.

She was ready. She wanted him. Now. Her moans and passionate whimpers should have told him, yet he continued to torment her with his hands and mouth. Her hand slid lower, over his abdomen, finally encountering his thickness. As her hand closed around him, she heard him groan. Delight flowed through her, mingling with the fire in her veins. Two could play at this game.

"Amanda," was all she heard before his mouth claimed hers. She was beyond hearing when his body moved over hers. Sliding her arms around his broad shoulders, she welcomed him into her heat, exploding mere moments later.

Jon lay in the pre-dawn darkness, his sleeping wife curled trustingly against his side, her head resting on his chest. It was fortunate that she slept. Otherwise she might have wondered at the frown marring his features.

It wasn't supposed to happen this way. He'd planned carefully to ensure it wouldn't. Sophie was supposed to be his destiny, his true mate. The other half of himself. His great-grandmother had been adamant he marry the woman with his statuette. She, and no other, would make him complete. He had avoided the trap. Avoided snare of caring too much and too deeply. So, why was he beginning to wonder if he might be falling in love with Amanda?

The little Season was well underway when Jon and Amanda arrived back in the capital in late September. They had spent an idyllic summer and both had been loath to return. Jon had promised to support the Earl of Shaftesbury in the fall session of Parliament with many of his social reform bills, as had Jay, Brand, and Gerald, in return for allowing Amanda to run the school as she saw fit. Once apprised of the school and Amanda's role in it, her father had also been persuaded to join in. With her marriage, he no longer seemed uncomfortable with her educational pursuits.

Amanda was ambivalent about returning to the city. On the one hand, she missed the school, although not nearly as much as she thought she would, but her time with Jon was still new and precious to her and each day spent with him seemed to bring new wonders. Once back in the capital, however, her days were filled with the school, Jon's grandmother and shopping for fabrics and furniture to accomplish the refurbishing she was doing not only to Kent House, but also to the Abbey.

Tina and Felicia were glad to see her upon her return, sweeping her into the rounds of balls, parties, and routs Society never seemed to tire of. The girls at the school were elated at her return as well, but she missed Eliza. With no one to chaperone, Eliza had elected to stay at The Barrows with the children.

She could have stayed at the Abbey, but she knew Jon would have stayed with her if she had.

"Your grandmother has invited us to tea tomorrow," she told him as they left the theatre one evening. "I told her I wasn't sure whether you would be available."

He smiled. "I will make the time."

Amanda snuggled closer to him and closed her eyes. She was more tired these days, but that did not bother her. She and Jon had decided they need not share their secret just yet. It was still so new.

After years of severe pain and discomfort every month, she had instantly noticed when it didn't occur. And so had Jon.

She had no other symptoms yet. Her body didn't feel any different, and she had no sickness in the mornings. It was a good sign, Jon had told her.

So far, the one argument they'd had revolved around her current state. He had told her she should no longer wear her corset and stays. They were not good for her in her condition. She had been scandalized at the thought of appearing in public without the required fashionable undergarments. He had threatened to leave her at the Abbey if she didn't relent— accusing her of putting herself and her appearance before their child. She had been insulted he thought her so shallow, but unwilling to allow him to dictate her wardrobe.

They had been at an impasse until Mary suggested she just let out some of her dresses and gowns and not lace her stays as tight. Not that she had worn them laced very tight in the first place, but the solution had been so simple she and Jon both laughed at the logic. Making up their quarrel had kept her walking on air for a number of days afterwards.

She was asleep when they reached Kent House and Jon carried her inside and up to her room. Mary no longer waited up for her in the evenings. Jon had told her it wasn't necessary.

Life is full of surprises—some wonderful and some not so wonderful. A week after he and Amanda had taken up residence in London, Jon remembered how much he hated surprises. More so, he was reminded that eavesdropping didn't always provide reliable, accurate or complete information.

White's was quiet in the afternoon. In the late hours of the day, many were already home primping for the night to come. Not so Jon and his father-in-law, who were sharing a bottle of port in one of the smaller salons.

"No news yet?" the Earl of Barrington asked him.

"Not yet," Jon lied.

Lying was something he normally eschewed, but he and Amanda had decided they would tell their family together about their impending addition. His sisters and grandmother wouldn't ask, but Amanda's father had no such qualms. He'd hinted more than once that he was ready to be a grandfather.

"Well, let's hope she tells you first, and not JoJo."

The mouthful of port Jon had been in the act of swallowing went down the wrong way, causing deep racking coughs to jar his body for several minutes.

"Who?" he wheezed.

A waiter passing through turned his head momentarily, then hurried on.

The earl pounded him on the back, and soon Jon was feeling better—on the surface. Inside, dread rose and began to spread, thickening the blood in his veins to sludge, and congealing in the pit of his stomach. A coldness settled in his chest.

"Who's JoJo?" He could barely force himself to say the name. Only he, Tina and Felicia knew the significance of that name.

Amanda's father didn't seem to notice Jon's stillness, as he answered airily, "Her black cat." Taking a leisurely sip of his drink, he continued, "She has this small statue of a black panther. I'm surprised you haven't seen it. She used to take it everywhere. Although," he paused for a moment, "the last time I saw it, Cassie had it. So, perhaps it remained at Barrington House. You have no idea how much trouble JoJo has caused over the years."

Jon stared at his father-in-law in disbelief but Trent blithely continued.

"She says a gypsy gave it to her and that it's a prince or some such thing. All I know is that she and JoJo have been inseparable since she was seven or eight. I even sacked a governess over it—but that was Barbara's fault."

Jon sat back in his chair, his mind in a whirl. The statuette. Amanda had his statuette? How was that possible? He was sure he'd overheard Tina and Felicia discussing it and Sophie. Moreover, she'd told him she'd never seen such a figurine. Hadn't she? Perhaps he *should* have asked.

Doing a quick calculation in his head, the pieces of the puzzle began to fall into place. And suddenly he was sixteen again. He, Tina and Felicia had spent that summer with their great-grandmother's gypsy band up in the Lake District.

He hadn't even wanted to be there. His mother and stepfather insisted he go that year and Nona had promised him something special would happen that summer. His parents only wanted him to ensure Felicia didn't come to any grief.

Once back at home in Devon, he remembered thinking he'd enjoyed himself after all, but except that they had gone further north than they had ever gone before, nothing out of the ordinary had occurred. But apparently something had.

Scenes passed before his eyes. Felicia playing in the lake near the camp; inviting him to meet her new friend. Felicia's new little friend with the big blue eyes and blond hair clinging to him in the water as the two of them taught her to swim. And the time Felicia had thrown her arms around his neck and given him a noisy wet kiss on the cheek and her friend had done the same. He had pushed the two of them away with the disgust of a teenager, but heard them giggling as he climbed the bank and headed back toward camp. Then there were the times the two of them had wandered off—trying to give him the slip. They had turned it into a daily game of hide-and-seek. He always found them. What was that little girl's name? It hadn't been Amanda.

"Katie."

He hadn't realized he said the name aloud until Amanda's father stared at him in shocked silence.

"What did you say? Where did you hear that?"

At the intensity of the earl's tone, Jon was jolted back to the present and scrambled for an appropriate reply. "I believe my sister once mentioned it was an old nickname of Amanda's."

Jon watched his father-in-law age before his eyes. Trent's face fell, his shoulders slumped, lines seemed to appear around his mouth and eyes, and he seemed to shrink into his chair. His grey eyes focused on a point somewhere above Jon's head.

"Her mother was the only person ever to call her that."

Jon said nothing, waiting for him to continue.

"I should never have married Katherine," he said in a tired voice. "But if I hadn't, I wouldn't have Amanda. She has more than compensated for the hell of my first marriage."

Jon was in a foul mood. His father-in-law had left White's shortly after his revelation, unaware of Jon's building ire. Jon had remained long enough to finish his drink, then left as well, opting to walk home. He needed to think.

Fate was laughing at him and he didn't like it. He'd been duped. Deceived. Amanda had *lied*. Why? The betrayal cut deep. Had she conspired with his sisters against him? Did she know what the statuette meant? She had to. What else would Nona have told her? He should have suspected something when she'd agreed to marry him despite the flimsy excuse he'd given for proposing. Trent wasn't unreasonable. Jon knew he could have been talked into allowing Amanda to continue at the school—and even helping her out by speaking with Lord Shaftesbury. But he'd been so sure of himself, he'd leaped without considering all the options first.

She had used him. Yet he had to admit, he'd used her as well. Hadn't he known when he proposed that she was in love with him?

As he reviewed the last few months, he realized the clues had been there—not the least of which was Amanda's dowry. Summersea, an estate in the Lake District, had come to Trent as part of her mother's dowry. His father-in-law had told him when they discussed settlements that he was including it in Amanda's dowry because he felt she was attached to it. He'd also told Jon neither he nor Amanda had been there in over ten years.

It had been fourteen years since the summer he'd spent in the Lake District with his great-grandmother. He couldn't have known the estate they camped on was Summersea, but shouldn't the very mention of the Lake District have jogged his memory?

His lips firmed as he remembered Amanda's innocent wonder on their wedding night and throughout the summer. She had finally attained her heart's desire—he could read it clearly in her face. If she believed Nona, she had fulfilled her destiny.

He took a deep breath of the cool evening air. He needed to calm down, but he couldn't. Fear kicked in as he thought of all he'd tried to avoid, but now had to face. He refused to fall in love. He had acknowledged his growing feelings for her, but he'd allow them to go no further. Fate. Love. Destiny. Those were for others, but not him.

As a man of science, he knew that what others considered signs of love were nothing more than a physical reaction to something the body found pleasing and enjoyable. That women labeled it love only meant they were susceptible to the softer emotions. Men, however, were not. He was not. Amanda was his to protect and cherish. If someone else wanted to call it love, so be it.

Love, it seemed to him, was unpredictable and arbitrary. That those two words tended to also be attributed to women was not a coincidence in his mind.

Unaware of the approaching storm, Amanda dressed early for dinner then sat at the escritoire in her sitting room to pen a letter to Eliza. She'd decided to stay in tonight, telling Felicia she wasn't up to the Dodgesons' soiree. She was only a few sentences into the missive when the door crashed open. Startled, she jumped and whirled around in her chair to find

Jon standing in the opening staring daggers at her. Apprehension rose in her throat.

"Well, well," he drawled, "if it isn't little Katie. Have you been swimming lately?"

Amanda stared at him in shock. He knew? How? And if he knew, why did he seem angry?

Jon leaned against the doorjamb and crossed his arms over his chest. The movement reminded her of what it felt like when those arms closed around her, as they had this morning.

"Nothing to say?" he demanded.

She didn't know what to make of his mood. Was he disappointed to remember her? Standing, she started toward him.

"Stay there!" His voice was cold. "Don't come near me. I'm not fit company right now."

"Jonathan? What...?"

"What's wrong?"

A flicker of fear kept her still, and she shivered at the ice in his tone. She nodded.

"Why, nothing," he replied in a silky voice. "Except I've just discovered I'm married to a liar."

She flinched. "I-I can explain."

"Save it for someone who'll believe it."

Tears burned at the back of her eyes, but she refused to let them fall. Why was he so angry? Shouldn't he be glad he'd found the person his great-grandmother had selected?

"I don't understand. Why are you angry?"

"What makes you think I'm angry?"

She shook her head, trying to clear her thoughts. "I-I don't understand," she repeated.

He levered himself away from the door and sauntered into the room. She watched him prowl the room, his long, lean frame moving with feline grace. He moved as silently as she might have expected a panther would. The room was not that large, but he managed never to come within arm's length of her.

"Don't you?" he asked. "No, I don't suppose you would." He stopped before a high, arched window and stared out at the gathering darkness. "You would think I should be ecstatic to

213

know Nona proved true."

"I-I didn't..."

"You would be wrong." He turned to look at her and the glance sliced right through her. "Do you know why I married you?"

She couldn't answer him. She could only stare at this man who resembled her husband, but looked at her with distaste. What happened to the lover of this morning?

"Do you?" he demanded, his voice rising.

Unaware of her actions, she took a step backward. "N-no."

"It was because you told me you had *never* seen a carved panther figurine."

Pain lanced through her and she caught her breath as a heavy weight settled in her chest.

"But you lied." He strode across the room to the door, pausing to look back as he reached it. "I would never have married you had I known you had that damned statue."

Then he was gone, leaving her frozen in place.

The slamming of a distant door jolted her out of her trance. Blindly she groped for the chair she had occupied earlier and sat.

When Mary came to tell her it was time for dinner, she was still there. The tears she had successfully held at bay while Jon had been in the room falling unchecked.

Amanda awakened the next morning with a deep sense of loss. Last night had been the first night since her marriage she had slept alone. Tears welled again, but she refused to let them fall. She had cried enough tears last night to fill a small pond. Today she would talk to Jon. Today she would explain to him why she'd lied. Would he understand?

Sliding from the bed, she washed her face, erasing all traces of last night's tears. The eyes looking back at her from the mirror were still red and swollen, but there was little she could do about them. She needed to see Jon now, before her courage deserted her. Crossing her room, she opened the door to Jon's and stepped into an empty room.

The bed had not been slept in. It was still turned down from the night before, Jon's dressing gown laid neatly across the foot. She stood at the end of the bed for a few minutes, feeling as if she held the weight of the world on her shoulders. Where was Jon? Where had he spent last night? And what should she do now?

She looked around the room a little desperately, as if there was some clue to be found that would tell her what she wanted to know. Silence greeted her. And closed in on her. The sense of loss intensified. When she could bear the quiet no longer, she fled back to her room, a sob rising in her throat.

For the next two days, Amanda waited. Every carriage, every horse, every pedestrian that went by on the street had her flying to the window, but Jon did not appear. Hopelessness deepened by the hour. During the day, she refused to leave the house, and each night she fell into an exhausted slumber tormented by dreams of Jon never returning.

Each time she remembered the night he left she shuddered at what he had revealed. *I would never have married you had I known you had that damned statue.* Had he really only looked for JoJo to ensure he did not marry the woman with it? Had he truly meant it? Did the statuette represent something he wanted to forget? Did he really not want to marry his destiny? Why?

Digging it out from beneath her gowns in the dressing room, she cradled the familiar figure to her chest. She had planned to give it to him for Christmas. Now she didn't know what to do with it. Should she even keep it? Cassie liked it. Perhaps she should send it to The Barrows with her father.

By the third day, anger had replaced despair. As she rose that morning, she decided she had waited long enough. She didn't know if he planned to return, but she wasn't going to mope around as if her life had come to an end. She might feel dead on the inside, but no one else need know. Besides, she had another life to care for and she refused to endanger her baby's life with her continual blue devils. When Jon returned, she would explain, if he would listen. Until then, life would go on.

With that decision made, she rang for Mary and made plans to go to the school. She needed to be around happy faces. And tonight, she would attend the Hathaways' soiree. A little dancing would chase the doldrums away.

Chapter Sixteen

Jon stood before the small carved stone that marked the spot where Nona was buried. The small grove on the northern edge of the Abbey's property was secluded, shady and cool. Neither Tina nor Felicia knew of it. Gypsies did not have many rituals for death and burial, but he was only part gypsy, and he found himself unable to keep the one which dictated they not mark a final resting place. He had been at her side when she died and, after directing Carlo and Mira to this spot to bury her, had returned a week later with the small stone. Still remembering the feeling of sorrow that had settled within his soul at her loss, he had set the stone in place himself. Another death. Another loved one gone. Another life over. Another piece of him forever out of reach.

Exhaustion pulled at him and he dropped to his knees before the stone. He'd been riding for three days—running from Amanda and fate. He traced the lettering lovingly, but his mind was not on the name he traced. Weariness settled on his shoulders like a heavy blanket. He wasn't even sure why he was here.

"Why?" he whispered. "Why, Nona? Why did it have to be Amanda?" He was beginning to question all the feelings he'd developed for her. They were only friends, he kept telling himself. Married, yes, but friends all the same.

The late afternoon sun did not penetrate the canopy of trees above the small clearing. A light breeze caused him to shiver lightly and the damp seeped through his breeches, but he was oblivious to the discomfort. Lost in his own private misery, he was unaware of the passage of time.

When you find the figurine, you will find your destiny. Then you will be complete. Nona's words echoed in his head. *You are not always comfortable with who you are, but she will need you just as you are. Do not be afraid to be yourself.*

Himself? He sighed as he thought of all the things Amanda did not know about him. Was that what Nona meant? *She will need you just as you are.* She had certainly needed him at Collingswood, but her nervousness over his treatment of her problem kept him from telling her more. Once again, fear had kept him from revealing a part of himself, while she was an open book.

Not quite an open book. She'd kept her own secrets too. The one secret he wanted to know—and she hadn't told him. His thoughts whirled. If she had told him, would he have married her? Would he have been there to stop her maid from giving her too much laudanum? His stomach clenched at the thought and he dropped his head into his hands.

Had he fallen in love with his wife? He had been so sure of himself and his ability to thwart Nona's wishes. He knew the woman with the figurine might become his weakness, that she would ensnare him in a way that no one else was able. Despite his belief in science and logic, he knew there were things in the world beyond man's control. Nona believed in the mystical; believed she could divine some things, but leave others to fate. She had taught him much over the years. So why couldn't he accept her otherworldly knowledge as easily as he accepted her explanations concerning herbs and their healing properties?

He closed his eyes and Amanda's face swam before him. For too long society had labeled and categorized him and his sisters. There were still mothers out there who would have never entertained his suit for the hand of their daughters. But neither Amanda nor her family cared about his background. All they had cared about was that she had wanted the match. Granted, he had used the reason of the school to propose in the first place, but he knew it had only been an excuse.

Now that he knew when she had received the statuette, he also understood she knew more about him than he would have ever allowed anyone else to know. She had known him before he became the shell everyone else was conversant with, before he had perfected the mask of the bored young nobleman. And while he never considered himself a rake by any means, he was not without transitory conquests—"transitory" being the operative word.

When his mother died, he had decided then and there never to care for another person outside of his sisters. He was too invested if he cared. Losing himself a piece at a time was too painful, yet he couldn't help but remember the joy he experienced with Amanda. She completed him. Had given him back those lost pieces of his soul. Was that love? Perhaps it was time to stop trying to control everything around him and let go of the past and the fear.

Life would go on regardless. Perhaps that's what he needed to learn, what Amanda was there to teach him. He had no control over who passed through his life, but he did have control over the interaction he had with those who did. He hadn't wanted to fall in love, but now having experienced Amanda, he wanted more. His parents, his stepfather, his great-grandmother; they were all gone now, but they had left him with a legacy. A legacy of love, and it was his responsibility to pass it on to the next generation—to the child Amanda already carried.

He opened his eyes to find that night had fallen. Rising to his feet, he looked back down at the small stone. He still doubted what he felt was love, but he knew he needed to get back to Amanda. He owed her an explanation. Turning, he left the copse and mounted his horse. The moon silvered the area and just for a moment, his great-grandmother's face swam before him. "Goodbye, Nona." Then he turned his mount and headed toward the Abbey. He would spend the night, then head back to London.

Amanda slipped from the brightly lit ballroom into a small deserted parlor and sank onto a sofa. Taking a deep breath, she breathed in the cool night air coming in from an open window, and closed her eyes. Moonlight streamed in, casting silvered shadows over the furniture. Leaning back against the cushions, she waited for her world to return to an even keel and her heart to stop racing.

The cool October air caressed her heated cheeks. The ballroom was a complete crush tonight, and the press of bodies and stale air had nearly caused her to faint. It wasn't the first time and she had to be careful no one else noticed. With Jon still gone, she continued to attend social functions without him. Felicia had been the only one to ask after him, but she had managed to turn the inquiry aside with a tale of Jon being busy with Parliamentary business.

"Amanda?"

She looked up at the sound of Felicia's voice.

"Are you unwell?" Felicia asked.

"No. I just came in here to get some air. The crush tonight is almost unbearable."

Felicia glanced around the small parlor, then sat beside her near the open window.

"It is much more comfortable in here, isn't it?"

Amanda knew she'd raised Felicia's suspicions. Perhaps it was time to go home. Evading Felicia's questions had become tiring. Sooner or later, she would figure out about the babe, if nothing else.

"It is," she agreed with a sigh.

Felicia looked at her closely. "Are you sure you're all right?"

"I suppose I'm a little fatigued," she finally admitted. "Perhaps I ought to go home."

Felicia's eyes narrowed suspiciously. "Do you need help? I could ask Brand—"

"No," she replied quickly. "I will be fine." She rose to her feet and felt a sharp twinge in her side. She was still a bit warm, but forced herself to stand firm and not swoon.

Felicia followed her from the room, but she could tell her friend was not convinced that she would be fine.

The anger that spurred her into action three days after Jon's departure had gradually resolved itself into acceptance. He left with no indication when he would return. He hadn't even told his valet. What was she to make of that? She was certain he'd left the city because he'd taken his stallion. Had he gone back to the Abbey? Maybe she should consider going there herself. At least she'd have some quiet.

Once home, she sent Higgins to bed and climbed the stairs

to her room. A sharp pain in her side had her stopping at the top for a moment to catch her breath. Perhaps she had overdone it tonight. With Jon gone, she had thrown herself headlong back into the rounds of frivolity trying to forget. Unfortunately, the parties were only distractions, holding the memories at bay for a few hours at a time. Back at home, alone, they returned.

Mary was waiting to help her undress and into bed. She toyed with asking Mary to bring her some laudanum to help her sleep, but the memory of Jon's reaction at Collingswood kept her silent. Once the maid was gone, she stared at the ceiling above her bed.

"Nona said once JoJo came for me all would be well," she whispered brokenly to the room, "but she was wrong."

Another twinge of pain in her side caused her to stiffen and wonder if the babe was the cause. Once it subsided, she drifted into a restless sleep.

Rosy fingers crept across the sky, heralding the arrival of another day as Jon rode into the mews behind Kent house. Both he and his horse were exhausted. Handing the animal over to a sleepy groom, he trudged toward the back of the house, letting himself in with his key. As he climbed the back stairs, he debated with himself whether to look in on Amanda first, or make himself more presentable.

Riding through the night, he admitted to himself he had no idea what to expect. There was no doubt he'd hurt Amanda horribly, then disappeared for a nearly a fortnight. She had never struck him as one who might hold a grudge, but then again he was different. He had been the one to lash out at her in anger and frustration, destroying a fourteen-year-old dream. How badly had he damaged her feelings and what would it take to put things to rights?

He frowned as he climbed the stairs. He'd done the same thing three years ago at the Abbey, but she seemed to have forgiven him. Would she do so again?

He stopped at the door of Amanda's room, listening intently. Unable to stop himself, he turned the knob and slipped inside.

The room was in shadows, the early morning light beginning to filter around the closed drapes. Approaching the bed, he stared down at his wife—and sucked in a sharp breath at the sight.

Amanda lay on her side facing away from him, her hair woven into a long golden braid. She had kicked away the coverlet and he had an unobstructed view of long, slim legs beneath her bunched up nightgown. Drinking in the sight of the smooth skin of her cheek and jaw flushed to a rosy hue from sleep, he reached out to touch her. She shifted and a small cry escaped, one hand going to her side. His heart skipped a beat, but the next moment nearly stopped altogether as his hand encountered an inferno. She was burning up with fever!

Turning her over gently, he shook her. "Amanda! Amanda, wake up!"

He shed his coat, allowing it to drop unceremoniously to the floor, and sat beside her. Guilt assailed him again as Amanda moaned.

Brushing back damp tendrils of hair, he spoke to her again and was rewarded when she opened her eyes in response. "Jonathan?" Her voice was uncertain, clogged with an emotion he was unwilling to put a name to. "Hot. Hurt." Her eyes closed again.

"Where?" He shook her gently. "Where does it hurt?"

Her hand moved, indicating her right side. "Here," she whispered.

Jon crossed the room to ring for her maid, then ran into his own room. Digging in the bottom of his own dressing room, he came up with a case and hurried back into Amanda's room. Mary entered at the same time from the hall door.

"Oh, my lord! You gave me a fright!"

Jon ignored her momentarily, putting his case down on the bed and opening it. The maid approached the bed as he searched the case. Pulling out a small pouch of herbs, he handed it to her.

"Take this down to Mrs. Barrett. Tell her I need it steeped into a strong tea quickly. Tell her the countess is sick. She'll know what to do. And send Higgins up."

Mary hesitated, looking down at Amanda for the first time, noting her flushed cheeks. "My lord, is she..."

"Go quickly, girl," Jon snapped. "Your mistress is quite ill."

Mary bolted, leaving Jon beside Amanda. Crossing to the washstand, he dipped a cloth into the cool water and wrung it out.

Returning, he reached out to shake her again as he laid the cool cloth on her forehead. "Amanda! Amanda, I need you to wake up."

Her eyelids fluttered again. Glazed and feverish eyes looked up at him.

"When did the pain start? Do you remember?"

"Didn't hurt...that...much," she said slowly. "Hurt yesterday...day before a little."

"Were you hot before?"

"No. Not hot. Last night."

Higgins entered. "My lord, the maid Mary said..."

"Yes, yes," Jon said testily. "Send one of the footmen to find Dr. Reynolds. It's early enough that he probably hasn't left his home yet. I need him now! And send Mary back up here with a basin of cold water."

The butler hurried out and Jon took the now warm cloth from Amanda's head and re-wet it in the basin on the washstand.

Jon ran his hands over her side and abdomen. *Dear God, don't let her lose the baby.* Not now. She cried out when he pressed a particularly sensitive spot, but otherwise found nothing else he considered wrong.

Sitting back, his mind catalogued the symptoms. There were only two possibilities, and he dreaded both.

When Mary returned with the basin of water, he sent her back for some ice to put into it, then stripped Amanda's nightgown from her, careful of the painful area. Bathing her with the cool water calmed her a little, but she seemed to be sliding in and out of consciousness. When Mrs. Barrett arrived with the tea, he and the housekeeper spoon-fed it to her until she'd taken in enough to suit him.

She seemed calmer by the time Mary returned. Leaving Mary to watch over her, he hurried down to the library. A

223

sucker punch would not have taken his breath away as violently as the sight that met his eyes. In the center of his desk sat his statuette. The wide, unblinking emerald eyes looked at him accusingly. Turning from the evidence of his guilt, he went to a bookshelf and began removing texts. When Dr. Reynolds was shown in not much later, he'd come to a distinctly unpalatable conclusion.

"Jon, m'boy. What's amiss?"

Jon shook hands with the doctor, then ushered him over to the desk, where several books lay open. "I returned home this morning from the country to find my wife feverish and with severe pain in the right side of her abdomen. I think it's an inflammation of her appendix, but I'm not sure since she's also increasing."

Dr. Reynolds put down his bag and bent over the books Jon had open. The two discussed several possibilities for a few minutes, referring to the medical and herbal texts in front of them. Then Jon led the doctor up to see Amanda. After a cursory, but thorough, examination the doctor confirmed Jon's diagnosis.

"I'm afraid you're right," he said. "I was hoping you weren't, but you've never been anything but thorough."

Jon sagged momentarily against the bedpost, watching as the doctor pulled the sheet up over the fitfully sleeping Amanda.

"Now what?"

Dr. Reynolds removed his spectacles and polished them with his handkerchief. "I'm not sure," he replied. "There have been some successes with removing the offending organ, but I've never tried it on someone who's with child. Even though it's early days yet, there is always the possibility she could lose the babe."

Amanda shifted restlessly, drawing both sets of eyes to her. To Jon she looked small and lost in the large bed.

"What about herbal treatments?" Jon asked hopefully. "I know I've read some papers regarding how the Chinese treat it with herbs. Although I don't know if all of the herbs are available here in England."

"We don't have much time," the doctor mused. "What you've given her so far will reduce the fever and dull the pain a little, but not for long. There's a new doctor on staff at the hospital who has spent some time in the Orient." He picked up his bag. "I'll go see what I can find out from him and get back to you within the hour. In the meantime, another dose of that tea wouldn't go amiss to keeping her comfortable for now."

An hour later, Jon and the doctor once again stood beside Amanda's bed. Jon had washed, shaved and eaten during Dr. Reynolds absence, but not rested.

"I spoke with Whyte," Dr. Reynolds began. "He's not optimistic about the use of the herbal treatments. He thinks the preparation and potency might differ greatly and cause more harm than good."

Jon nodded in resignation. He had considered the possibility that even if they could find the right herbs, not knowing how to prepare them and what strength to use would make treatment difficult.

"It looks like surgery is our best option," the doctor informed him. "I spoke with Clover too. He's the current expert on anesthetics. Unfortunately, his apparatus for administering chloroform is too cumbersome and complicated, and I didn't think you wanted to try to take her to the hospital. He and I both agreed the best method would be to use the mask. I have one in my bag."

It took Jon a moment to realize his friend had already made the assumption Amanda needed to be operated on. Unfortunately, he also assumed Jon would be the one doing the operating. The thought filled him with dread, but the alternative was worse. He refused to take her to the hospital and let one of the surgeons there do it. Too many people died in hospitals from infections and he would not expose her to the possibility. After studying Semmelweiss' theory on childbed fever, he was doubly sure the last place he wanted to have her operated on would be the hospital. Lister had made inroads, but too many doctors scoffed at both he and Semmelweiss and still refused to take cleanliness seriously.

"I would have preferred," he said at last, "it not come to this."

The doctor was not unsympathetic. "I know, m'boy. But we don't have the time. And you've done it before," he encouraged.

Jon shook his head. "Not this particular surgery." The gravity of the situation was beginning to catch up with him and not for the first time, he tasted fear.

"There must always be a first time."

Dr. Reynolds rummaged in his bag and came up with a small linen-wrapped bundle while Jon crossed the room to ring for the housekeeper.

When Mrs. Barrett arrived, he sent her downstairs with a list of things he needed and told her to unlock his workroom. Shedding his coat and neckcloth, he approached the bed where the doctor was checking on Amanda.

Still and white in the great bed, she moaned slightly when the doctor pressed her abdomen, but otherwise showed no response to the doctor's prodding, pressing and tapping on various parts of her anatomy.

"She's healthy," he said, turning to look at Jon. "Shouldn't be any trouble at all."

Jon's smile was more of a grimace. His own gut was already tying itself in knots. Reaching over, he wrapped Amanda carefully in the sheet, then lifted her in his arms. She was still light as a feather, the babe seemed to have added no new weight as yet. She whimpered when he first picked her up, then settled again. With Dr. Reynolds following, he led the way down to his workroom.

The room at the bottom of the back stairs was long and narrow with a wall of windows overlooking the small kitchen garden, a wide counter jutting out from the sill. Along the short wall at the very end stood a washstand with two bowls and pitchers and a large stack of clean towels. The wall opposite the windows housed floor-to-ceiling shelves filled with a variety of gadgets, books, bowls, beakers, utensils and even a few bones. In the middle of the wall a small kettle hung over a cheery fire in the small fireplace. The center of the room was taken up mostly by a large table, around which sat four haphazardly placed stools. Mrs. Barrett was just finishing up covering the table with a layer of sheeting as they entered.

"Thank you, Mrs. Barrett," Jon said. Glancing around the

small, but clean space, he was satisfied with what he saw.

"'Tis good I scrubbed in here just yesterday," commented the housekeeper. She reached the door and turned just as Jon was putting Amanda down on the table. "I'll be nearby if ye need me, m'lord."

Jon nodded and the housekeeper went out, closing the door softly behind her.

Dr. Reynolds was pulling items out of his bag and placing them on the counter as Jon carefully unwrapped Amanda's still figure, then re-covered all but her face and the painful area on her abdomen. She was still slightly feverish and he could tell the tea was beginning to wear off.

An onlooker would have been forgiven for assuming Jon and the doctor had done this many times before, so quickly and efficiently did each prepare for the task before them. Dr. Reynolds approached with the mask, an oval metal frame to which was attached a multi-layered cloth of flannel and cotton designed to fit over the patient's mouth and nose. This he left sitting on Amanda's chest, then returned to pick up two bottles, which he handed to Jon.

"I ran into Lister while I was there and told him what was going on. He gave me these. This one—" he handed Jon a brown bottle the size of a whiskey decanter, "—is for you to thoroughly wash your hands in, and this one—" he handed him a smaller green bottle, "—is for the dressing when you're done." He turned away, retrieving another even smaller brown bottle. "Are you ready?"

Jon rinsed his hands in the carbolic acid solution and picked up the items he had laid out. Bringing one of the basins with him, he set it down on one of the stools next to the table. He watched as the doctor fitted the mask over Amanda's nose and mouth and, removing the stopper from the brown bottle, allowed just three drops of the solution inside to fall on the mask.

Amanda had begun to writhe in pain, but Jon held her steady. "It's all right, love. Just relax," he crooned to her. She seemed to respond to the sound of his voice, the tension easing from her body. Dr. Reynolds added another drop to the mask. Minutes later she was completely limp and unresponsive—even when Jon gently pressed the exposed area. Dr. Reynolds nodded.

Jon took up a very sharp knife. For a moment he merely stared at the implement, wondering what he was doing. How could he cut Amanda? Could he really mar that alabaster skin? Sweat broke out on his brow. He knew he had no choice, but fear spiraled through him nevertheless, twisting in his gut with almost painful intensity.

Doubts attacked him. What if he made a mistake? What if he accidentally cut where their child grew? What if he damaged her irreparably? What if he lost her?

He couldn't bear to lose her now, but what if he did? He had worked hard to save his mother, but still hadn't. Dr. Reynolds had been a wonderful mentor, but the good doctor hadn't lost a piece of himself with every death. His hand shook and pain sliced through him at the horrifying possibility. He took a deep breath, but still could not stop his hands from shaking.

If he lost her now, he wouldn't be able to live with himself. It would be all his fault. If he hadn't left her, he might have noticed something earlier.

Dr. Reynolds' voice came to him out of the past. *You did everything you could, son. No one will fault you for it.*

But he had. He blamed himself for not knowing more, for not trying something different, for not moving his mother to a hospital, for not asking another doctor for his opinion, and a myriad other things. Back then, his doubts had been magnified by his stepfather's death a mere two years earlier. Discovering years later his stepfather had actually been murdered eased his misgivings over losing him, but his mother's death nearly had destroyed him. He had been confident of his ability to save her, but couldn't in the end. He knew so much more now, but was it enough?

He hadn't wanted to fall in love for just this reason—but it had all been for naught. He loved her. She was his life. His reason for living. And now he had no choice. He was her best hope at the moment. No one else was available and he didn't know if they had the time to wait for a surgeon he trusted to be free.

How would he live with himself if she died at his hands? If he never told her of his love?

"It's all right, son." Dr. Reynolds' voice shook him from his paralysis. "Try not to think of who she is. At the moment, she's a patient who needs your help, nothing more."

Jon nodded, took a shaky breath to calm himself, and applied the knife.

Two hours later he sat beside a still-unconscious Amanda, but his heart had finally returned to its normal tempo. She was no longer in the deep, chloroform-induced senseless state which had allowed her to lie quietly while he cut her open and removed her appendix, and for that he was supremely thankful.

Dr. Reynolds had left a full half hour ago, telling Jon he would check on them around tea time. Jon had merely nodded, too exhausted to do anything more than sit on a stool and watch his wife. Mrs. Barrett knocked lightly and entered.

"The doctor says I'm to sit with her ladyship while you get some rest. No, don't argue," she said firmly when Jon looked up and started to speak. "He said you was to go straight to bed, and I was to remind you that you'll be no good to anyone if you collapse from exhaustion."

A ghost of a smile lightened his features for a moment before he turned dull eyes back to Amanda.

"Very well," he conceded, "but perhaps we can make her ladyship more comfortable by returning her to her own bed."

"It's all ready."

Checking the dressing over the incision, he was satisfied all was as it should be. Tenderly lifting Amanda in his arms, he followed Mrs. Barrett out of the workroom with his precious burden and back up to the master suite. Before he laid her back on the clean sheets, he brushed his lips across her forehead. "Get well soon, love. I have much to explain yet," he whispered. To Mrs. Barrett, he said, "Awaken me if there's any change." Then he entered his bedchamber and succumbed to the ministrations of his valet.

Chapter Seventeen

Pain in her side roused Amanda from a deep sleep. Too groggy to even open her eyes, she was vaguely aware of someone else in the room. Moving to try to ease the pain, a strong arm suddenly slipped beneath her head and raised her gently.

"Drink," a disembodied voice directed as a cup was pressed against her lips. She drank. A few sips were all she could manage, then her head was returned to the pillow. Moments later, a sickly sweet smelling cloth covered her nose, and she was sliding back into unconsciousness.

"I guess that will have to do for a few days," Dr. Reynolds said to Jon as he removed the chloroform-soaked cloth from her face. "You'll have to keep her under until the incision begins to heal enough that you can use laudanum to control the pain."

"Not laudanum," Jon contradicted him. "She's had too much of it over the last few years. I don't want to use it unless I really feel it's necessary."

"I know you prefer to use the willowbark, but I don't think it's strong enough. Do you want some more of the hemp preparation?"

Jon thought for a moment. The stuff he had given her for her monthly cycle pain had worked quite well—and faster than the willowbark tea would. Perhaps it would work as a medium-strength painkiller.

"Yes, I think I would. Perhaps I'll use it for a week and see how she does."

"When she's stronger and can take in more of the broth, then you can start giving her small amounts of it as well."

"Hopefully by then I won't have to keep her under as much."

Dr. Reynolds nodded. "The sooner she can stay awake for longer periods of time, the better. You want to get her back on more than beef broth for the babe's sake."

Jon stood outside Amanda's room and listened to the laughter coming from within. Had it only been seven days ago he'd returned and found her burning up with fever? His heart still skipped a beat when he remembered all that happened that morning. He was grateful the appendix, which had turned putrid, hadn't leaked its poison into her system before he removed it. But it had been a close call.

Her recovery was just short of amazing. A short week later and she was awake and alert, receiving company, and needing only small doses of the hemp preparation to keep away the pain. The incision, while still red and angry looking, was healing nicely. No infection. No fever. And the babe hadn't seemed affected either. He could not be more thankful—unless she stopped regarding him with extreme wariness.

He wanted to talk to her, to explain, but her recovery was more important for now. Two mornings ago, Dr. Reynolds had made his last visit.

"You don't need me looking over your shoulder any longer. She's doing remarkably well."

Four days ago, Felicia had come to call. After being put off by Higgins with the excuse that "Her Ladyship is unwell," for two days before that, she finally threatened to cause a scene on the front step if he didn't let her in and call Jon down.

She had taken him to task. "All it would have taken was a note, and I would not have bothered you. You might want to let her father know, however," was her parting shot.

Trent arrived the next morning. Unwilling to accept Jon's explanation, he insisted on seeing Amanda for himself.

Felicia had become a regular visitor, offering to sit with Amanda frequently. Yesterday she'd brought Tina with her, and they had returned today.

Hearing footsteps coming up the staircase, he looked up as

Higgins approached with Trent following. He smiled. Trent had been by every day since Jon had written him. If he needed further proof of Amanda's family's devotion, it was given quickly when he had, with difficulty, talked Trent out of sending for Eliza.

"We have a crowd today," he said to Trent, opening the door to allow his father-in-law to precede him into Amanda's room.

Amanda looked up as the door to her room opened. Her face brightened considerably when she noted it was her father, followed by Jon.

Her father approached the bed and bestowed a kiss on her forehead. "How are you feeling today, poppet?"

"Much better, Papa. My side doesn't hardly hurt at all."

"Good, good. Thought I heard laughter before I came in."

"Tina was just telling us about the time Shana jumped into the lake at Collingswood but hadn't learned to swim yet."

He laughed. "Did you tell them you swim like a fish?"

Felicia's shout of laughter had all heads turning in her direction, but it was Jon's statement which caused them all to look at him.

"I certainly hope so."

"And why is that?" her father asked.

Jon lounged against one of the bedposts, arms folded across his broad chest. He was dressed casually in only a shirt and trousers, his collar open to reveal the strong column of his neck. When Amanda looked up at him, surprise clearly written on her face, he smiled, then winked at her. The playful action doubled her heartbeat and left her slightly breathless, but his next words nearly caused her heart to stop altogether.

"Because I taught her."

Felicia and Tina both stared at him as if he had lost his mind. He knew what they were thinking. A statement like that could not go unexplained, and he had never publicly spoken of his gypsy roots, of Nona, Carlo, Mira or any of the others. He most certainly never opened the subject himself. He had too many hurtful memories of scathing remarks and condemning looks to deliberately open himself up for more. Yet Nona had told him Amanda would accept him for himself and knowing Trent and Eliza much better than he had before, he knew they would as well. There was just that one little problem of the reason Amanda had been at the camp in the first place.

He'd spent much of the last few days debating with himself how to open the subject with Amanda. Having not come up with a satisfactory way, he now took the opening presented by her father. He hoped she would understand the step he was taking by talking of it in front of him.

As expected, Trent's reaction was one of stunned amazement. "You? But how? And when?"

"The summer I was seven, Papa," Amanda responded, drawing her father's gaze. "At Summersea."

Trent seemed to be at a loss for words, a myriad of questions in his gaze. Felicia saved him the trouble of deciding where to start.

"It took me a whole day to coax her into the lake, then she wouldn't get any more than her feet wet. Once I realized it was because she couldn't swim, I enlisted Jon to teach her. Three weeks later, you couldn't have kept her out." She grinned.

"It wouldn't have done any good for me to stay out. I would have ended up wet anyway," Amanda returned. "Besides, the first leg of nearly all of our excursions started out in the lake. Learning to swim was the only way to keep up with you."

"Remember the fish?" Felicia asked, barely containing her laughter.

"It did not bite me and I did not scream," Amanda answered indignantly.

"Yes you did. Mira was only being nice. Even Nona protected you and disclaimed all knowledge."

Jon watched Amanda's father, understanding his confused silence as the earl looked from Amanda to Felicia to Jon and back. He wondered if Trent had connected them to the statuette yet.

"You should know that both Nona and Mira were thankful for you." Tina joined the conversation.

"Me? Why?"

Jon answered her question. "Because without you there, it

would have been a very lonely summer for Felicia. If you'll remember, there were no other children your age in the camp and Felicia running wild would have driven us all to Bedlam."

Jon and Trent left the ladies to gossip over tea and headed downstairs. When Jon invited his father-in-law into the library to chat, he accepted, waiting until they were settled with drinks before breaking the silence.

"I assume you wanted to explain what the conversation upstairs was about," he began, "but I assure you my curiosity could have waited until Amanda was recovered."

Jon chuckled. "I'm sure it could have, but there are some things I'm not sure she knows."

"Such as?"

"Why she was at my great-grandmother's gypsy camp in the first place."

Trent did not follow up on the statement. Instead, he commented, "So, at least some of the rumors are true."

"The one which says my sisters and I are related to gypsies—yes, *that* one is true. Some of the others..." Jon shrugged, indicating how little importance he attached to the rest.

"Yes, well, we know what people are like. Most of the gossip is constructed from whole cloth, with not even a single rumor to build from." Trent's voice was hard, but not bitter. "You needn't dance around the issue. I can guess for myself why Katherine might have taken Amanda off to a gypsy camp, then left her to her own devices. Perhaps it is I who ought to be thankful for Felicia."

Jon laughed outright. "You may think so all you want, but do not even hint at it to Felicia. The three weeks I spent chasing those two around the Lake District still provides me with ammunition to needle Felicia with occasionally."

A sandy eyebrow rose. "Were they that bad?"

Jon shook his head. "In truth? No. But you might remember I was but sixteen."

"Ahh. Now I do indeed understand." He paused for a few moments, then said, "I came into my title at fifteen. By sixteen,

I was confident that I knew everything. I suspect Felicia would have taught me differently."

"I had no excuse," Jon added. "I came into my title at six, but I had a good role model and mentor in Felicia's father. I should have known I didn't know everything."

Trent chuckled. "And the statuette?"

Jon reached over to the corner of his desk where the statuette sat. Picking it up, he put it down on the small table between them and ran his hand across the smooth contours of its back. He'd resolved to tell Trent as much as he wanted to know, but where to begin failed him for a moment.

"JoJo," he said unnecessarily. "The first time Tina and I spent a summer with our great-grandmother, she was very cautious. Protecting our identities was important to her," he began and launched into the story of Nona and her firm belief in everyone's destiny.

The telling was cathartic for Jon. He never realized how much he wanted to tell someone more than just the superficialities of living with his great-grandmother. It was satisfying, he discovered, to tell his father-in-law about his great-grandmother. About her life, and how theirs intertwined with it. With Nona, everything had a purpose, a destiny. She lived by her cards, and they gave her answers which made little sense to others at the time, but always worked out in the end.

By the time Amanda's father left, Jon was feeling better about his past. No longer was it a millstone around his neck he tried to ignore. It had finally taken seeing Amanda and talking to her father to realize there was little he could do about the rumor mill. Entirely too much of his previous time and energy had gone into cultivating the required image. No more.

His stepfather had been right all along. There would always be those who would not accept him, but that was true for nearly everyone. That it was because of Nona for him had been more acute because his paternal grandmother once refused to accept him for that very reason as well. Her ultimate acceptance after Tina's marriage had turned many around. Those who still refused to see him for the person he was, he would simply ignore from now on.

Denise Patrick

Amanda rolled over, trying to get comfortable. The small twinge in her side reminded her that a little over a week ago, she had been very ill with a fever and radiating pain in her side and back. She remembered little except pieces of a strange dream, then Jon shaking her awake.

She discovered she had been ill enough to require surgery. That explained the ugly, puckered scar now forming low on her right side, but little else. What, exactly, had happened?

Gingerly sitting up, she swung her legs over the side of the bed. The room was warm, a fire burning brightly in the grate. She knew she was alone, having sent Mary off to find her bed it seemed like hours ago. Now she was just restless.

Heartened by only the barest feeling of tenderness in her side, she stood, and was rewarded when she felt no dizziness or weakness. Moving slowly, she approached the door connecting her room with Jon's. Opening it on well-oiled hinges, she peered into the darkness beyond.

Was he there? The fire was banked, but the room was comfortable, although not quite as warm as hers. Should she disturb him? She'd wanted to talk to him for a few days now, but he was never alone with her. If Mrs. Barrett wasn't there, it was Mary, or his sisters or her father. Somehow, he managed never to be in the same room with her unless there was someone else present. Fleetingly, she wondered if he did it on purpose.

She sighed. They needed to talk. She wanted to know what he was thinking.

A part of her wanted to have it out with him. To force him to acknowledge his great-grandmother hadn't been a candidate for Bedlam. But another part of her dreaded the possible confrontation.

His admission to her father this afternoon gave her hope, and she prayed it wasn't misplaced. Had he come to an understanding with his past? Would he talk about it now? About Nona? About the statuette and the reason she had it?

Suppose he insisted she had married him under false pretenses?

She was comforted by the thought that she was his wife. He

236

was not likely to put her aside—especially since it was possible she carried his heir. She didn't want to dwell on what might have happened had he learned about JoJo *before* they married.

Straightening as best she could with allowance for the tightness in her side, and squaring her shoulders, she approached the massive bed.

Empty!

Her shoulders slumped as she stared at the space where Jon should be sleeping peacefully. Blast it! Didn't the man ever sleep in his own bed? She giggled at her thoughts, and clapped her hand over her mouth as she glanced around the dark room. Now what?

"I'll wait," she muttered to herself. Lighting the small bedside lamp, she climbed into the big bed, and settled beneath the covers. Snuggling into the pillows, she took a deep breath and was calmed by Jon's scent clinging to the linens.

When Jon entered the room mere minutes later, she was fast asleep.

His tie already hanging loosely, Jon shrugged out of his jacket and tossed it and the neckwear over one of the chairs near the fire before noticing that the door to Amanda's room was open. He was removing his shirt when he noticed the bedside lamp and wondered why his valet left it burning.

Shucking the rest of his clothing, he crossed to the end of the bed. Spying Amanda's sleeping form, his hand stilled as he reached for the silken trousers he had recently been sleeping in. Myriad thoughts flew through his head as to why she would be in his bed, the first of which was that she was in pain and had come to find him. It was quickly dismissed once he asked himself why she would bother to come all the way to his room when she could have called someone from her own. More suggestions emerged and were discarded until he began to feel a chill on his backside and remembered he was standing in a cooling room with not a stitch on.

Grabbing up and donning the trousers, he moved around the side of the bed and sat beside her. For a few moments, he looked his fill. The soft glow of the lamp turned her skin golden and he reached out to stroke lightly down her arm. The satiny texture was smooth beneath the pads of his fingers, reminding him of how soft and feminine she felt when he took her in his arms.

She stirred and her eyelashes fluttered sleepily.

"Jonathan?" The wariness in her tone bordered on fear and his heart contracted in pain. Had his outburst made her afraid of him? He rubbed a hand over his eyes, squeezing them closed tightly for a moment, before looking back down at her. She shifted on to her back, wincing slightly, then moved to sit up.

Helping her up, and settling pillows at her back, he watched her push stray strands of gold out of her face, then fold her hands in her lap.

"Why are you here?"

Amanda glanced down at her hands and didn't answer.

He slid two fingers under her chin and lifted her face to his. "Amanda?"

"I-I wanted to talk to you, but you've avoided being alone with me."

His lips quirked. "I have?"

Her lower lip trembled and she stilled it by worrying it with her teeth, then nodded slowly.

He sighed and dropped his hand. She was right, of course. He *had* avoided being alone with her once she was no longer unconscious and sleeping regularly. When he realized she was healing just fine, hadn't developed a fever, and was conscious most of the day, he'd deliberately never been alone with her. He told himself it was because he didn't want to upset her, but he knew better. He didn't want to talk about the night he'd confronted her about JoJo. The night he'd lost his temper and stormed out of the house like a child having a tantrum. Just thinking about his actions made him ashamed of himself.

"I wanted to tell you," she began, her voice trailing off as she raised clear blue pools to his.

"Don't..."

She could not have missed the pain in his voice, but she took a deep breath and continued anyway. "I'm sorry I..."

"Amanda..."

"...lied about..." Her voice trailed off and tears spilled down her cheeks.

Jon groaned and pulled her into his arms, pressing her

face into his shoulder. Hearing her apologize made him feel like a cad.

"It's not your fault," he groaned into her hair. Inhaling the sweet scent of honeysuckle, he blinked back the moisture gathering in his own eyes. "It's not your fault," he repeated.

"But...but I...you...we...wouldn't be married if I..." She hiccupped and sniffed. Hot tears scalded a path down his chest. Calling himself every kind of fool he could think of, he held her while she sobbed. He knew tears did not come to her easily. That he had reduced her to them told him just how deeply he'd hurt her.

Unconsciously his arms tightened around her. When he felt her stiffen, then begin to squirm, he remembered her side and released her.

"Does your side hurt?" He held her away from him, his hand going to her side, pressing lightly through the material of her nightgown. "Did I hurt you?"

She shook her head, wiping her eyes with the back of her hand.

He pressed her back into the pillows and pulled the covers up to her chin. "You need to rest. We will talk another time."

"No." There was a hitch in her voice. "I'm not tired, and I-I want to talk now. I need to know."

Jon did not want to have this conversation. He loved her, but it was too new, too fresh. He did not want her delving too deeply into feelings he was only just becoming accustomed to. Talking about JoJo would bring too many insecurities to the surface. Things he still needed to process before he could talk about them.

"I need to know," she said in a stronger voice, "what you intend to do."

He turned away from imploring blue eyes and turned down the lamp. Rising to his feet, he walked around to the other side of the bed and climbed in.

"Right now, I intend to go to sleep."

She shouldn't have come. She should have known she couldn't force him to talk to her. He would do what he wanted regardless of what she wanted, or needed. She turned into the pillow as a sob rose in her throat. How would she ever face him again after tonight?

Closing her eyes against a fresh wave of tears, she wondered if she should go back to her room. Would he prefer to sleep alone now?

Yet it felt oh so good to be lying next to him again, even if they weren't touching. She could feel his heat, the comfort of his presence. Despite her confused feelings, a soothing calm descended upon her. Now if she could only hold back the tears. She sighed. What was wrong with her? She never cried. Well, only rarely. Perhaps it was the babe making her so emotional.

Yet, as a fresh wave of tears surfaced, the feeling that she'd lost everything enveloped her, bringing the raw feelings of loss and loneliness to the surface. It was like losing her mother all over again. As the tears fell, soaking the linen beneath her head, she held herself still. Once he fell asleep, she would return to her own bed.

Gentle hands grabbed her shoulders and turned her as Jon's shadow rose above her.

"God, Amanda!" His voice was ragged. "Please, stop!" She was drawn into a warm embrace, her face pressed against his chest. The dusting of dark hair tickled her nose and she could hear his heart racing.

She slid her arms around his waist and pressed the length of her body against his. As if holding him close could chase away the feelings of despair threatening to overwhelm her.

"I'm sorry," he said as he threaded his fingers through the hair at her temple. "I can't. I just can't talk about it right now." He took a deep breath and his voice hitched. "Too much has happened and I want you to make a full recovery first."

His voice soothed her—something in the tone giving her hope. Perhaps he was right. Her body relaxed against his as he sank back onto the pillows, taking her with him. She wanted to believe him. Wanted to believe he only wanted the best for her. She clung to the thought as she laid her head on his shoulder and allowed her body to melt against him. Emotions drained from her, leaving her weak and exhausted with heavy lids. She succumbed to the moment and closed her eyes.

Jon held her for a long time, listening to her breathing and enjoying the feel of her softness pressed against him. He was an emotional wreck. Never had anyone been able to delve so deeply into his soul before. Frankly, it scared him, but he recognized his need for Amanda. He wanted, no needed, her to bring light into those dark places he'd kept hidden for so long. The door inside his heart was wide open, but only Amanda knew the way in. It was terrifying and satisfying at the same time. Tomorrow, he promised himself before he followed her into slumber. Tomorrow they would clear the air.

Chapter Eighteen

Amanda moved slowly as she descended to the dining room the next morning. Jon had already been gone when she awoke, but she hadn't felt deserted. Remembering his revelation of the night before, she was heartened by his words, understanding that her recovery was most important for now. It was why she insisted on getting up and venturing downstairs for the first time in nearly two weeks.

Higgins was closing the front door as she descended. When he turned, he held a large vase of red and pink hothouse roses. A smile broke across his normally stern features when he noticed her.

"These just arrived for you, my lady."

A thrill went through her as she opened the card he handed her. The words nearly jumped out at her and she drew in a deep breath to still her racing heart.

I've been told many times that flowers speak when the heart is unable. I'm sorry about last night. Love, Jonathan

She resisted a sudden impulse to hug herself. Instead she turned a brilliant smile on Higgins and instructed him to put the flowers in the morning room.

She and Jon still needed to talk. If he needed her to be fully recovered before he could do so, then she would be fully recovered as soon as possible. That meant today. She *was* feeling better. Only a small twinge in her side occasionally reminded her of her illness.

Her efforts were appreciated by the staff and Felicia. Jon did not return home until shortly before dinner, but his flowers kept her company. Evincing surprise that she was up and about, he hurried upstairs to change.

"I did not expect you to be up," he told her when he joined her a short time later.

"I was tired of lazing about in bed when I no longer felt ill."

He chuckled as she handed him a glass of wine.

"Thank you for the flowers. They're lovely."

"You're welcome."

Did you mean it? The words hovered on her tongue. All day long, she'd kept the card close, desperately wanting to believe the hidden message in the words he'd written and the flowers themselves, but unsure.

Insecurity around Jon was new to her. She'd always been able to tell him what she was thinking. Until now. Their relationship had taken a turn the night he disappeared, she acknowledged. The path they'd been on before then was gone forever. Was this new one better?

Higgins announced dinner, saving her from a decision.

Dinner was quiet, with limited conversation about casual friends and acquaintances.

After dinner, they were leaving the dining room for the salon when Higgins approached with a note on a salver.

"A note for you, my lord."

Jon picked up the missive and frowned at the handwriting on the front before he unfolded the sheet.

"Is there someone waiting for an answer?" he asked when he finished scanning the contents.

"Yes, my lord."

Jon turned to Amanda, and she saw the disappointment in his expression before he spoke.

"I'm sorry," he said with a small smile. "Dr. Reynolds has requested my help with a problem. I hate to leave you..."

"I am fine," she assured him. Understanding that Dr. Reynolds was a special friend, she knew she could not keep him here tonight when he was needed elsewhere.

Jon turned to Higgins and gave him a set of instructions before turning to escort Amanda into the salon.

Once inside, Jon closed the door and pulled Amanda into his arms.

"I would have preferred to stay with you," he told her with a quirky smile. "Reynolds isn't nearly as agreeable on the eyes."

She smiled back at him. "I certainly hope not."

His hand slid up her spine, pressing her closer. Bending his head, he whispered her name against her lips, then kissed her.

She could do nothing more than respond. Jon's heat enveloped her, yet his passion was kept firmly in check. His arms held her close, but his hands stayed on her back. Lifting up on her toes, she slid her arms around his neck and closed her eyes. The wonder of being in Jon's arms again, of having him kiss her with tenderness and love, brought a lump to her throat and a melting sensation in her heart.

When he raised his head, she lifted her eyes to his and knew then he'd meant every word he'd written. For now, it would be enough. They still needed to talk, but she was content. His friend needed him, so she would let him go.

A knock on the door drew them apart.

"Don't wait up for me," he told her. "John doesn't often ask for my help, but when he does it's often something complicated and likely to take some time. If you plan to attend the masquerade tomorrow night, you will need your rest."

Then he was gone, but she was not alone.

Upstairs she breathed deeply of the fragrance permeating her room. As she prepared for bed, then dismissed her maid, she looked at the vase of roses and said a small prayer of thankfulness.

JoJo had finally come home to her.

"I received the most wonderful note today from your grandmother," Amanda told Jon the next evening. He hadn't returned home until just before dinner and she had informed him that his sisters and their husbands would be joining them. Now that the family had left, they had repaired to the library. "I thought I might venture out to see her tomorrow."

"You have made a remarkable recovery, so I don't see why you shouldn't. Just don't overtax yourself." He hoped he sounded encouraging.

She curled up on a sofa near the fire as he crossed to the decanters near the window. "Do you think I might become ill again?"

"Not with what you had before, but your system may not have completely recovered. Even something as small as a chill could have adverse effects, and you must continue to think of the babe."

Jon nearly winced at the imperious tone that crept into his voice. It was the same tone he often used with patients when giving them instructions. He wondered if Amanda noticed.

"Yes, Doctor," she replied cheekily.

He willed himself not to react as he poured himself a brandy and said in a grave voice, "These last two weeks have not been easy and I would never have forgiven myself had I returned too late to save you."

"I do not understand. What did you mean, 'had you returned too late to save me'? Surely, Dr. Reynolds would have—"

He took a sip of his brandy, allowing the liquor to slide smoothly down his throat before turning to her. "Sherry?"

She shook her head. "No, thank you."

Picking up the figurine off his desk, he crossed the carpet and joined her. In the meager light of the fire, he noted her confusion at his comments. He was doing a poor job of explaining himself, but there was so much he needed to tell her.

"Was I in terrible danger, then?" she asked when he settled next to her, having put the statuette on the side table. "I only remember pain in my side and being feverish. Was there more?"

"No, but the pain in your side was the result of a putrid appendix, which had to be removed."

"That explains the scar," she murmured unnecessarily.

"It is very likely that my staff would have contacted Dr. Reynolds had I not been here. They know he is the physician I would call. But he does not perform surgery unless he absolutely has to." He smiled, thinking of his friend's probable reaction. "He would have taken me to task for not being here."

"I see." She shifted and laid her head against his shoulder.

He chuckled as he finished off his brandy and put the glass down. "No, love, you don't, but it matters not. I have something for you."

Surprised, she turned toward him as he picked up the statuette and held it out to her. For a moment she merely stared at it, then she reached out as if afraid it might be real enough to bite.

"But I...I left it for you," she said haltingly. "Felicia said Nona promised it to you."

He nearly groaned. What, he wondered, had she told Felicia?

"Besides," she raised tender eyes to his, "I don't need it anymore."

A heaviness settled in his chest as he put the statuette back down on the table. Rejected. His world was suddenly out of alignment. She didn't need JoJo anymore. He should have anticipated it, but it still hurt. Would she ever need JoJo again?

She shifted closer and slid her arms around his waist. Her warmth gave him comfort he hadn't realized he needed and he reciprocated the gesture, turning to hold her against him.

"I don't need the figurine anymore," she repeated softly, "because I have you."

The world realigned and he looked down into pools brimming with love.

There was still much he wanted to explain. Nona and his medical training for starters, but at this moment only one thing needed saying.

"I love you."

A brilliant smile appeared, topped by a mischievous twinkle in sapphire eyes.

"I know."

Taken aback, he merely stared down at her. Then he threw back his head and laughed. Holding her close, he buried his face in her hair.

"I don't know why," he finally said, "I thought Nona couldn't possibly have understood what she was doing. I should have known better."

"I won't tell you what your sisters would say to such a statement."

He shook his head. "You don't need to. I can figure it out all by myself."

"I do owe you an apology, I suppose." She reached up and stroked his jaw. "I probably shouldn't have lied to you about the figurine."

He couldn't contain his chuckle. "Nona would have approved." A question rose in her eyes. "When she told me of Felicia's ring, she told me I was to use any means necessary, force if it was needed, to ensure Felicia married the right person. I think she might have said the same thing regarding deceit if you'd been older than seven."

Her smile made him want to laugh again. Not since he was a boy had he felt so in love with life. So in love with *his* life—and the wife Nona had chosen for him.

"She promised me a prince, you know."

"Then I'm sorry you had to settle for me."

"Even though she wouldn't tell me, I knew it was you. When I told her JoJo was my prince, all she said was that I would know when I found him." She sighed deeply. "I can only hope our son will not be as stubborn."

Jon stood and lifted her in his arms. "You must be tired. It has been a long night." As they left the library, she wound her arms around his neck and laid her head against his shoulder. Her warmth seeped through his coat and shirt and the scent of honeysuckle surrounded him. He breathed deeply, savoring the moment.

"Even more so for you. Were you able to help Dr. Reynolds?"

"Yes."

"How?"

He put her down once inside his room and shut the door behind him.

"You might not believe me if I tell you."

She looked up at him and pouted. "Does that mean you won't tell me?"

In response, he turned her around and began unfastening the hooks down the back of her gown. He bent and brushed his lips across a satiny shoulder and felt her tremble slightly. Glancing over his shoulder to the bed behind him, he was relieved to see his valet had followed his instructions and left one of Amanda's nightrobes beside his own dressing gown. He'd not ask the man how he'd managed to procure the garment. Some things were better left unknown.

Amanda's skin prickled in the cool air as the gown slid into a puddle at her feet, followed by her corset. She stood mute in the partially darkened room as Jon undressed her, peeling away layers of clothing with a gentleness she remembered from the summer. His large hands skimmed over her skin, heating it with just a touch. Excitement shimmered in the air.

She turned and reached for his tie but he stilled her hands.

"Not yet," he murmured. "I need to know you are truly healed."

Then he reached behind her and, to her surprise, picked up her dressing gown. She wanted to ask how it had come to be there as he helped her into it and lightly tied the belt, but the moment passed. Ushering her to the bed, he bade her lie down, then shed his jacket and retrieved a small case from beside the bed.

"Tell me if this hurts or is uncomfortable," he said as he used two fingers to press the area around her scar.

"No, it doesn't hurt." She squirmed. "Jonathan, what are you doing?"

His hand slid over her abdomen and pressed again. Ordinarily that action would have started her blood singing, but the touch was so impersonal, it did nothing for her. She frowned.

"What about here?"

"No."

When he parted the lapels of the robe and pulled an oddly fashioned, three-pronged object from his bag, her eyes widened. Fitting two ends in his ears, he then put the other end on her chest between her breasts.

"Jonathan, what *are* you doing?"

"Shhh."

She frowned again, but remained silent until he finished and put the device away. Then she sat up.

"Will I live?" she demanded peevishly.

His chuckle only annoyed her further.

"You are as healthy as the proverbial ox," he replied.

Leaning closer, he stopped a hair's breadth away and continued, "But much easier on the eyes."

Then his mouth covered hers. Amanda was still irritated at his unwillingness to answer her questions, yet she could not stop herself from responding. Sliding her hands up his chest and tangling her fingers in the hair at his nape, she fell back on the pillows, drawing him with her.

When he raised his head, breaking the kiss, she shivered at the fire in his eyes. But she still wanted to know.

"You still haven't told me how you helped Dr. Reynolds."

He straightened and began removing his shirt. "John is personal physician to Her Majesty. When she demands his presence, needless to say, he goes, regardless of the time or any other patients who might need him. The other night he was attending a woman about to give birth and having a difficult time of it."

He finished undressing and slid naked into the bed beside her. Reclining on his side, he propped his head up with one hand while sliding the other across her still flat abdomen. A thrill shot through her at his touch.

"So, he did what he usually does when I'm in town and he needs a stand in. He sent for me."

Amanda stilled and stared at him in wide-eyed astonishment.

He gathered her close and lay down beside her. She could hear his heart beating heavily against his chest.

"Despite how it might have appeared, I did not spend most of my summers with Nona chasing Felicia around. Gathering herbs and learning about them consumed most of the time. I was fascinated by them and Nona indulged my curiosity. After I learned all I could from her and graduated from Oxford, I attended the medical school at London University."

"Is that where you met Dr. Reynolds?"

His chest shook with laughter. "No. Actually, I met him some years before that, after a brawl."

"A brawl?" She knew she sounded incredulous. She could not see Jon brawling with anyone.

He nodded and launched into a tale. "While at Oxford, I occasionally came down to London—usually with Ted Hartwell.

He and I have been friends since Eton. Unfortunately, I was still inordinately sensitive about my background then and it didn't take much to set me off.

"It was the year before my mother died, so it must have been fifty-seven, Ted and I came to London during the Season. We didn't attend any parties or balls. He actually didn't want his mother to know he was in town, so we mainly frequented a few gaming hells and taverns.

"One evening we went to a favorite tavern and there were some other chaps there we knew from Oxford. I discovered later one of them was the younger brother of one of Aaron's close friends, and we know what Aaron thought of me. We ended up in a brawl. When it was all over, the tavern owner sent for a doctor for the injured, but the doctor took so long to come that I began patching people up. By the time Dr. Reynolds arrived, I had taken care of the worst of it. He was duly impressed and suggested I might consider a career in medicine. He didn't know, then, who I was and Ted and I did not bother to enlighten him. I told him I would think about it, and contact him after I was finished at Oxford."

"And did you?"

"No. Actually, I threw his card away." Jon was silent for a long time. His fingers threaded through her hair, but she knew he wasn't aware of it. The tenor of the silence told her he was thinking. "Then my mother fell sick and nothing Nona had taught me seemed to help. When she died I felt as if I had failed." His voice changed, and she heard the determination behind his next words. "I vowed never to let it happen again and contacted Dr. Reynolds."

Jon released her and rolled onto his back. She followed, leaning up on his chest and looking down into his face. His eyes were open, staring upward, unseeing.

"When I approached him and explained I wanted to learn more, he understood, but he was brutally honest." His lips twisted. "'Death is a part of life,' he told me. It was something Nona had told me as well. 'We cannot stop it.' Then he said, 'Come back when you want to make a difference. When you want to help, not only by curing, but also by accepting that we cannot cheat death. It always wins, eventually.' I was stunned and a little angry that he would dismiss me as he did. But it was for the best, for it made me realize that not everything would fall into place just because I wanted it to."

Amanda leaned down and kissed his chin. "I'm sorry." She didn't know what else to say. She knew his mother's death had affected him deeply.

The smile which curled his lips was genuine this time. "There's no need to be," he reassured her. "Dr. Reynolds might have refused to help me at first, but I eventually persuaded him of my sincerity. He taught me, however, that doing the best I could to save my mother was a worthy endeavor all on its own. That she died anyway was not my fault. Medical science, he has reminded me more than once, is still a work in progress, and probably always will be."

She tilted her head to the side, gazing down into soft green eyes. "So you really are a doctor?"

He nodded. "But only the family knows. When I made the decision to learn all I could about healing and medicine, I never expected to practice. I just wanted to know."

The sudden movement startled her and she squealed as he pushed her onto her back and rose above her. Dipping his head, he brushed his lips across her throat. "But I have been very thankful for the training these last few months." His tongue trailed across the top of a breast, then he blew on the wet trail. She quivered, but his voice as he continued was little more than a tortured whisper. "I don't think I have ever been more afraid of a result than I was when I removed your appendix. I couldn't believe I actually cut you open. It was the most frightening thing I have ever done. If I had caused you to lose the babe, or..." He buried his face in the crook of her neck, tightening his arms around her. "God, Amanda, I would not have been able to live with myself had I lost you. And I would have had no one but myself to blame."

Her arms slid around his shoulders and she savored the feel of his body pressed against hers.

"But you didn't, and because of you I don't need the laudanum any more. Nona must have known I would need you to help me."

He took a ragged breath and raised liquid-filled eyes to

hers. "One wonders how, but I suspect you are right." He stroked her cheek with his fingertips. "I love you." Then he kissed her again, his mouth opening over hers as his tongue slid inside.

Jon suddenly became the center of her world. Nothing else mattered beyond the small space occupied by the two of them. Passion flared as his tongue stroked hers, rubbing sensuously against it, and exploring her mouth.

"I love you too," was all she was able to gasp when he raised his head momentarily before he took her mouth again. The heat had been simmering between them for most of the evening, alternately flaring and being tamped down while they talked. Now it exploded and became an out of control fireball, capable of incinerating everything in its path.

Jon's hands smoothed away the robe, baring her to his view. His gaze scorched a path from her neck to her toes as he threw off the thick coverlet and studied her. No longer was he the impersonal doctor; the eyes that roamed her body were those of a lover and her senses responded accordingly.

"When I made the decision to ask you to marry me, I told myself it was because you did not have the statue and you were easy on the eyes." He grinned down at her. "At least I was right about something."

She curled into his arms and slid her hands across his chest and down lower to his abdomen. The skin was hot beneath her hands and she wanted him more with each passing moment. "I hope you still think that in fifty years."

"Nothing would give me greater pleasure than to remind you of that in fifty years." Then his mouth and body covered hers and the rest of the world ceased to exist.

Epilogue

August 1878, Lake District

The two little girls ran into the small clearing, squealing with laughter as they came. Seated on a log before a fire, Amanda looked up as the youngest of the two, her blond curls streaming down her back, made straight for the two men standing beside one of the wagons and launched herself at the tallest of the two. The other little girl, a dark-haired sprite with large dark eyes, grabbed him around the waist and hid behind him, peeking out to watch as a boy came tearing into the camp. His ebony hair was plastered to his head, and although he wore no shirt or shoes, the breeches he wore were soaked through, as if he had been swimming in the lake.

Jon looked up from his discussion with Carlo, just in time to see his six-year-old daughter, Lecia, fling herself at him. Catching her, he lifted her up to ask a question, but was forestalled as she threw her arms around his neck and held on tightly. When Carlo's granddaughter, Cara, grabbed him around the waist at the same time and squeezed herself behind him, he was not surprised to look up just in time to see Richard emerge from the trees in rapid pursuit. What surprised him was that Richard was soaking wet. Keeping a straight face with difficulty, he looked down at his ten-year-old son and noted the outrage sparking in his green eyes. It did not take much guessing to know what happened, even before his son's indignant accusation.

"They pushed me in the lake!" he cried.

"Did not!" Lecia shot back, tightening her arms around her father's neck.

"You tripped," Cara said defiantly, and Jon heard Carlo chuckle beside him. He had no doubt that Richard had, indeed, tripped and fallen into the lake. It was likely, however, that Cara and Lecia had helped him along.

"Did too!" Richard insisted.

Mira emerged from the *vardo* behind Amanda, and put down a small girl whose blond tresses hung down her back in unruly waves. Hearing the commotion, she looked up and exclaimed, "Cara, what have you done now?"

"Nothing that can't be remedied by a towel and some dry clothes," Jon answered. "Isn't that right, son?"

Richard was not so easily appeased. Folding his arms across his chest he fumed for a moment before he grudgingly replied, "I suppose so."

Amanda watched the interaction fondly. She didn't doubt Cara had something to do with Richard's trip into the lake. There were times when she felt the same way about her husband. High-handedness ran in the blood, it seemed, and while Lecia and four-year-old Katie often hung on their big brother's every word, Cara, at eight, was not so inclined. Her method of dealing with a self-important young lordling was to knock him off his high horse every so often.

Mira said nothing further and joined her on the fallen log. Jon and Carlo would handle the three scamps. The blond tot sat on Amanda's lap, talking excitedly about the small wooden carving Mira had given her.

"She reminds me of you many moons ago," Mira said to her. Amanda smiled in memory.

"I'm not sure you would have recognized me at four. Lecia, however..." She allowed the sentence to taper off as she watched her daughter and Cara standing together giggling.

Mira looked over at them and agreed. "They remind me of you and Caro." She sighed as she turned back to Amanda. "Nona would be pleased," she said. "Life has come full circle."

"We will miss you," Amanda told her. Tomorrow, Mira, Carlo and Cara would head south to meet up with Cara's family. At Southampton, they would board the *Gypsy Star,* and leave England for good. The cards, Mira told her, said it was time to go.

Just as Nona had lived by her cards, Mira had learned the same. It had been nearly one hundred years since Nona, her parents, and a small band of gypsies left France during turbulent times. But now the cards decreed it was time to return, and while Mira did not question it, Amanda knew Jon, Tina and Felicia would be sorry to see them go.

"Although I was born and raised in this land," Mira had told her, "I do not feel a part of it. It's as if the land of my parents and grandparents call to me. Carlo and I will join our sons in France to live out our days."

Cara and Lecia joined them by the fire, using sticks to poke at the pieces of wood being turned to ashes. She looked at the two girls. They had become fast friends in a short period of time and she knew Lecia would miss her friend.

Mira spoke again. "Lecia is very much like her namesake."

"In temperament, at least," Amanda agreed. "But she looks very much like her great-grandmother, who also had blond hair and green eyes. Felicia and Brand both warned me that naming Lecia after her would turn her into a hellion." Glancing over at her daughter, who was whispering something to Cara at the moment, she laughed. "They were right."

Jon and Richard emerged from the other wagon. Richard was dry and wearing a clean pair of breeches. He was obviously still out of sorts from his dunking at the girls' expense. As they reached her, she looked up into her husband's eyes, a question in hers.

Jon bent down and whispered to her, "He's fine. His pride is damaged more than anything else." The laughter in his voice assured her. "We will discuss the problems engendered by the combination of little girls and lakes."

For a moment Amanda was seven years old again, then she giggled. "Tell him it could have been worse. He could have been teaching Lecia, or Cara, to swim."

Jon grinned. "At least then they all would have been wet."

Katie chose that moment to show her father her new toy. "Kitty," she told him.

Jon looked at the small woodcarving. It had not been painted, but its shape said that it was unmistakably a cat. "Very pretty," he commented.

Once he and Richard turned away, Lecia came over to see the small carving. "It's not as nice as JoJo," she said.

Amanda turned to look at her, as Katie defended her new acquisition. "I like it," was the tot's reply, then she scooted off her mother's lap and went to show Cara.

"It's still not as nice as JoJo," Lecia repeated.

Amanda smiled at her daughter. "That's because JoJo is one of a kind." Glancing in the direction her husband and son had gone, she said to herself, "And he's mine—all mine."

Author's Note

In the late nineteenth century, modern health care was in its infancy, and women's health care was still in the womb. New strides were made daily; however, women still died in childbirth in large numbers.

Most were claimed by childbed fever, or pleurisy, an infection usually caused by the use of unsterile implements. Ignaz Philipp Semmelweis (1818-1865), an Austrian physician, was one of the first to link the two. While doing studies on childbed fever, he began to note some similarities between women who contracted it and those who didn't. But it wasn't until a young, *male*, medical student contracted it and died that he put the information together. He published a paper on it in 1861. Unfortunately, the establishment laughed at his theories and drove him out of the medical profession. He eventually died in an asylum.

In the thirteenth century a woman who requested pain alleviation for childbirth was put to death. By the middle of the nineteenth century, she was no longer put to death, but the answer was still no. With the Bible as the basis for much of the learning and culture, society took the directive in Genesis literally, and the use of anything to lessen the pain of childbirth was considered evil. Queen Victoria changed all that when, in 1853, she gave birth to her eighth child with the use of chloroform. Although a few doctors had been using it for a number of years, they had been considered outside the mainstream and looked at as less than competent. With the royal nod, life suddenly changed immensely for women suffering through labor and delivery.

Sir John Russell Reynolds (1828-1896), personal physician to the Queen had, indeed, participated in the historic birth in 1853, but he is, to a greater extent, known for his experiments with the painkilling properties of the Indian hemp plant, or marijuana, as we call it today. The movement to legalize marijuana for medicinal purposes will proudly inform one and all that Queen Victoria took it to alleviate the pain of menstrual cramps with much success and no side effects. Whether there were truly no side effects is debatable, but it is well documented that she used it under the guidance of Sir John for many years.

Anthony Ashley Cooper, seventh Earl of Shaftesbury (1801-1885) was a major proponent of reform during this same time; however, his target was the uneducated poor. His initial attempt at setting up schools eventually became what were known as "Ragged Schools". Although set up to teach *all* children, it was difficult to convince the ruling classes that girls needed schooling as much as boys did. Often girls were taught in private schools or at home if their mother was capable. Schools like the fictitious Wynton School in this book were prevalent, funded solely by generous members of the upper classes. It was not until the early twentieth century that Shaftesbury's reforms began to take hold and education began to be offered to all children—regardless of sex or social standing.

About the Author

To learn more about Denise Patrick, please visit www.denisepatrickauthor.com or her blog at www.denisesden.blogspot.com. You can also send an email to denisepatrick@gmail.com.

He doesn't need a wife. She doesn't want a husband.
Destiny's not listening.

Gypsy Legacy: The Duke
© *2008 Denise Patrick*
Book 2 in the Gypsy Legacy *Series*

As children, Brand Waring, heir to the Duke of Warringham, and his brother were kidnapped and sold to a plantation in the West Indies. Now Brand is back to wreak vengeance on those responsible for his brother's subsequent death. The last thing he wants, or needs, is to be distracted by an instant attraction to a flighty Society belle.

Felicia Collings has found it easy to refuse every marriage proposal, thanks to a ring left to her by her gypsy great-grandmother. Reportedly it will lead her to the man whom she is destined to marry. To her relief, the ring has been blessedly silent on this issue. Until Brand recognizes it, and sparks fly.

In spite of himself, Brand finds himself drawn to the beauty, and to the wounded soul reflected in her eyes. At his gentle hands, Felicia begins to learn what it means to be cherished and loved.

Then the past rears its head to threaten their fragile happiness. As Brand begins to doubt whether vengeance is as sweet as a lifetime with Felicia, he finds himself racing to save them both from not one cold-blooded killer—but two.

Available now in ebook and print from Samhain Publishing.

After one daring act, two worlds collide

A Reason to Rebel
© *2009 Wendy Soliman*

Duty has always been Estelle Travis's byword. But every woman has her limits, even a recently widowed one with few prospects. Her father's coldly calculating plan to force her into another marriage is the final straw. In an act of rebellion, she takes up a position as companion to Lady Crawley. She soon realizes she may have just exchanged one peril for another, in the guise of Alexander, Viscount Crawley.

Alex is beguiled by the aura of mystery that surrounds the beautiful new governess. Her air of vulnerability brings out his protective instincts in spades. He discovers her well-hidden reckless streak when her sister goes missing and, rather than do what's expected and return to her father's austere household, Estelle embarks on her own search.

Amid a thickening cloud of suspicion and whispers of murder, what choice does a gentleman of honour have other than to offer his assistance? Then there's the allure of her company, even if it exposes him to dangers that have little to do with her sister's plight...

Warning: This title contains a Regency heroine who abandons conventional behaviour, breaches the social divide and renounces her inhibitions.

Available now in ebook and print from Samhain Publishing.

Mystery, murder, and an old menace.
It's enough to damage the strongest love.

Harley Street
© *2009 Lynne Connolly*
Richard and Rose Book Four

Lord and Lady Strang return from their adventure-filled honeymoon, more than ready to settle into married life. After a few weeks living in his parents' Piccadilly mansion, Richard and Rose are restless for their own home, a space where they can work out the pattern of their new life together.

House-hunting will have to wait. A maid in the household of Rose's aunt has been murdered, an act that forces Richard to reveal a dark secret from his past. Despite the desperate passion they share, marriage requires disclosure—something at which Richard has never excelled.

In light of his revelation, Rose must find the strength to delve deep into the bedrock of their relationship while simultaneously facing the height of London society. As they work to unravel the clues that lead to a murderer, an old enemy launches an attack on their already fragile hearts...

This book was previously published.

Warning: This series is addictive. Danger, excitement and hot, hot sex might give you ideas. But you'll have to find your own man.

Available now in ebook and print from Samhain Publishing.

GREAT
CHEAP
FUN

Discover eBooks!

THE FASTEST WAY TO GET THE HOTTEST NAMES

Get your favorite authors on your favorite reader, long before they're out in print! Ebooks from Samhain go wherever you go, and work with whatever you carry—Palm, PDF, Mobi, and more.

Samhain
Publishing, Ltd

WWW.SAMHAINPUBLISHING.COM

LaVergne, TN USA
31 May 2010
184489LV00011B/1/P